MURDER
ON THE
MENU

Also by Alex Coombs

The Hanlon PI Series

Silenced for Good

Missing for Good

Buried for Good

The DCI Hanlon Series

The Stolen Child

The Innocent Girl

The Missing Husband

The Silent Victims

MURDER
ON THE
MENU

ALEX COOMBS

NO EXIT PRESS

First published in the UK in 2023 by No Exit Press,
an imprint of Bedford Square Publishers Ltd,
London, UK

noexit.co.uk
@noexitpress

ISBN
978-1-915798-72-5 (Paperback)
978-1-915798-73-2 (eBook)

2 4 6 8 10 9 7 5 3 1

Typeset in Janson Text
by Palimpsest Book Production Ltd, Falkirk, Stirlingshire

Printed in Great Britain by CPI Group (UK) Ltd, Croydon CR0 4YY

MIX
Paper | Supporting
responsible forestry
FSC
www.fsc.org   FSC® C171272

To JAW
xx H

Chapter One

I first met Slattery on the day I had my very low-key opening. Any less low-key, and it would have been invisible. I'd bought the restaurant, the Old Forge Café, and officially completed the deal on 31st December. I guess I wanted my new venture, which was essentially my new life, to begin on New Year's Day. It felt right, and there is always that optimistic sensation that everyone has at the beginning of January – this will be my year! This is my time! I was no exception. Or in my case, this will be a year of no regrets, of positivity, of expunging the past. Emerging from the wreckage of a failed relationship into a brave new world.

I'd been in the village of Hampden Green in the Chiltern Hills for a week. Just one week. It felt an awful lot longer. In the past few days, I had brought in painters and decorators to give a more contemporary feel to the restaurant than the chintz and cream decor favoured by the former owner. I had not expected my first customers at the Old Forge Café to be two uniformed policemen and a Detective Inspector. It most certainly wasn't the demographic that I had in mind when I bought the place.

The café had previously been owned by a Mrs Cope, an archetypal fluffy-white-haired lady in her late sixties who smelled of face-powder and rosewater and had eyes like a cobra. I had looked over the books and the operating costs. The Old Forge Café turned a reasonable profit but I could see big room for improvement. It also fitted all the personal criteria that I was looking for: location, accommodation and tranquillity. Additionally, it had a very well-equipped kitchen with a state-of-the-art oven and gas range. I decided to keep the name, partly because people would know where it was, and partly because I couldn't think of a better one.

For the poet TS Eliot, April might have been the cruellest month; for the hospitality industry that's not the case. The cruellest month is the beginning of the year. I had officially opened the place on a Friday in January, the hardest time to make money in catering. Everyone's broke after Christmas, everyone's depressed, and the weather's usually awful. It's not weather for going out. Out here in the South Bucks countryside, it was no exception. Mind you, my staff bills were low, for the simple reason I didn't have any. I was a one woman band.

It didn't take me long to realise that Mrs Cope not only had the eyes of a snake, but the morals of one. Buy in haste, repent at leisure. The kitchen equipment, now I came to actually use it, instead of being hurried around it by an estate agent, was in a terrible state. For example, the door fell off one of the fridges on about the third use and I had to wedge it shut with a sack of potatoes. A lot of the restaurant furniture was quite literally falling apart and the less said about the structure of the building, the better. The painters and decorators had had a field day pointing out more and more horrors revealed by their work.

But despite these setbacks, I was happy. It was my own place and I'd had enough of London where so many things reminded me of my past life with Andrea. Here he had bought me dinner, there we had argued in a pub. Those were the offices in which he'd worked. The geographical terrain of London was overlaid with a psycho-geographical grid on which I could plot my career in catering as well as our relationship, and I wanted a fresh start. I didn't care that I was unknown here. Start off small and grow with the business, that was my short-term plan. I figured that as profits grew I could rebuild the place around me. I wasn't even too concerned about the potential lack of customers – it's always a problem in January, it wasn't unexpected.

I put together a simple menu with a few clever touches. It was a café menu; I had no liquor licence yet. Things had to be made from low-cost ingredients so I could make a decent profit margin as I couldn't get away with high prices and there was no buffer of profit from alcoholic drinks.

Not being too busy suited me for the moment. I felt that I would rather take a low footfall and turnover on the chin and work through the bad times of January and February, growing organically, than start out when things traditionally went well. Battling adversity, well, I was kind of used to that. And it was undeniably pleasant to wake up in the flat above the restaurant and savour the silence.

For the last two years I had been living in noisy central London kitchens, eighteen-hour days, working with kids who were twenty years my junior. My one-bedroomed flat in Kentish Town had been equally noisy. I was getting too old for clubbing, too old for the wafts of weed that kept seeping up from the flat below and the street outside, and London night life had long since lost its appeal. Gone were the days of finishing work at eleven and then going clubbing until four. Making the move to the Chilterns was not a hard decision to make.

I also didn't mind the fact that I had hardly any personal effects in the flat that came with the restaurant. Not now that Mrs Cope's stuff had gone. It wasn't just the furniture that she had removed. She had taken not only the lampshades, but the lightbulbs too. That seemed a bit excessive, but, I reflected, Mrs Cope was a thoroughly vindictive woman.

Still, I was enjoying the space. Just as well since I had so much of it. Uncluttered by things I couldn't afford, I pretended I was enjoying the minimalist life. Who needs tables and chairs and a sideboard? Who needs a bed and a chest of drawers? In a symbolic act I'd junked all my old furniture, a gesture of severing links with the past. Who needs a wardrobe, I had thought, I wasn't looking to go to Narnia. I was regretting it now, that was for sure. That's what you get for being impetuous.

I led the police into the restaurant area, gave them a table, asked them what they wanted to drink – two cappuccinos for the PCs and a double espresso for the man I assumed was their boss, and busied myself behind the counter. At least the old Gaggia coffee machine still worked.

The two uniforms were festooned like paramilitary Christmas trees with the tools of their trade: batons, Tasers, radios, other bits and bobs of equipment. They clashed horribly with the chintzy furniture of the restaurant which I couldn't yet afford to replace.

I brought them their coffees. They looked me over in a markedly hostile way. Perhaps they missed Mrs Cope. Perhaps it was because I wasn't from round here. Or maybe they just didn't like my face.

The winter rain beat down unceasingly.

Through the glass I could see the green itself (or the common as it was sometimes called); the children's play area, the fitness/arts studio, twenty or so houses and the village pond. There was also a pub, the Three Bells, a rough kind of place with a pool table. It was one of two pubs in the village. Houses of various shapes and sizes fronted on to the green. The road bent around to the left out of sight, leading to the King's Head, the other village pub.

The two pubs were indicative of the social divide of the place: BMWs and Mercedes at the King's Head, pick-up trucks and vans at the Three Bells.

In short, a typical Chilterns village. And carrying on the good old country traditions of surly hostility to incomers.

'What brings you gentlemen to Hampden Green?' I asked. The uniforms glanced expectantly at the DI, their spokesman. He had a tough, good-humoured face, somewhat battered and quite tanned. He also had a powerful physique under his suit, running somewhat to middle-aged fat, and a very obvious 'don't mess with me' attitude. He looked hard as nails.

He stood up and pointed out of the window.

'You see that house, the one with the blue door?'

I could, and I did. I nodded.

'That's my place.'

It was said more in the tone of a warning than anything else. That's my house, this is my turf, this is my patch. Like a dog cocking its leg, the DI was marking his territory. He looked at me in an intimidating way to underline the message. Satisfied, he carried on.

'I'm DI Michael Slattery, by the way. Now, I am here to investigate a burglary that occurred down at Andy Simmonds' place last night. Do you know Andy?'

'No,' I said. I didn't know anyone.

'Well, he's a pig farmer and butcher and he has a farm shop where he sells his meat. Last night someone forced the lock on his walk-in fridge and nicked about two grands' worth of sausages and mixed meat. I'm investigating the crime.'

Blimey, I thought. What did he expect to find here? If I were the sausage thief, how would I get rid of them? A menu composed of nothing but sausage dishes? January is sausage month?

'A DI?' I said. Quite senior for this sort of thing. Years ago I had dated a policeman and I seemed to recall DIs were fairly important. Not to throw any shade on sausages but I would have thought he would have had more important things to do than look into a meat robbery – and why did he need two uniforms?

'Slow day at the office?' I asked.

He scowled. I think my comment had been unwise. There'd been two shootings and a fatal stabbing round the corner from where I had last lived in the month before I'd left.

I was sorry for the farmer's loss, but really? Anyway, I felt that somehow I was failing to connect with DI Slattery.

I went back to my sausage musings. Mrs Cope would have shifted the sausage. That sounds like a dreadful double entendre, but what I meant was, bangers and mash, sausage casserole, sausage sandwiches, sausage and onion gravy. Or continental *bockwurst mit kartoffeln salat*. Homemade sausage rolls. . . I suddenly thought, my God, why am I mocking her? All of that sounds good, maybe not the casserole. All locally sourced, so good for the environment, and from free-range pigs. When I'd been out running I'd seen them in their muddy field standing around their little corrugated-iron pig houses. Good for animal welfare! Hearty food for this abysmal weather. I made a mental note.

'*Investigate sausage possibilities.*'

But that was for later; right now I had the police to deal with. I waited for Slattery and his not so merry men to break the silence.

Outside the windows of the café the village of Hampden Green carried on its peaceful, unremarkable existence. It continued to rain.

I looked at the trio of cops. Three pairs of eyes stared back at me with naked suspicion. I stopped looking at them and looked out of the bow-fronted window behind them instead. A kind of horrible silence ensued. Periodically one of the uniform's radios would squawk into life. He would ignore it.

Through the glass I could see most of the village. The green was deserted.

Slattery was the first to move. He stood up and pointed at the common.

'Well, let's just say that this is very much my patch' – his gesture encompassed the whole village – 'and I'm a tidy man and I like to keep things clean. Now, you're new around here,' he said, with a distinct lack of enthusiasm, 'so I would like to officially extend the hand of welcome, but if anyone should swing by offering prime pork goods at knockdown prices I'd be upset if you failed to inform me.' He looked menacingly at me, so did his colleagues. 'In fact, I'd be very upset.'

This was, I decided, nothing to do with a break-in. This was DI Slattery showing me who was boss, who ran Hampden Green.

'Sure,' I said, 'coffee's on the house.'

He nodded, took his wallet out and handed me his card. 'I'll see you around,' he said, as he stood up to leave.

It was a threat rather than a promise.

I wondered what I'd done to upset him.

I guess I wasn't local.

Chapter Two

My next visitor was altogether more charming than the forces of law and order. It was only by chance that I actually heard her. I was making a coffee and walnut cake and had to go back into the restaurant to make an espresso that I was going to use for flavouring. It was then that I saw her through the glass of the front door. She waved at me to get my attention. I went over and let her in.

'Hello,' I said, 'can I help you?'

I was talking to a girl who I guessed was in her late teens, early twenties, who had been trying without success to ring the bell by the restaurant door. I say 'guessed' because she was mainly concealed by a large umbrella that the heavy rain was bouncing off. It was ten o'clock in the morning but almost dark under the cloudy, black sky.

'I'm sorry,' she said, gesturing helplessly, 'I've been ringing the bell. . .'

Another thing that didn't work, thank you, Mrs Cope, I thought. I'll add it to the list.

'It's temperamental,' I lied, which sounded better somehow than 'broken'. 'Broken' was unprofessional, defeatist.

'Do come in,' I said, ushering her inside. I took the umbrella from her and her coat, sodden and heavy from the hideous weather.

'I've come about the job.' She looked around. 'Is the chef, Charlie Hunter, around?'

'I'm the chef, Charlie Hunter,' I said. Bet this doesn't happen to Monica Galetti, I thought.

She looked stricken.

'I'm sorry. . . I thought. . .'

'That's ok. Have a seat.'

We both sat down and weighed each other up. I had put an A board outside saying that I needed waiting staff. I was amazed that the writing hadn't been washed away. The marker pen for A boards was supposed to be weatherproof to a degree but it must have been undergoing a pretty severe test out there. I hadn't been too confident that I would get any takers. There was not a lot of footfall in the village and the rain made people concentrate on the road rather than signs outside restaurants.

'I'm Jessica, by the way, Jessica Turner, but people call me Jess.'

'I'm Charlie Hunter, as you now know, chef proprietor.' I smiled at how pompous that sounded. It was true, it was an accurate description of my job, but it sounded quite grandiose. You could be chef proprietor of a burger van when you think about it.

I examined my applicant appraisingly. Jessica Turner was about five foot five with dark curly hair, large brown eyes and an attractive, lively face. She was well-spoken and was dressed down in a baggy jumper, jeans and Cuban-heeled boots. She looked intelligent and good-humoured.

10

I explained my plans for the restaurant, she listened attentively and asked a couple of sensible questions.

I asked Jess about herself. She was a second year student at Warwick University studying Computer Science. She was staying at home temporarily as a combination of industrial action and building work at the uni had shifted that term's work online. I nodded. IT, I was impressed. I had a website that I'd bought off the shelf but I lacked the time to be organising it properly, let alone updating it. In my hands it looked decidedly amateurish. Jess could help there when we were quiet. Her skills would come in handy. I could write a menu, but I couldn't use spreadsheets with any degree of competence, or even coherently organise a simple-to-use drag and drop website. Did she have waitressing experience? Yes, she did.

'What kind of food are you going to do?' she asked.

I made her a coffee and explained not only the menu, but its rationale. There was nothing too fancy or too expensive.

So, on the menu as well as restaurant dishes there were old warhorses like caramelised red onion and steak baguette, baked potatoes, quiche and various sandwiches. It was still predominantly a café menu, but a café menu with artistic flourishes, and from these little seeds mighty things would grow.

There was the inescapable ploughman's (we were in the country, there were fields), but made with good cheese, homemade pickled red cabbage and piccalilli. I had added plenty of things that would not go off – I couldn't afford the luxury of waste – so there were quite a few cutesy preserves and frozen desserts, parfaits, semifreddo and sorbets that would last and not have to get binned if unsold. Occasionally I'd add mysterious touches: compressed pine-apple, a potato foam on the soup, that kind of thing. Stuff like that was old hat in London but still novel out here. There was only me, it couldn't be too adventurous; I didn't have the luxury of time, but it was good, it was honest and it represented reasonable value for money.

It was more like I was pitching for a job than she was, but I guess she was about the first person I'd had a chance to talk to about it.

'That all sounds very interesting,' she said. And the strange thing was, she sounded like she meant it.

The job was hers.

'I'm afraid it's only minimum wage, but you get tips, which you share with the kitchen staff.'

She nodded. 'How many kitchen staff are there?' she asked.

'None, other than me. But I don't get tips, since I'm the owner, so currently they're all yours. But you will have to help with the washing up.'

She smiled. 'I can wash up, Charlie.'

She had a great smile. I think she was amused by the shoestring nature of the business. We agreed that she could start the following day.

'So I guess I'd better take my sign down then,' I said.

She looked puzzled.

'What sign?'

'The A board.'

'I didn't see the A board sign.' She looked confused, as did I. I stood up and glanced out of the window to see if it was still there. It was, it hadn't been stolen, that was my suspicious London mind at work; she must have just been blinded by the godawful rain.

'Then how did you know I needed a waitress?'

Her face cleared. 'Oh, that. Well, someone told me last night.'

'But I hadn't put a sign up last night.'

She shook her head sorrowfully. 'Oh, Charlie, you're not from here. This is a village, everybody knows everything about everyone else's business. Don't worry, you'll get used to it in the end.'

We shook hands and I watched her back disappearing across the green as she trudged home through the rain.

I thought about what she had said. I suppose I thought it was quite sweet that everyone knew what everyone else was doing without Facebook, TikTok, Twitter or other social media.

After all, it was a pleasant, friendly little village. What could go wrong?

Chapter Three

The following day, twenty-four hours after DI Slattery's visit and Jess's hiring, there was the arson attack.

Coincidentally fire, in the form of smoke, had gone into what I was cooking at the time. I had just made and served a customer a smoked venison sandwich on rye with a small garnish of curly endive, beetroot and cornichons.

It would be fair to say that the customer, bald, overweight, tattooed (not a great look – the flab, not the ink, I have a couple of discreet tattoos myself, not on public display) was not shaping up to be one of my favourites.

Jess arrived as things started getting heated between us. I hadn't been overly impressed with the look of him when he walked in and my opinion of him was getting progressively lower. Jess gave me a sympathetic glance as she passed by, heading for the kitchen to change into her apron.

'What's that?' he pointed aggressively at the garnish. Most things about the guy were aggressive as well as his mannerisms: his bald (aggressively so) shaved head, his tattoos, visible on his arms and flowing up his neck, lots of red and blue and green (bright, vivid colours, no delicate Korean style ink for him), his general demeanour.

I patiently explained. How it would enhance his eating experience, how the flavours were cunningly paired, how the vinegar that the small cucumber (which is what a cornichon is) was pickled in would cut through the richness of the meat. And didn't it look good! He was having none of it.

'Bollocks to that,' he remarked judiciously. I doubted he was a professional food critic, so his opinion was not worth taking on board. At least I hoped he wasn't a food critic. Although, 'Bollocks to that,' would make an arresting title for a food review in a paper.

'No offence, darling, but when I want crap on my plate I'll ask for it, OK?'

Idiot, I thought. I gritted my teeth (darling! Would he have said that to Angela Hartnett? I think not), shrugged and fetched a plate, and deftly scraped off the offending items with the blade of a knife. For a mad moment I would willingly have plunged it into him.

Actually, I'd have changed tools first.

I was using the back of my long, broad-bladed chef's knife to clean the plate. For stabbing Whitfield (that was his name I learnt later) to death I'd have gone for a long, thin but sturdy boning knife. It would have slid in much more easily.

As my old head chef used to say, *'Always choose the right tool for the right job.'*

The question of what is right and not right, a perennial problem. They say that the customer is always right. Not in the world of good food. There, the customer doesn't know best, the customer is entitled to their opinion, but that's all they're entitled to. Not to demand changes to the menu. I'm quoting a chef I once knew; well, it was OK for him, he had the luxury of fame and money. I had neither. I did what I was told. I felt belittled, sad and dirty, complicit in Whitfield's vandalism of my food. And angry.

The sandwich sat forlornly on the plate. He switched his baleful attention from me and the food to jabbing messages into the keyboard of his phone.

I went back into the kitchen. Jess walked in with an order in her hand.

'Cheque on, one steak baguette, one minestrone soup with parmesan and rosemary focaccia. . .'

I thought of the guy again and I picked up a frying pan and crashed it down on the range. Arsy customers really upset me; it shouldn't, but it does. Jess flinched.

'Are you OK?'

I told her what had just happened.

Her face cleared. 'Oh, that's Dave Whitfield; ignore him, he's a knobhead.'

I put another pan on the heat and took a rump steak from my fridge and a tub of pre-cooked caramelised red onion.

As I seasoned the meat she said, 'Whitfield lives across the common, you'll probably be seeing quite a lot of him.'

My heart sank.

'Oh, great.'

'Yeah, he lives in the house with the obelisk.'

I knew immediately which house she was talking about. Outside of discussions as to the real meaning of *2001 A Space Odyssey*, you rarely hear the word 'obelisk'. You did in Hampden Green, courtesy of Dave Whitfield.

She disappeared back into the restaurant. I attended to the steak and thought about Whitfield and his house. It really did have an obelisk, a kind of blue Perspex tower in the front garden that was illuminated, like a miniature version of the Shard in London. It must have been nearly three metres tall. This cast an eerie blue light over the green at night. In a village with no street lighting, it was quite the thing. It was disconcerting, the way it glowed, an unmissable blue beacon. I could even see it through my curtains. So, the mystery was now explained – that was Whitfield's house, his plastic tower, his turquoise aura. His own personal advert for his construction business. The letters, DW were etched into it for all to see. I had been wondering what they stood for, now I knew. Perhaps the purple phallic tower in his garden was making up in metres what he lacked downstairs in the trouser department. Maybe I should ask him.

'How on earth did he get planning permission?' I asked Jess later. Planning was a sore point. My window frames were rotten (thank you Mrs Cope!) and needed replacement. They were listed though, and this added insanely to the cost. The point was, any form of deviation from the norm was fraught with difficulty and had to be 'in keeping with the village'. You couldn't just put any old window in, it had to be identical. And not just looking the same, the material had to be an exact match. God alone knows how Whitfield had managed to get his huge, glowing pillar through the council planning department. It certainly was not 'in keeping with the village' in any way, shape or form.

Jessica had said darkly, 'That's the question everyone here asked. Let's just say, money talks.'

I left the kitchen by the back door to get some more panna cottas from the fridge in the store room on the other side of the kitchen yard. One of the double doors of my gate to the road had swung open and I had a clear view over the common and the houses on the far side.

Right now Whitfield's tower, clearly visible, wasn't talking but it was certainly communicating. In smoke signals. Maybe this was an example of sympathetic magic; he was eating smoked venison, here was more of it. A whole lot more. His front garden was ablaze and was emitting a huge black column of the stuff. Not just smoke, big yellow flames licked up into the cold grey January sky. It was very dramatic, like an illustration I had in my Children's Bible when I was very young. A fiery pillar. I stared at it in fascination, a tall, burning mass of fire.

I ran back into the kitchen and into the restaurant. Whitfield, earbuds in his ears, was sitting in the restaurant with his back to the window, oblivious to the towering inferno in his front garden, still scowling at his phone.

The other customers were all, as one, staring at the conflagration. Their conversation had ceased, they were transfixed. I should have told him about the fire, but I was still annoyed with him from earlier. Karma, I thought.

I could now hear the sound of sirens. Someone had obviously phoned the fire brigade. Then I heard the sound of the bell as the front door of the restaurant opened.

'Oi, Dave!'

Whitfield didn't hear. The man who had just entered,

19

strode across to Whitfield, leaned over and pulled the earbuds from his ears. I recognised him; he was one of the many builders who lived in the village, a tall, good humoured grey-haired man, Chris by name.

Whitfield transferred his scowl from the phone to Chris. 'What?'

'Your tower's on fire, mate,' Chris said, cheerily.

Whitfield put his phone down, his back still resolutely turned to the window.

'What are you on about?' he said angrily. The other man pointed and only then did he turn round and look out of the window. 'JESUS!'

He did a double take and literally rubbed his eyes with disbelief. Then he moved; for an overweight guy he was surprisingly quick off the mark.

He leapt to his feet and was out through the door, running over the green in the direction of his house, its position clearly marked by the thick plume of smoke and the fire engine. We all watched him go.

As if a spell had been broken, the dozen or so people in the restaurant started talking animatedly to each other.

I cleared Whitfield's plate away.

The bastard still owed me for his sandwich.

Chapter Four

A week passed. Jess had gone and I closed the restaurant for the day. All in all I was not dissatisfied with the start of my business. Everyone seemed happy with the food, except for Whitfield, and the universe had punished him by burning down his obelisk. Good.

When I had designed the format of the menus I had mentioned that I did outside catering for events and parties. I was pleased that already I had received a couple of enquiries from women who had eaten here and were interested. If I could get that side of things working it would help tide me over when business was quiet mid-week and during the rest of the winter. When spring came, I reasoned, I'd start to get the walkers or people who would actually want to venture into the countryside, as opposed to just the locals.

My mind wandered to other things. I thought of the burning pillar on the other side of the green. I wondered who had done it. I shrugged; there was nothing I could do about it. I put it out of my mind; Whitfield's troubles were nothing to do with me.

Nothing to do with me at all.

I moved my mind back to work. Back to outside catering.

Outside catering is a pain. For a start, you have to work out of someone else's kitchen. I've only done it a couple of times but I've had to move washing out of the way, children's toys, all sorts of junk, just to get at a sink or a stove or a work-surface. I can't stand clutter. For me, a kitchen is a place to cook, pure and simple. In a lot of houses though it's like an annexe of the living room.

Then too, you're out of your comfort zone; you have to bring everything with you. And you lack the amenities of a professional kitchen: large ovens, hot-plate cupboards, space to work. The latter is particularly infuriating when you don't have it.

Another problem that would only be recognised by professionals, is that for a chef your kitchen is your kingdom. You are in charge, nobody can set foot in it without your say so. In someone else's house a kitchen is a public space; people wander in and out, jostle you, run taps, open fridge doors, poke around, move things, behaviour that would not be tolerated for a second in a commercial kitchen. So outside catering, being in someone else's space, is, all in all, a tricky thing to do.

The plus side is, if you get it right, it's easy money and you get to show your wares, your ability to a wide audience. It's a great advert if it all works well.

Upstairs in the flat that was above the restaurant, I pulled off my chef's whites and did some basic yoga exercises, down dog, sun salutation and a bit of Tai Chi to relax my tired muscles. Standing upright for twelve hours a day is not good for you. It was fantastic to stretch my cramped body. I luxuriated in the stretches. I like yoga, so long as it's done slowly and thoughtfully. I can't stand the idea of Hot Yoga, I get hot and sweaty enough in a kitchen without wanting to do it for fun.

I looked around my bedroom. The plus side, it was very big, plenty of natural light and a view over the common. The downside, it was depressingly furniture free. The restaurant had swallowed my money. I was sleeping on a mattress on the floor, my clothes in a built in wardrobe. The wardrobe was large, the clothes depressingly few. Mind you, I wouldn't be going out much, but it would be nice to dream. I sighed, my empty wardrobe to go with my empty social life.

I tried to kid myself that I liked this minimalist look, but in truth, it was rather depressing, and the carpet that Mrs Cope had bequeathed me, well, threadbare would be a euphemism. It was stained and moth-eaten. Frankly, it was nasty. I could always take my mind off the carpet by looking out of the window. In the daylight I could see Dave Whitfield's house with the charred mess of his obelisk and behind it, trees and fields.

I finished my yoga, and as I did so the front doorbell sounded. I rolled my eyes, pulled a tracksuit on and went downstairs. I could see who it was through the glass; I was less than thrilled.

'Do come in DI Slattery,' I said, as I opened the door.

'Thank you.' He didn't sound terribly thankful. I had forgotten his intimidating bulk; he filled the door frame.

Slattery was a big man. I'm five foot eight, and I guess that he was considerably taller. He looked at me coldly. His eyes were brown and hard.

'Any luck with the sausage thief?' I asked politely.

'No.' Another glare.

There was no back room at the restaurant, no manager's office. Just the eating area, toilets and kitchen. We could have gone upstairs but there were no chairs and while I couldn't speak for DI Slattery, I personally had no great wish to sit next to him on my mattress.

I waved him to a table in the restaurant. I did not want to switch on machines that had been cleaned for the day. He would have to do without the offer of hospitality. No coffee or cake for you, Mr Policeman.

'How can I help you?' I asked.

He sat opposite me, giving me a sardonic once over. It was such a classic policeman's look, polite scepticism with a hint of amused contempt.

'We received an anonymous tip-off that someone answering your description had been seen exiting Dave Whitfield's garden earlier this morning.'

I stared at him with incredulity.

'What!'

He repeated the sentence. He raised his eyebrows expectantly.

'Well,' I said, 'I was nowhere near his garden.'

It was one of those moments when you are accused of something that you haven't done but you feel strangely ill-equipped to deal with it. My denial, true as it was, rang hollow in my own ears. I felt myself starting to go red.

'Ok,' he said, 'you were nowhere near his garden.'

'Well, I did run past his house.'

I go running daily, three to five km and a ten to fifteen km long-run once a week. There is a footpath by the houses on the other side of the common and I had run there today. I explained this to Slattery.

'So,' he said, wearily, 'you were near his garden.'

'Well, maybe I was,' I said hotly, 'but I never touched his obelisk.'

'Fine,' he said irritably and stood up. 'I'm glad we've got that cleared up.' He looked at me and shook his head. I could see that he didn't really believe me.

I saw him out and closed and locked the door behind him.

I went into the kitchen and looked at my prep list for the morning. I was now out of sorts because of the accusation that I had something to do with the arson attack. Coupled with that was, I couldn't really understand what Slattery had got against me. Nobody enjoys being disliked and I was no exception.

I gave up on brooding. When in doubt, cook something. I had a prep list as long as my arm and I decided to make a base for some cheesecakes. I reached for a couple of packets of digestive biscuits and tipped them into a steel bowl and smashed them to crumbs with the end of a rolling pin. While I did so, I imagined bringing the rolling pin down hard on the faces and heads of Slattery and Whitfield.

Serve Whitfield right for being so snarky about my food and calling me 'darling' and Slattery for persecuting an innocent woman.

Cooking can be so therapeutic.

Chapter Five

While the three cheesecake bases set, I crossed the road and walked around the village green. I say, walked. I squelched. The rain was still falling; whipped by the wind, it seemed to be coming at me sideways. It was ferociously cold, particularly after the warmth of the kitchen.

I looked at my watch, half-four. For the time being I was only opening at lunchtimes. Gradually I would phase in evening meals. Slow but steady growth was what I wanted.

I kept my head down as I walked. The green was a rectangular piece of common ground that houses and a few businesses fronted on to. On my side of the road there was my place, the Old Forge Café. I was in the middle of the left side of the rectangle and my neighbours were a small car repair business that also did MOTs, and a few houses. More or less diagonally opposite from me at the top right corner of the common was the Three Bells pub and next to it the village hall which doubled as a fitness centre and arts studio, and several more houses. On the opposite side of the green, the right side of the rectangle

27

if you will, was Whitfield's house and of course, DI Slattery's. The road to Frampton End, the next village ran along the bottom. It was an attractive place, compact and down to earth, not full of second homes and retired business people.

The green, being at the top of the hill and surrounded by buildings, made the sky overhead seem vast. A couple of red kites soared overhead in the darkening sky. Soon it would be completely dark. There was a playground for children on the far side, but there was no one around today, it was too cold to play. There was a pond near there too, sometimes it had ducks. Not today. The only person I saw was a man, head down, buried in the hood of his anorak, leaving the house next to Whitfield's with its charred obelisk in the front garden.

I thought, the village committee will be up in arms about that. It was like a sinister beacon of civil unrest, not suitable for a South Bucks village.

I walked up to the Three Bells and went inside. It was, quite frankly, as a country pub, disappointing, more than that, a bit of a dump. People have an image, rooted in reality, of what a nice countryside pub is, from the low-beamed ceiling, to the inglenook fireplace and cosy, homely charm. The Three Bells certainly fell short of the kitsch ideal. It fell far short of it.

The pub was basically one long room with the door at one end, the bar at the other and a pool table in the middle. The pub was defiantly not chocolate-boxy. It was never going to feature on *Location, Location, Location*, when Kirsty and Phil go for a drink to discuss something. It had as much atmosphere as a motorway service station. At this time of day it was quite busy, early doors. Half past four was knocking-off time for the local builders, and there were half a dozen scaffolders in there who worked for a company based just up the road, Marathon Scaffolding. They all wore company sweatshirts saying 'Marathon'.

They nodded at me in a condescending way.

Strangely, I wasn't the only chef in there. The catering trade was present in the pub in the form of four young male chefs from the pub round the corner, the King's Head. I say pub, it was now a four-rosette restaurant. The King's Head was knocking on the Michelin star door, asking to be let in. The chefs looked very young, very frail and very pallid compared to the muscular, weather-beaten scaffolders.

They must be on split shifts, the nightmare side of working in a kitchen, 10.00 to 3.00, 5.30 to 11.30 and there was nothing for them to do in the couple of hours off that they had, other than come here. I could sympathise, I'd done enough of those killer shifts in my time. And, of course, if someone's off – sick or holiday – you work straight through, making your day stretch from ten in the morning to eleven or midnight. Fine if you work for Goldman Sachs and get paid a fortune, soul-destroying when you're in some shit-hole kitchen, on minimum wage, desperately trying to keep the show on the road.

There was an enormous Scottish guy with them, six-foot-four, overweight, Dougie by name, an affable bear of a man. He was the King's Head's sous chef, the man directly below the head chef.

'Afternoon, madam,' Malcolm, the landlord, said to me as I walked up to the bar. It's one of the oddities of life that many landlords seem to detest the general public, and Malcolm was one of them. He looked at his customers with an expression of total dislike, boredom or irritation. He was a red-faced, cadaverous man, reticent but when he spoke it was in a hoarse whisper, as if from beyond the grave. I had never seen him smile. I'm not saying he didn't do it, perhaps he was a closet laugh-a-minute kind of guy.

I wasn't complaining. I didn't want a successful pub with an affable landlord just across the road from me. They might start doing food and I would suffer. Malcolm only did crisps and nuts; the occasional packet of pork scratchings was his idea of a gourmet treat, that and a 'seafood snack' that stank like cat food. He was no threat to business at all.

I said hello, ordered and watched as he fetched me a Coke.

'I'll get that,' said a voice behind me.

I turned. It was a young guy I'd seen before in the pub before; short, stocky, good-looking and balding. Like Whitfield who I'd seen him drinking with when I came in, a devotee of tattoos, although he favoured ones that were more abstract (tribal, Maori-style) and monochromatic.

'Thanks,' I said. His eyes were half closed and he smelled strongly of weed; he looked extremely stoned. He extended his hand. 'Hi, I'm Ollie.'

'Charlie.' We shook hands.

'Do you want to come and join us?' he gestured at the table. Whitfield too looked the worse for wear, eyes glazed. I guessed he'd been smoking weed too. Maybe it was the stress of having the obelisk burn down. Join Whitfield? Christ no.

'No, I'm fine,' I said. 'I've got to get back to the kitchen in a minute. I've got a cheesecake to make.'

Ollie nodded vaguely, patted me amiably on the arm and wandered back to his table and Whitfield. He hadn't asked me what flavour it was, or even if it were New York style, that is, baked. Maybe he wasn't a cheesecake kind of guy.

I drank my Coke by myself, listening to the clack and bang of pool balls from my fellow chefs, the rumble of manly conversation about football from the scaffolders, Ollie and Dave Whitfield in catatonic silence, the landlord staring into the middle distance, avoiding eye contact with everyone. Then the door opened and a very tall man of about sixty with iron-grey hair and wearing an expensive suit came in, accompanied by a girl a third of his age, hanging on to his arm. Despite the cold and the rain, she was showing a lot of flesh, wearing a very short skirt and vertiginous heels. She too was heavily tattooed. The two of them joined Whitfield and Ollie at their table.

I sipped my Coke and looked around at the pub bar and its clientele. I could have joined the other chefs but the last thing I wanted to do was talk shop, or play pool come to that, which I can't do anyway. I'd had enough of what passed for atmosphere in the place and I left soon afterwards. I guess I'd only been gone about half an hour from my place. As I walked towards the Old Forge through the darkness, I noticed from a distance something about the place that didn't seem right. As I got closer I could see what it was.

In my absence, someone had graffitied the double wooden gates that opened on to the small courtyard to the side of the building. It was more than graffiti, it was a message, spray-gunned in a shaky hand, 'Go Home Townie Bitch'.

I stood there in the cold night air and the driving rain staring at the insult. I felt a mix of anger, sadness and revulsion, then I unlocked the gate and let myself into the courtyard, closing and locking the gates behind me.

I'd deal with it in the morning.

Later that night I turned the lights out and got ready for bed. As I lay there on my mattress all I could think about was that somewhere in this village someone disliked me enough to try and get me in trouble for the arson attack on Whitfield by telling Slattery they'd seen me leaving his garden, and now this.

I had managed to make an enemy and I'd only been here just over a week. It was a disturbing thought. Disturbing too was the scene at the Three Bells.

Before I left the pub, I had turned and looked back at the red-faced, probably alcoholic landlord, the aggressive, rowdy scaffolders, the shattered-looking chefs by the pool table, the stoned forms of Whitfield and Ollie – and the sinister, ageing businessman and his youthful mistress. It was like some morality play: drunkenness, violence, exhaustion, greed and lust all in the one room.

It hadn't taken me long to realise that, pretty though it might be, Hampden Green was certainly no paradise.

Et in Arcadia Ego.

Sleep was a long time coming.

Chapter Six

The following day I made lime jelly in an ice cube mould and used slightly less liquid than the recipe suggested so the jelly cubes were quite firm and easy to handle. There was a healthy drop of tequila in the mixture. I had some meringues that I'd made to use up some egg whites left over from making sweet pastry for tarts, Bakewell and fruit. I carefully placed a circular meringue on a plate, piped Chantilly cream over it, added some passionfruit compote, some passionfruit pulp, some raspberries for colour and three of the tequila and lime jelly cubes and a jaunty little meringue hat. I garnished this with a twist of kiwi.

'Ta da!' I said, pleased with my handiwork.

'That's beautiful,' said Jess admiringly.

'Thank you,' I said.

'A work of art. I'm sure the Earl will appreciate it.'

'Well, take it away then,' I said, and got on with the next order. The Earl? Had I heard right? The door swung to behind Jess as she carried my artwork out.

I had now learned quite a bit about her. She was twenty. She had a Giant Schnauzer called Siegfried. She had studied maths, further maths, physics and chemistry at A level and had straight A-stars in all four. She liked the theatre, she still swam competitively. She had liked middle distance running. 'But I grew to be totally the wrong shape. . .' she sighed.

She also loved eating cream. 'I'm Miss Dairy Queen,' she confided to me and if I had been whipping the stuff would clean the mixing bowl with a spatula and eat it.

God knows how she kept her waistline down. Maybe all that swimming. I was envious; I had to calorie count and fast to keep my weight where I wanted it.

I carried on making soup – green pea and parsnip. I blitzed it with a stick-blender, it was certainly vivid. I tasted it – well, if you liked that kind of thing it was lovely – I seasoned it with salt and pepper.

Later I would make slightly curried mini pea fritters as a garnish and when I served it, I'd float one in the centre of the bowl so the brown of the fritter contrasted with the emerald of the soup.

'So we've got an earl in?' I said.

Jess had returned. She put the plates down by the dishwasher and I started cleaning them. A commercial dishwasher has a cycle that takes around three minutes but you have to give what goes into it a quick clean in the sink first, otherwise the machine would break down under the weight of leftover food. In a busy kitchen the dishwasher's sink ends up looking like a particularly horrible minestrone. There never seems to be enough time to empty it before refilling.

I was spending a great deal of time washing up. I thought,

God we need a kitchen porter. Then I suddenly recalled, with alarm, Jess would be back at uni all too soon when the next term started. I'd need another waitress.

She answered my question regarding the aristocracy. 'Of course there's an earl.' She shook her head at my stupidity. 'Earl Hampden, he lives in Marlow House, on the Hampden estate,' she added.

I nodded. I'd passed the place several times when I'd been out running. It was a very large red-brick mid-Victorian place. I felt a twinge of disappointment; I was expecting something along the lines of Blenheim Palace.

'I thought you were Earl of something or other?' I asked.

Jess shook her head. 'Our one is just called Earl Hampden,' she said decisively.

'What's he like?' I asked.

'Mean,' she said, slightly irritably.

I couldn't resist going to have a look myself. I knew it was ridiculous but I had never met an earl, or a lord, or any form of titled person. I wanted to go and see what he looked like. I muttered some excuse to Jess about needing some coffee and I went into the restaurant, made myself an espresso and returned to the kitchen.

It was the grey-haired man I had seen coming into the Three Bells.

'I saw him the other day, in the pub,' I said. I hadn't liked what I'd seen. He had seemed slightly sinister; his age contrasted with the youth of the girl clutching his arm, her hair very blond against his dark suit. His choice of drinking companions made him seem Mafiosi-like too. An ageing, lecherous Don.

'Bet he was with some floozy,' Jess said sniffily. 'He's on some rich man's dating agency database.'

The words 'dating agency' came heavily italicised.

'He likes going to East Asia a lot.' The way she said it made me think it probably wasn't for the food, the temples or the beaches.

'Bangkok?' I asked. For no reason other than it was the first name that came into my head.

'You said it.' She went back into the restaurant, annoyed at the aristocracy's lack of morals and I carried on cleaning.

Later, during a lull in food orders, while a couple of tables studied dessert menus, I asked her if she knew Ollie. I described him to her.

'Well, Charlie, you *are* getting to know the village, aren't you?' she said, rolling her eyes. 'If you want to buy drugs in Hampden Green, Ollie's your man.'

'Really?' I said. I don't know why I should have been surprised that a country village should have its own resident dealer. Drugs are everywhere.

'Yeah, and he is to dealing what Whitfield is to construction, that is, crap. He nearly got beaten to death a couple of years ago when he tried to rip off a couple of guys from London.'

Jess paused, in exasperation. 'He's an idiot,' she carried on, 'he got found in a lay-by on the Speen road. He said it was a mugging.' She shook her head disbelievingly as if anyone would be so stupid as to fall for so transparent a lie. 'Yeah, right, Ollie, in the middle of nowhere,' she said scornfully. 'The only things off the Speen road are fields with cows and livery yards. Who did that then, who put you in hospital for a fortnight, the Pony Club?'

Time passed. I prepared seventeen meals as well as a fair amount of cakes. It was a pleasantly busy morning. All in all, I was doing a lot better than I'd hoped for. Some of it would be down to curiosity, but I was providing very good food at bargain prices. When I made more of a name for myself, I could build in bigger margins, but right now, getting myself established was the driving factor.

While I was cooking I reflected on Slattery and his attitude to me. If he was so worried about crime and keeping his village – this village – free of it, why wasn't he concentrating more on Ollie and less on me? It was puzzling.

'What are you going to do about the graffiti on the gate?' Jess was back. She put her tray down.

I looked up from what I was doing.

'Paint over it I suppose.' It was a sore point. I hate painting, any form of DIY really. I'd have to sand it down, find paint that matched the grey the gates were painted in – come to think of it they needed repainting completely, I couldn't afford the time and I couldn't afford a professional painter.

'My cousin Francis would do it for you, he's cheap,' Jess said.

'Is he any good?'

'Good enough. It's not the Sistine Chapel,' she said. 'He's a handyman and landscape gardener, he'd do a reasonable job.'

'If you could ask him. . .'

'Sure.'

She took away the food for Table Three. Later she came in and said, 'One of the customers said he would like a word about doing some catering for a party.'

Great, I thought, with satisfaction. 'Oh, good,' I said, then, 'do you know him?'

I immediately thought, stupid question. Jess seemed to know everyone in the village, but that's obviously part of the village way of life. Hardly surprising.

More Jess facts that I had learned during service: she'd been born in the maternity department of the local hospital in Wycombe, the nearby big town, grew up in Hampden Green. She had been educated in the village primary school, then back to Wycombe for a grammar school education.

Her reply to my question entailed a rolling of her expressive, dark-brown eyes. Not a good sign.

'Him. Justin West.' The name was delivered with the sort of enthusiasm with which you open a buff envelope marked HMRC.

'What's he like?' I was curious to know what Justin had done to attract Jess's obvious ire.

'He's a yoga teacher, very New Age.' Jess's voice was sniffy. Four A-stars at A level in science subjects and the legacy of relentless, Boolean mathematics had left their mark on her view of the value of mysticism. She clarified, 'New Age in terms of beliefs, not years on this planet.'

'Well,' I said, 'I'm no spring chicken myself.'

She looked at me. 'I suppose he is younger than you, now I come to think of it,' she conceded. Cheers Jess. She continued, 'And he's a hypocrite. He owns or part-owns a very swanky health club in Slough that's supposed to be incredibly expensive. I don't think catering for the rich is very eco-friendly, do you?' she added sniffily.

Frankly, if the rich wanted to come and eat here they

were more than welcome. Provided they tipped. I've met more than one skinflint millionaire.

I went through into the restaurant to meet the object of Jess's ageist, rationalist scorn.

I'd never met a male yoga teacher and was curious. Plenty of female ones. In my limited experience yoga teachers are women and they tend to be cut from the same cloth. Often with a background in dance or gymnastics, they are genial, usually fairly affluent, good-humouredly bossy, and obviously very flexible physically. I wanted to see the male version.

First impressions: wide, sincere eyes, long, dark hair – held in a top-knot, quite tanned or naturally brown, slim, wiry body, boho kind of dress sense, silver jewellery, late thirties so, as Jess had kindly pointed out, slightly younger than me. He was quite good-looking.

He was drinking herbal tea. To be expected.

'Hi, so good to meet you,' he said. His voice was low-pitched and husky. He made eye contact with me, as if I was super-important.

I listened as he spoke, giving details of the proposed party. A hundred people, mid-February, a fifteen hundred-pound budget. I liked what I was hearing. A chance to showcase and show off. I was delighted.

I was aware of a kind of stiff-backed resentment from Jess as Justin and I ran through proposed menus. Jess moved around the restaurant deliberately clattering things. If she'd been an animal, a cat say, her fur would have been on end, angrily bristling.

'It's for the feast of Imbolc,' he said, meaningfully. 'Perhaps you have heard of it?'

I confessed my ignorance of pagan festivals. He leaned forwards towards me and said, 'Maybe you'd like to come over tonight to discuss the menu, we could finalise things, get that over with.'

'Yeah, that'd be great. Where do you live?' I said.

He pointed out of the window. 'On the green, the Kiln House.' He stood up with an easy athleticism. He was slightly taller than me. 'Eight-thirty suit you?'

'Fine, I'll see you then,' I said.

He smiled at me then moved lithely out of the restaurant. I went back into the kitchen. Jess stood at the fridge, her arms folded. Her expression was as cold as the machine that she was leaning against.

'What!' I protested. Judging by her face Justin and I might as well have been kissing passionately in the restaurant.

'So, eight-thirty, his place' – her eyes narrowed – 'alone'. She stressed the word.

I frowned. 'Stop it, Jess. What's the matter with him? He only wants me to do a party.'

'Oh, I'm sure he'd love a party with you.'

'Not that kind of party, Jess,' I protested.

'Huh.' Frowny face.

At this point I grew slightly cross. 'He's a customer, Jess. It's business, not a date.'

'That man has a reputation, Charlie you should steer well clear.' Jess's voice was haughtily dismissive. 'He made a pass at my auntie once. Mummy was furious. She's boycotted his yoga class ever since.'

Oh, grow up, Jess, I thought, uncharitably.

'Look, Jess. It really is none of your business, and, by the way, I'm not your aunt and I'm more than capable of looking after myself.' That was certainly true.

'Yes, it is my business,' she said serenely, 'this might be *your* business' – she waved her arms to encompass the kitchen, and she emphasised the '*your*' as if there was some doubt about it – 'but as *your* employee it's part of my duty to inform you of potential hazards, such as the lecherous Justin.'

I made a placatory gesture. I didn't want to upset Jess, even if she had seemed to have decided that she was running my life.

'Well, Jess, if he makes a pass at me, I shall refuse ever to go to his yoga class. I'll boycott it like your mum.'

'Hmm,' said Jess as she pulled off her apron and shrugged herself into her coat.

'Bet he tries to get you to do down dog.'

Chapter Seven

I walked across the common in the driving rain. The ground squelched underfoot and freezing water ran into my shoes. I tightened my grip on the bag I was carrying containing food samples, my chef's knife and a steel, the tool with a handle used for sharpening knives. A good chef never goes anywhere professionally without their knife or knives. It's so dispiriting if you are in a civilian's kitchen and you need to cut something, you borrow a knife and it's sooo blunt.

I cursed myself for not having taken my car even though it was such a short distance. A couple of days ago the houses where Justin lived would have been lit up by the eerie blue light from his neighbour Whitfield's garden. No longer. I rather missed the obelisk and its eerie blue light filtering through my curtains.

It struck me once more that it was an odd village: the sex-addicted earl, the resident drug dealer, the misanthropic publican, and other social undercurrents of which I was completely ignorant. Still, I didn't need to worry about any of that. I was neutral, I provided food, I was like a utility company, above the fray. All I needed to do was worry about whoever it was in the village who'd got it in for me, the anonymous graffiti artist/hater.

I rang the bell and Justin opened the door.

'Shoes, please,' he said.

I gave him the bag I was carrying to hold, and, balancing awkwardly on one leg, then the other, removed my mud-covered footwear. Justin watched my mono-legged teetering critically; it wasn't very yogic. I bet he could take his shoes off elegantly, perhaps I should sign up for a class. I followed him into the hall. The house was more or less as I had expected: dimly lit, with wall hangings and several Buddhas, fat Chinese ones and slimline Thai. The living room was a profusion of Persian rugs and framed Chakra diagrams. Jazz music played discreetly in the background. Miles Davis, 'Kind of Blue'. Incense was burning in a holder.

I wondered if it was really the kind of atmosphere for a business discussion. Perhaps Jess had been right.

After her lurid warnings, I was half-expecting, no, fully expecting Justin to be wearing some kind of come-hither clothing, something certainly provocative if not positively tarty. A loincloth?

He gestured at a sofa and I sat down. He was wearing sensible black trousers and a baggy jumper, his hair held back in a man bun. He didn't look like a tiger about to pounce. There was though, undeniably, a romantic aura about him. He was fine-featured with large, dark eyes. Time had given him just the right amount of lines to suggest not only maturity but a man with a poetic soul.

'Thanks for coming,' he said brightly and asked if I wanted some wine. I accepted a small glass of red. After that, he sat cross-legged on a chair opposite me, a low coffee table between us. A more or less perfect lotus pose. He got straight to business, no romantic small-talk.

'Now, the party,' he said briskly, 'what did you have in mind?'

'Canapés,' I said, unzipping the food-bag, putting boxes and the knife and steel on the coffee table, 'I brought a selection as examples.'

I opened a container that held asparagus twists with puff pastry, assorted crostini on homemade ciabatta, homemade rye bread, duck rillettes, capers, beetroot gravadlax and celeriac remoulade. Oh, and a selection of vol-au-vents. I think the Seventies are due for a comeback.

Underlining the point, Miles Davis moodily trumpeted away in the background.

Justin leaned forward. 'Oh, God, this so good,' he said, nibbling a disc of rye bread with a very thin circle of goat's cheese topped with a beetroot mousse. He had excellent teeth, I noticed, and a wide, attractive mouth. He filled my wine glass up, and said, 'What then? I mean, after the canapés?'

He stood up in a smooth, effortless gesture. All his movements were sinuously graceful and I noticed how flexible he was. He picked a cushion off the floor, bending over so I could see that he could place his hands flat on the ground. Show-off, I thought.

'A buffet, I think. I've got a few ideas here,' I said, producing a sheet of paper with a flourish.

I had printed off about twenty items which I thought we could narrow down to half a dozen. He took the paper and peered at it in the dim light of the living room.

I was enjoying my evening out. It was nice to be in warm, pleasant surroundings. When I went upstairs at the Old Forge Café it was to yellowing, peeling wallpaper and silence. The legacy of years of neglect. You could see where things had been before Mrs Cope moved out so it was like being haunted by the ghosts of dead chests of drawers and armchairs past. The radiators in my flat didn't work very well and it was bitterly cold. Sometimes I slept in a jumper. Shivering on my mattress.

I sat back and stared at the fire while Justin went through my suggestions.

My flat smelled indefinably of old lady (maybe that's why it was so cold, her malign aura still lingered). Not so this lounge. The burning incense and the effect of the drink, the dim light, smell of patchouli joss-stick, was oddly evocative of student years a quarter of a century before.

He joined me on the sofa and tucked his long legs underneath himself so he was sitting on his heels, facing me. His head was bent studiously over the sheet of paper.

'I like the idea of the chicken and apricot tagine with Moroccan spices,' he said. So did I, it was easy to make and practically foolproof. 'We'll need a vegetarian dish,' he said looking up from the paper, 'about half the guests don't eat meat.'

'It's on the other side. The tagine comes with a harissa sauce to give it a zing for those who want heat. The harissa will go with whatever vegetarian dish you choose, too, it's quite versatile.' He turned the piece of paper over. 'Do you like the idea of the smoked aubergine moussaka?' I asked.

'Yes, but it's a bit too exotic for them,' Justin said, 'as is the Caribbean jerk vegetable curry.'

Oh, I thought. I was disappointed; I had thought both of those would be quite interesting and different.

He put the paper down. 'What about roast vegetable lasagne?' he suggested.

I groaned mentally. How dull was that! No bloody way!

Justin moved slightly closer to me. I wondered if he was about to make some kind of a pass. He refilled my wine glass. Maybe I should have been worried after what Jess had said but I was enjoying my role as expert chef and problem solver.

'Umm, Charlie. . .' he began, but suddenly our cosy tête-a-tête was interrupted.

The ear-splitting noise of a car alarm rent the night, drowning out Miles Davis's trumpet on Justin's expensive Bose stereo system.

'Oh, for heaven's sake. . .'

He glared irritably in the direction of the window. It wasn't a very spiritual, yoga recommended look; Justin was very angry indeed. The moment, if indeed it had been a moment, was ruined. There was the sound of shouts from outside, somewhere on the green, and then a pounding on the front door. He jumped athletically off the sofa and left the room.

I heard voices raised from the hallway: 'Where is he. . .?' An angry male.

'Calm down, Dave.' Justin's voice, exasperated but firm. I sat where I was; I didn't think it my place to interfere with whatever was going on.

'I'll kill the bastard! Where's he hiding!' Then the door of the living room flew open and an enraged figure of a man burst in.

It was Whitfield. I looked at him in astonishment. He was wearing very little: a white silk kimono open to reveal a hairy, flabby stomach and man boobs with a Union flag tattoo across his heart, and a pair of saggy black briefs from which his large, hairy balls hung out of one side on prominent display. He was an eye-catching figure.

He saw me, jabbed an accusing finger. 'You, what are you doing here! Was it you?' He was trembling with rage, his eyes bulging. His balls too, come to that.

Was what me? I wondered, not unreasonably. The trouble was, Whitfield was not a man that you could reason with at the best of times. I'd already tried with the sandwich garnish and failed, and right now was obviously not the best of times. It would be fair to say he was enraged.

I stood up. 'Why don't you calm down and. . .'

'Calm down!' he shouted in outrage, pointing a finger at me. 'You're having a laugh, aren't you? "CALM DOWN!" You bitch!'

I wondered what on earth was going on in Whitfield's mind. Maybe it was the drugs, weed-induced paranoia. Or the booze; you could have stripped paint with his breath.

'Just calm down, Dave,' added Justin. He looked totally helpless, if not panic-stricken. It contrasted very much with his earlier attitude. It struck me that when things kicked off, on the whole you didn't really want a yoga teacher on your side, you wanted someone a bit more robust.

Whitfield advanced on me, like Nemesis, pop-eyed with anger, fists clenched, then to my surprise, tried to grab hold of my collar. I could smell the whisky on his breath, it was overpowering – he was fearsomely drunk. All our advice to calm down had gone unheeded. His flabby builder's tits bounced angrily, the Union flag prominent – patriotism, the last refuge of the scoundrel, I thought. I had no idea what had got into him; quite frankly, the state he was in, neither did he probably.

The time for discussion, I felt, had somehow slipped away. Years of working in fraught kitchens when, back in the day, it was far from a politically correct haven – more like a weird jungle – kicked in. Better men than Whitfield had tried to intimidate me and failed. I grabbed the steel from the coffee table and brought it down hard on Whitfield's head. He stopped in his tracks, stunned and maybe shocked, and I slammed my fist into the side of his head and knocked him down.

Textbook! I thought proudly.

Whitfield made an odd noise, like a loud groan, his legs buckled and he collapsed in a sitting position on Justin's oak coffee table. Fortunately it had been built to last and it withstood the fifteen stone or so of Whitfield crashing down on it.

I rubbed my knuckles; the human head is quite hard.

'My God!' said Justin, staring at the fallen builder, eyes

wide. I wasn't sure if he was impressed or shocked. Maybe he wasn't sure himself.

Whitfield got shakily to his feet. He rubbed the top of his head, then his jaw, looked angrily at me. I can't say I was worried.

'You've got celeriac remoulade all over your balls,' I said, calmly, pointing at his groin with my steel.

'Do what?' He seemed confused. Perhaps it was because I'd nearly knocked him unconscious, perhaps it was the concept of celeriac remoulade. Maybe it was because he'd never been hit by a woman. The element of surprise had most certainly been mine.

I was feeling elated, all that adrenaline coursing through my body. I hadn't hit anyone in seriousness for about three years, not since a huge argument with a restaurant manager turned nasty.

'It's that stuff like coleslaw that's hanging off your bollocks,' I explained patiently. Perhaps he'd like the recipe. We all looked at the offending area of his anatomy, hanging out of his baggy pants. Bits of shredded celeriac in a garlicky, lemon mayo clung to his hairy testes. It was like some kind of horrible sex game. He'd sat down in the remoulade, dunking his balls in the stuff. A sort of mayonnaise tea-bagging.

'I think you should go home and change.' I added, 'It's not a good look.'

Whitfield nodded. He was almost docile now. The blow to the head had quietened him down. He looked down at his groin again and then at us. He seemed somewhat at a loss.

'I'll take him back,' said Justin, rolling his eyes upwards in a 'God give me strength' sort of way. He turned to me. 'Someone's chucked paint over his Ferrari. He chased them and thought they'd hidden in here.'

Well, that explained both Whitfield's presence and his rage. The various Buddhas in the room regarded us with tranquillity, as they would do.

I frowned, puzzled. 'Why would they do that? Hide in here I mean.'

'God alone knows. . .' he said, despairingly, then to Whitfield, 'Come on, let's get you home.' Half supporting the drunk and possibly now concussed builder, he set off out of the living room. 'Back in a minute,' Justin called to me.

A few minutes later he returned, sat down opposite me and poured us both some more wine.

'Where did you learn to fight like that?' he asked, wonderingly.

'Highgate boxing club. My dad ran it, he used to be a pro,' I said. Well, that was true as regards the hook that had felled Whitfield – hitting people with kitchen implements had been my idea. Fusion, I thought, just like cookery. Justin shook his head in admiration.

'I'm so impressed,' he said. I was very pleased with his reaction. Some men don't like independent women, let alone ones who can handle themselves in a fight. It obviously didn't bother Justin.

'So someone chucked paint over his car?'

Justin nodded. 'That's his pride and joy, no wonder he went ballistic. First his pillar thing, now his car. . . I dunno. . .'

'This village is weird,' I said.

He looked surprised. I told him about the 'go home bitch' incident and before that someone reporting me to Slattery for the arson attack on Whitfield.

'Maybe he got to hear about that,' Justin said, 'then when he saw you here. . .'

'Possible,' I agreed. Maybe Slattery had tipped him off. I asked Justin what he thought the policeman had against me.

'Well, I rather think it might be your job,' he said, somewhat sadly. My job?

'What's wrong with being a chef?' I asked, baffled.

'Well,' Justin said, 'the ex Mrs Slattery ran off with a chef. They'd hired him to do the outside catering for a party, ironically to mark their tenth wedding anniversary. It was going to be a big do, a marquee and everything. . .' He looked at me critically, 'And you look a bit like she did, so I think, at a subconscious level he's not favourably disposed towards you.'

He yawned, showing those excellent teeth again. I stared at him, somewhat hungrily.

'Anyway, thanks for coming over. . .'

No moment of attempted seduction had happened. And even if that were on the menu, the moment had obviously passed. There had been no down dog.

Jess would be pleased.

It was time for me to go. We said our goodbyes and as he closed the door I opened the garden gate to cross the common. I looked back at the row of houses. There were no lights on at Whitfield's but in the upstairs window of one of the other houses I could see a silhouette. Slattery, standing in his bedroom surveying Hampden Green like Batman looking out over Gotham.

I squelched home across the fields.

Chapter Eight

At 7.30 that Tuesday morning in January, over three weeks since I had taken ownership of the Old Forge Café, with no inkling of what was about to happen, I pulled my trail shoes on, zipped up my waterproof fleece and started running out of the village along the main road. Lights were on in several houses; it was nearly sunrise but still dark and no one was about. The driving rain stung my eyes as I splashed through the puddles on the tarmac.

I thought about the previous night, the drunken Whitfield and wondered vaguely if Justin had been going to try something on me. I was also thinking about who might have graffitied my gate. I pushed these thoughts away and concentrated on trying not to slip over in the mud of the footpath.

Just out of the village was a single-track road on the left and I ran down this. I hadn't seen a single car, and then as I turned right I heard the flat explosion of a shotgun. That didn't surprise me, the woods and fields around here often echoed with gunfire. It was still pheasant season and, of course, there were always wood pigeon.

I thought nothing of it.

I turned right off the road, through a small gate, over a stile and then on to a footpath that ran diagonally across the huge grass field where about a dozen horses lived. I could see them through the rain over to my right, huddled together. The sky was a deep grey overhead, but there was enough light to see the path, a squelchy brown strip of mud ahead of me. In about an hour's time you might see a dog walker, but right now, the field was deserted.

I started running across it and I heard a second bang, this time much closer. I remember thinking at the time how loud shotguns were. I jogged on, slowly, mindful of my balance, my feet slipping and sliding on the wet mud and, as I approached the boundary hedge that marked the end of the field, I saw a shape lying on the grass near the stile that was let into the hedge on that side.

I slowed to a walk and then came to a horrified standstill.

I had never seen a dead body before. Well, I had, I'd been holding my dad's hand when he died, he had slipped away quietly. This was not the case with what I was looking at now. This guy hadn't gone peacefully, far from it. He would have been face down in the mud, but there was little left of his head. One hand still held the shotgun.

It must have gone off while he was climbing over the stile; one Neoprene booted foot was hooked over the wooden lower step, so his leg was in the air at a 45-degree angle, the rest of him lying sprawled in the mud. The sleeve of his Barbour jacket had ridden up as he had pitched forward into the mud. I recognised the garish tattoos immediately.

Over the other side of the hedge was a private road, a tarmacked drive, which led to the Earl's estate. On the other side of that drive was another stile and another field where the footpath continued. I was in time to see a figure running away. I could make out no details other than the fact it was a person; it could have been a man or a woman.

I stood staring at the body. I remembered Slattery's words: '*If you step a millimetre out of line. . .*'

I stared again at the remains of Whitfield. He'd been noisy, violent and obtrusive in life; his end had followed a similar trajectory. There was nothing that could possibly be done. I knew though that I wanted nothing to do with this. I didn't want Slattery to put two and two together to make five. I'd already been in trouble for running past his house the day his pillar had caught fire; a few hours before, I'd beaten him up, now this.

I also didn't want whoever was running away from the scene of crime to know I'd been a witness, even though I couldn't see who they were, just a shape in an anorak with the hood up, running fast.

I hadn't wanted to be involved in his life. I didn't want to be involved in his death.

Hear no evil. See no evil.

I turned on my heel and ran back to the Old Forge Café the way that I had come. The path was a sea of mud and water and the driving rain obliterated my footprints.

I wasn't going to get involved.

No way. It wasn't my fight.

Chapter Nine

Trying to pretend nothing had happened was not easy. I kept thinking that I had guilt written all over my face. It wasn't like I had actually done anything. I hadn't killed him, I just hadn't reported it. Whose fault was that? DI Slattery, you embittered woman/chef hater, I told myself. It's all down to you.

Anyway, Jess arrived at half-nine and asked how things had gone the night before. She lived at the other end of the village and hadn't noticed the sirens which had filled the air round about eight o'clock. Needless to say, I had. Any moment now, Slattery would be round.

I told Jess about the incident the night before with Whitfield. I left out his balls, leave the man with some dignity. She was delighted. Knowing what I now knew, I felt a bit guilty.

'You really hit him?'

'Yes, Jess, I really did.'

'That's the sickest thing I've heard in a long while! Good for you!'

I busied myself in work, trying (and failing) not to think

of Whitfield's bloody corpse. I carried on with the preparations for the sourdough. I weighed the sourdough starter (a gloopy natural yeast mixture that is mixed in with the flour to produce the carbon dioxide which inflates the dough). It had taken me ages to make; even though it was mainly just flour and water, it had kept going off until I found a recipe that worked. I had wasted kilos of flour. Only mulish stubbornness had kept me going. I'm a bit like that; once I start something I feel compelled to finish it.

I put the flour, starter, sugar and salt into the mixer, fixed the dough-hook on and started it. The battered old machine (another thing that could do with replacing) clanked and whirred into life. It was deafeningly loud.

Jess was pressing butter into small ramekins ready for service.

'Did you enter those figures on that worksheet in Excel?' she asked.

'Errrm, not as such. . .' I said evasively. I didn't really understand Excel, and I certainly couldn't touch type like Jess. She shook her head in exasperation.

I moved on to inspecting the sandwich fillings. Every day before service you need to check that you have everything you need to make what's on the menu. It's called the mise en place list, MEP for short. Even in an outfit as small as mine, this can run to a hundred odd items, from the simple, grated cheese for example, to the complex, langues de chat biscuits or lemon mousse. This was a problem for me; in reality it was my biggest problem. I had too much to do and I couldn't really afford to employ anyone to help me. Not another chef anyway. So I was still working eighteen-hour days, like in London.

I noticed that I'd need to roast off some more topside of beef and make some more horseradish. I added them to the list and groaned mentally. More work.

'And you beat him up!' She was still thinking about the incident the night before. Her tone was admiring.

'I didn't beat him up, I defended myself with reasonable force,' I said. I wasn't keen to get any kind of reputation for violence. That could be viewed as freakish in a woman. It had been hard enough to be accepted as a chef.

'Beefy!' Seemingly that was good, in this context.

'It was a fracas.' I added, 'A minor fracas.'

'He's supposed to be really hard.' She looked me up and down, dubiously.

'Beating up Whitfield will really put you on the map,' she commented. 'It'll be all over the village by now. You'll be famous.'

'Hooray.' I was far from enthusiastic. The shouting, the car alarm, the general pandemonium, had doubtless drawn the attention of neighbours wondering what on earth was going on. Curtains would have been twitched, tongues wagged. A half-naked, traumatised Whitfield being led back to his house with the vandalised car (not forgetting the charred obelisk) by the local yoga teacher. The new restaurant owner retreating to the Old Forge Café. Speculation would presumably run riot.

A threesome that had got seriously out of hand?

A food-related debate that had become heated?

Was I the kind of woman you'd want to do your catering after last night's lurid scene?

I started making meringues to calm myself down. Did you

know that you can make meringues in a glass vacuum bell jar? I've seen it done at a food demonstration: you pump the air out and the meringue swells and swells, but of course, it's utterly inedible. Sometimes the old ways are the best.

'Well,' she said, looking through the door into the restaurant, 'here's DI Slattery. I hope Whitfield hasn't pressed charges.'

I sighed. This was the moment I had dreaded. It was inevitable.

'You bring him in here, Jess, let's see what he wants.'

Jess led Slattery into the kitchen and discreetly left us to it. I looked up from my work, a welcoming smile on my face, the very picture (or so I hoped) of someone who had not come across Whitfield that morning.

'Have you been out this morning?' he asked.

'Did you know that undissolved sugar can lead to grittiness and weeping in a meringue?' was my reply. Anything rather than talk or think about Whitfield. I started folding the white powder into the very white egg mix. It's why I was using icing sugar rather than caster.

I was silent, concentrating on the meringue while I wondered what to say. Better keep it simple. Hope that no one had noticed me running, the dreadful weather had deterred even the die-hard dog walkers. I hadn't met anyone and I had been wearing a balaclava, my hair was hidden as well as my face, my body shapeless under a fluorescent green running fleece.

'I said, where were you this morning?'

'Here.' I tried my smile again. Slattery was impervious to its charms.

'Any witnesses?'

'I lead a lonely life, Detective Inspector, why are you asking?'

'Dave Whitfield was found dead this morning,' he said.

'Oh my God, where?' Shocked face.

'Do you know Five Acre Field?' demanded Slattery.

I shook my head.

'I know some of the paths by sight, from when I go jogging, but I don't know what they're called.'

'He was found by a stile, his shotgun had gone off, there was very little left of his head.'

'Poor old Whitfield,' I said, looking at Slattery with great sincerity. Or so I hoped.

I didn't want to think about Whitfield's head. Or his balls for that matter which kept intruding into my field of consciousness. What a thing to be remembered by.

'So where were you this morning?' Slattery was persistent, I had to give him that.

'Here,' I said again.

'Thing is,' Slattery said, 'I hear you beat Whitfield up last night, the night coincidentally his Ferrari got trashed.'

'Well,' I said, 'that was self-defence, and I had nothing to do with his car.'

Slattery said, casually, 'There is a plausible scenario in that an angry Dave Whitfield was lurking for you on your morning run, saw you, threatened you with his shotgun, there was a struggle and it went off. You would be wholly innocent of murder. . .'

I leaned forwards over the table that divided us.

'I am an innocent woman, Inspector, and I didn't shoot Whitfield, either on purpose or accidentally.'

We looked into each other's eyes. I could see he was itching to arrest me. I wished to God his ex had run off with someone other than a chef. Why not the guy who had put up the marquee?

'Lying to the police is a serious offence,' he said.

'Well, then, it's a good job I'm telling the truth,' I said, somewhat snottily. 'And now, if you don't mind, I'm a busy woman.'

He stared at me with baffled rage.

'I don't like smart-arses,' he said, drawing himself up to his full height, 'and I don't think I like you very much.'

You had to admire his honesty.

'I'm very lovable when you get to know me, DI Slattery,' I said, giving him what I thought was a winning smile. 'We should meet up more, perhaps we'd bond.'

'Well, I'll see you later,' said Slattery, darkly. 'Of that there is no doubt.'

He left, and the restaurant door banged to behind him. I sighed with relief as he disappeared.

Chapter Ten

After that unwelcome excitement, I could start to relax. The morning started slowly – some teas, coffees and cakes – then about twelve o'clock we started to get busy. It was shaping up to be a pleasant, if uneventful lunch, maybe twenty to thirty covers, all fairly straightforward. Not bad for a Tuesday, I thought, I was busier than I'd anticipated. Long may it last.

At half-one, Jess came into the kitchen, deposited some used crockery in the pot-wash area and leaned across the pass. She looked quite excited.

'There's a man out there who wants to speak to you. . .'

'But of course,' I said, nonchalantly, wondering who it might be, 'when you look like I do, Jess, you get used to it. . . What does he want?'

Jess said, 'He says it's personal.'

'That sounds alarming.' I wondered who it was. Various images of random people scrolled through my mind. I slid a sea bream fillet on to a plate and carefully spooned over some beurre noisette and sprinkled chopped dill over it. Sometimes the simple things are best.

'Table two please. . .'

As Jess picked up the plate, I asked, 'What does he look like?' That seemed a sensible question.

'He's gorgeous,' she said, almost open-mouthed.

'Could you be more specific?' I asked.

'Foreign,' she said.

Well, I thought, turning my attention to a dessert cheque, that was descriptive but unhelpful.

'That's a bit vague, Jess,' I replied. 'Is it Vincent Cassel?' I had a bit of a thing about the craggy French actor. I'd been secretly pleased when he split from Monica Bellucci. Being French, he was bound to appreciate good food; I was in with a chance.

'Who?'

'Never mind,' I said. Youngsters, eh! Jess carried on.

'He's very well-dressed, dark, kind of Italian looking. Great shoes.'

She disappeared into the restaurant. I turned back to the stove.

Perhaps it was *Grazia* magazine, perhaps it was Italian *Vogue* come to do a piece on England's hidden villages. I doubted it. Italian, eh? Well, there was one person, but no. No, it couldn't be. Not him. We were history.

Nevertheless, faint alarm bells started to ring.

When I looked up, there was my ex-fiancé on the other side of the pass.

'Hello, Charlie,' said Andrea, 'it's been a while.'

Later that day the butcher called to let me know he had some good venison haunch, was I interested? Yes, I most definitely was. In the afternoon I drove to the butcher's on the outskirts of Wycombe. My windscreen wipers were on full – it was raining again from granite grey skies – how could there be so much rain in one country? The car occasionally jolted badly as I hit yet another pothole in the road concealed by a puddle. I used the time to review the day.

Inevitably, the face of Andrea and all the attendant memories kept floating into my consciousness. To say my emotions were all over the place would be pretty accurate. It had been a year now since the split. Regret, for my past behaviour and what I'd lost; guilt, because I'd severed all ties with him, mainly out of cowardice. There had been another man. Not on Andrea's part, mine.

He was an agency chef with whom I had cooked in an incredibly busy kitchen, sixty-hour weeks, ten hours a day in each other's company in the noisy, cramped, hot-house madness of a Soho kitchen. We worked together drenched in sweat, like well-oiled machinery. Then one night, it just happened; our hands met, then our mouths, then our bodies. I had wrecked everything.

I hadn't wanted to face Andrea, to have an adult discussion. Basically I had run away.

I was amazed that a man as attractive, intelligent and successful as Andrea would even want to see me again. I'm not sure I would have wanted to.

But to be honest I didn't know what to think.

I concentrated on what I could comprehend: food, rather than the mysteries of life.

Lunchtime service had been busy-ish. I could feel my takings growing. It was a good feeling.

Every night I had done my accounts with a meticulous

attention to the bottom line. Not using Excel, sorry, Jess. I didn't have much wiggle room. Money was tight. But I estimated that I now had enough money coming in to hire a kitchen porter, or in more normal speak, someone to wash up for me.

Now it looked as though I might be able to afford to share the load.

I mentioned it to Jess before she left.

'So do you know anyone who might be interested? You mentioned your cousin a while back.'

The gate still needed painting. I had run a brush over the offending words in the interim. It looked a mess, but at least the message was hidden.

'I'll speak to him.' She had another go at the question she had wanted answered all day long. 'So are you going to tell me about him?'

I had endured four hours of Jess's silent curiosity which had taken the form of hints and reminiscences about former boyfriends – 'but he was like. . . way too clingy. . . do you know what I mean?' – in the hope I would follow suit. She was obviously fascinated by my ex.

I put my chef's knife down and said, 'OK, Jess, his name is Andrea Di Stefano, he's Anglo-Italian, his dad's from Ancona, that's by the seaside in Le Marche in central Italy, he's an investment banker and we were together for four years and then we split up. A year ago.'

And since then my personal life had been an extended train wreck – apologies to all trains for the comparison.

Jess's eyes were alive with excitement; all I had managed to do was to whet her appetite for more.

70

'And what's he doing here?'

'He was in the area, Jess, and he thought he would pop in and say hello, which he did.'

Jess made a snorting noise. 'Nobody is ever "in this area". Not unless you've got a damn good reason.'

I considered that, it was true.

'Anyway,' I said in a tone that drew a line under the discussion. 'Kitchen porter positions. . .'

'No need to get aggressive.'

'I am not "aggressive",' I said, in an aggressive tone. 'Kitchen porter?'

She harrumphed irritably at the termination of our Andrea discussion, but she could see that I had no intention of taking it any further. She conceded defeat and frowned thoughtfully.

'My cousin, Francis. He's not the brightest though. . .'

'That's fine, I mean it would suit someone who. . .' Who what? Who wasn't over-burdened with brains, was what I was going to say, but that seemed a bit cruel. It did have the advantage of being true though. Being a kitchen porter is not a particularly wonderful job. It's not something you aspire to. If, at school, you were to say, 'When I grow up I want to wash dishes for a living', then your horizons would have been considered disappointingly narrow.

'I'll get him to come tomorrow. He's a nice guy; you can see what you think.'

I finished doing my prep for the next day and cleaned the kitchen. Soon I'd have someone to help me do that. Unless he had the brains of a snail, the job was his.

As I swept, cleaned and mopped the floor I remembered

with a wry smile the first night of my professional career when I'd worked in a busy restaurant, and being surprised that we, the chefs, had to clean up after service.

'Do we have to do that?' I'd asked.

The sous chef had looked at me like I was insane. 'Well, who else did you think would clean the kitchen, the elves?'

'Cleaners,' I had said.

'Idiot,' he'd said, shaking his head. 'You're not in a bloody office, get busy with that brush.' It had been a steep learning curve.

I put the mop away and looked with pleasure at the gleaming kitchen, its shining steel work-surfaces, its neatness, the pleasing sense of order and efficiency. That is, if you didn't look too closely at the malfunctioning equipment, but boy, was it clean! I have reached that stage in life where I find I can take a huge amount of pleasure in the small things that are on offer. Probably, given my hand to mouth existence, it was just as well.

I thought with regret of Andrea. God, had I made a terrible mistake. And been paying for it ever since.

After the butcher's I did some clothes shopping in the New Year sales. I came away with a new blouse and skirt. Halfway round John Lewis I realised that I was probably subconsciously buying something to wear if Andrea asked me out. I got angry with myself. 'I don't need any validation from you!' I muttered, slightly too loudly. A man standing in front of me turned and asked if I was speaking to him.

Later, still smarting from that incident, I went and ate an early, solitary meal in a restaurant in the centre of Wycombe.

As you drive into it there is a sign that says it is an historic market town. This makes it sound attractive. The reality is that any trace of historicity was long since erased. It is large, brutal, long and sprawling. Its centre is dominated by a roundabout surrounded by lots of mini roundabouts in a mandala-like pattern. It would be confusing but the roundabout is surrounded by landmark buildings of an unmissable size: an ugly Sixties-style hospital; a concrete fire station; and a university (formerly the Technical College), another large, less than architecturally inspired building.

The Raj was a fairly typical Indian, the menu could have been predicted by more or less anyone who regularly ate curries anywhere: all the usual suspects were there, but what it lacked in originality it made up for in quality.

I enjoy eating alone. Probably just as well these days. I nibbled a poppadom and thought about Andrea. It had been strange seeing him. He looked great as ever, sleek and expensive like the car he was driving. An Alfa Romeo, parked outside the cafe. His hair used to be long, well, long for investment-banking, now it was cut stylishly short; his eyes were still as beautiful as ever. I remembered how, occasionally, I used to run my finger over his Roman nose which he always thought was too big for his face but wasn't. When Jess had described him as gorgeous she wasn't wrong. He was class.

We had talked briefly, any awkwardness was on my part. I was conscious that my chef's whites were stained here and there with food, that I smelled strongly of the chargrill and sweat. I had an angry weal on my forearm where I'd brushed against the red-hot interior of the oven and a couple of fingers were adorned with blue sticking plasters where I'd nicked myself with a knife.

I was looking and feeling less than gorgeous.

He had said he wanted to see how I was doing, what I was up to. Our conversation, my part of it anyway, had been stilted and awkward. Andrea was, as always, coolly amused. As ever, he seemed very self-possessed, very self-contained. I asked him what he was up to. Engaged to be married. Oh, I had said, feeling suddenly sick in the pit of my stomach like I'd been kicked there – congratulations.

Part of me had been hoping that he wanted to re-connect, but it looked more like he was there to formally declare that we were irrevocably over. That he had moved on.

Well, good for you, Andrea, I thought bitterly. I am happy to know that. That was certainly quick off the mark. But, I reflected, that's often the way these things happen; people get married on the rebound from another. Nice of you to take the trouble to drive out and tell me.

Then I thought, maybe she was an old flame? Or maybe some woman in his office who'd been praying, lighting candles in church, for Andrea to leave me and notice her. Stop it, I told myself severely. What's happened has happened and fevered speculation is not helping any.

Perhaps he'd invite me to the wedding.

Maybe I'd win the catering contract.

I turned my mind away from the past to the present, back to what I was doing. Away from the 'might have beens' and 'if onlys'.

I ate my way slowly through my onion bhaji and lamb vindaloo. Andrea had never liked Indian food. Ha! And he hadn't been keen on me tasting of onion when we kissed. I ate some more onion and coriander salad. I can eat what I want now, Andrea!

It was also nice, ordering things I had no intention of replicating in my own kitchen. Whenever I eat out I inevitably find myself, assuming I'm enjoying it, assessing whether or not to copy it for my own menu. All chefs do it, that's why certain dishes or styles of cooking resemble the spread of illnesses. You can trace it like an epidemic.

Like the mania for fractions on a menu when it comes to pricing, for example, 5 for £5.50. Infuriating. Ditto the small plates/large plates schtick. A couple of years ago it was a kind of list of a dish's constituent parts – for example 'loin of pork, duchesse potatoes, rosemary, caramelised apple'. And lower case lettering on everything. Maybe even worse than comic Sans typeface on a menu in my opinion. That kind of thing. Or pork belly – decades in the wilderness, then it's everywhere. Or painting every gastro-pub grey inside.

Next year it'll be something different, God knows what but you'll know it when you see it.

The Raj, as its unrepentant, unmade-over, politically incorrect name suggested, was totally free of modern trends. They wouldn't be blow-torching lettuce here. With its flock wallpaper, plastic bamboo and palm trees, 'Indian' lager (brewed in Romford), it could hardly be more reassuringly clichéd.

I could enjoy it without too much analysis. Like I'd decided not to analyse my brief chat with Andrea.

If I could. . .

I still had my venison sitting in the back of my car. It was three degrees outside in the car park, about the temperature of my fridge. Rain was still beating down. All in all, a cold, miserable evening.

I had a book to read, *Saulnier's Repertoire*, which was a cookbook (of sorts, you have to know what you are doing – it is more a helpful list of ingredients). The *Repertoire* features Escoffier's recipes; he was a nineteenth-century French chef who really created what we now know as fine dining. There aren't many culinary geniuses around, but he was one of them. He said that the greatest dishes are simple. If you look at his recipe books, well, they don't seem that simple to me.

French cooking is still the benchmark for me, modern French is my preferred style.

Anyway, I looked up 'deer' in the book which appeared to be *chevreuil* in French. I wanted some new ideas to play around with. My edition is mostly in English but the headings and sub-headings are in French – and made a note that chestnuts were a good idea.

I had the haunch of venison, roe deer, and I was going to cut medallions from it (what was left I would use for stock) and pan-fry it, serving it with fondant potato. I was toying with how to work chestnuts into the dish.

I had my book propped up on the cruet set when I was distracted by someone leaning over my table.

'Fan of Escoffier, eh! You must be Charlie Hunter!'

I looked up. The voice was loud, confident, expensive and its owner – tweed jacket, tie, cords and brogues – belonged with it. Countrified, moneyed, assured. The kind of man who makes English people dislike the English.

He had a beard, neatly trimmed; not a hipster lumberjack beard, his was conventional, reddish brown that matched his thinning hair, and a bit of a paunch under the check shirt. His cheeks were finely cross-hatched with broken veins. Had I met him before? He seemed familiar, or was it just the type of person he represented?

'Luke Montfort.' I shook the proffered hand. 'I live near the village,' he explained.

'Oh. . .'

'Anything in here about mousses?' he slurred. I could smell the booze on his breath and then he picked up my copy of Saulnier, unasked. He leafed through it, squinting at the text. I felt a stab of anger at the way Montfort loomed irritatingly over my table. I fought down a desire to snatch the book back off him. His smile seemed unbearably smug, patronising.

'Interesting,' he said, weighing the slender, yellow-jacketed book in his hand, 'but nothing about mousses. I tell you what, show me a good mousse and I'll show you a good cook. Do you agree?'

'Sure,' I said. Anything to get rid of him. He was starting to make me extraordinarily cross. Part of it was the presumption on his part that I should want to share time and space with him. Part of it was the overwhelming waves of self-worth that billowed from him, like dry ice haloing a performer on-stage.

The silence prolonged itself.

'Do you want to join us for a drink?' he asked.

He indicated the rear of the restaurant. I looked the way he was pointing and in the reflection of a conveniently angled mirror I saw a man I didn't recognise, Ollie Scott and, of all people, DI Slattery. I could see him looking at us with alarm, obviously relishing the prospect of my company about as much as I did his. What on earth were they doing together? Especially Ollie, wasn't he supposed to be a drug dealer? I took a mouthful of Diet Coke. Join them? What a depressing thought.

It was quite tempting to tell the truth: 'No, I can't think of anything worse.'

'No, I'm fine, thanks' is what I actually said.

Montfort, unaware of my mental debate, looked down at me and smiled again.

'Well, I'll leave you to your cogitations. Put mousse on the menu, I'll come.'

Everyone's an expert, aren't they?

'Indeed,' I said, 'I'll make a note.' I made a mental note, *No mousse on menu, do not encourage Montfort at all costs.*

He re-joined his companions. I quickly called for the bill and left.

Chapter Eleven

It was Thursday and I began work in the kitchen at eight. I'd already been up for two hours, running through the South Bucks countryside in the cold drizzle for forty-five minutes. The going was very treacherous underfoot and sometimes I would have to squelch around flooded fields. This was followed by a tepid shower courtesy of the dreadful plumbing in my bathroom. The shower wasn't a shower per se, it was one of those rubber things, shaped like a Y that you fit over the taps. I'd last seen one of those when I was a catering student in a hideous student flat, many, many years ago.

One day, I promised myself, when I got rich, I would have a power shower. What a dream; some yearned for a super-yacht, others for fame and status – I just wanted hot water on my skin. Well, I thought, as I towelled some warmth into my skin, at least I had a fulfillable dream.

Then downstairs, yawning and tired, another huge mise en place list to complete before service.

Jess arrived half an hour early and we shared coffee while I told her about bumping into Slattery and the others the previous night.

'God, that slime ball Luke Montfort!' Jess was scathing.
'So you know him then?' I asked.

'I was at school with his daughter; she's a stuck-up bitch,
by the way.' She paused to accurately cut the coffee and
walnut cake that I had made into quarters, prior to cutting
each quarter into thirds. That was not for us, that was for
sale. She took a step back to admire her handiwork.

'Yes, I know him, he's just really creepy. Not the kind
of man you would want to sit next to if you're a girl. He
tried it on with a couple of my friends – and me come to
that, when I was fifteen. Mr Wandering Hands. . .'

She put two fingers in her mouth and mimed throwing
up, rolling her eyes at the horrible thought of the aged
pervert Montfort and his paedo tendencies.

'I didn't know Slattery knew him, but he was a friend of
Whitfield's – that's almost certainly how he got his permission to put up that tower thing in his garden.'

'The obelisk?'

She nodded. 'The obelisk. Montfort's head of the council
planning permission department. . . he wields a lot of
power, he lives very well on a not particularly high salary.'

Does he now, I thought. My mind filed that away in my
folder marked 'Whitfield'. In my mind his death and the
graffiti on my gate were somehow linked, as was the
complaint that had been made to Slattery about me.

By association maybe, my mind drifted to Whitfield's
neighbour. Justin hadn't called, but I wanted him to. I kind
of liked him, even if he'd proved ineffective during the
Whitfield incident and I'd had to take over. But I was used
to crisis management. I also wanted confirmation, with a

hefty deposit, of the Imbolc festival booking. Perhaps I should start going to his yoga class. I could see a lot more of him then.

'Moving on, Jess,' I said, briskly, 'let's think about work.' We went over to the kitchen work-surface.

'OK, talk me through today's specials.' She put on a serious face.

'This is the pan-fried venison.'

I quickly seared off some slices of venison for her in a small frying pan and while it rested made a speedy sauce from the juices in the pan deglazed with balsamic vinegar, madeira, reduced stock, juniper berries and cranberry sauce, served topped with blackberries. It came on a bed of kale with a fondant potato.

Jess ate it with relish, then the specials dessert which was pear and blueberry pudding with Chantilly cream. She had a surprisingly hearty appetite but her stomach seemed ironing-board flat despite the astonishing amount she ate. Mine is too, but the amount of effort I need to keep it that way is immense.

'That is bloody good,' she said, 'that meat melts in the mouth. How do you get it so tender?'

'I don't overcook it.' No great mystery.

'It's delicious.' She smiled, wistfully, 'Mummy's a dreadful cook.'

Thank God for people like your mother, I thought. I don't need home-grown competition.

'Well, if you could push it to the customers, I'd be grateful. Tell people it comes pink, it'll be tough if I cook it any longer. They can't have it medium or well-done.' I thought back to the question that I didn't want to ask but needed to. 'When do you go back to uni?'

'Summer term begins in April,' she said. I sighed. What would I do without her?

'You were going to ask your cousin. . . ?' I started to ask.

'Francis? I did. . .' she began, when there was an almighty bang on the kitchen door and I looked around, startled. It was like someone was trying to break it down. Slattery, I thought, come to arrest me.

'Ah,' said Jess, opening the door; it wasn't the police. 'Here he is. . . speak of the devil.'

Her cousin Francis was of medium height and solidly built. Very solidly built. He was red-faced, with eyes that were popping out of their sockets. His hair was straw blond. He had a head that seemed to be perfectly spherical, like a football. He looked like an amiable Viking, too good-natured to be of much use on the pillaging front, but a dab hand with an oar.

I had always thought of myself as strong and I had good grip strength. We shook hands and I suppressed a groan of pain. I had a rethink about my physical prowess. Francis was hugely powerful. He had old-fashioned strength, not like a gym bro, more like a powerlifter. He wasn't buffed, or toned, he wasn't jacked, he was just built like a proper, old-fashioned weightlifter.

'I'm Francis,' he announced, staring around him as if terrifically pleased to be there in my kitchen. He smiled at me, he smiled at Jess, he smiled at the Hobart oven, he smiled at the mixer. He smiled at the chargrill. He reminded me irresistibly of a large, friendly, none too bright dog, a Labrador or a Golden Retriever.

I gave him one of my chef's jackets to wear and his arm muscles packed the white cotton fabric of the sleeves like sausage meat does its casing. Arms like a blacksmith.

'Where do you work at the moment, Francis?' I asked.

'In a garden centre and nurseries, my Dad's a gardener' – he frowned –'but they've cut my hours so I'm looking for a new job.'

'Well, no time like the present,' I said. 'Let's get started.' He beamed at me. 'Have you worked in catering before?' I asked.

'No.' He smiled at me some more and didn't elaborate or add anything, the smile went on and on.

'Are you interested in food?' I asked, in a helpful way.

He frowned, thinking. You could hear the wheels turn.

'I like nuggets,' he said, after a long while.

'Oh well, that's a start,' I said, cheerfully. 'Let's begin with some basic vegetable preparation.'

The morning rolled on, with decidedly mixed results.

Francis was great, great at washing up. I tried to get him to cut vegetables for me, nothing fancy. Disastrous.

We surveyed his attempts to cut carrots into batons. A more irregular array of orange shapes would be hard to imagine. Hacked to buggery, as my former head chef would have said.

'I don't think I'm very good at this,' said Francis, surveying the carroty carnage.

I scratched my head; that was true. I tried to think of a way of conveying mild disappointment with an encouraging hint that maybe there was light at the end of a fairly dark tunnel.

'I'm as much use as a chocolate teapot,' he said gloomily. I was to find out as I got to know him he was a repository of these old-fashioned sayings.

'It's a wise man who knows his limitations,' I said, patting him on the shoulder. It was like touching the massive muscle of a carthorse.

Francis made to tip his efforts into the bin.

'Whoa, tiger,' I said, 'never throw anything away until you've cleared it with me. They'll do for soup. Now, let's try you on potatoes. . . maybe we'll have more success with those.'

We didn't.

The day wore on.

Jess bustled in and out, efficiently serving and charming about thirty customers. We sold all the venison and I had the satisfaction of crossing out several items that were on the specials board. I converted Francis's carrots into swede and carrot mash, and carrot and coriander soup.

'When we serve this,' I said to Jess apropos the soup, 'remind me to sprinkle it with fresh chopped coriander. If you don't remind me, I'll forget.'

She wrinkled her nose as she sniffed it. 'I can't say I care for it very much,' she said.

Francis dropped a couple of plates. I winced as the horrible sound of smashing crockery filled the room. 'Sorry! I was in a bit of a pickle with the dishwasher.'

I shrugged, and carried on with the coriander conversation. 'Coriander's not popular on the whole in Europe, but there you go. . . I'm not personally a fan of carrots myself, while we're on the subject, but it's not all about us, is it, Jess?'

A typical service, heads down, no nonsense gallop. I had the advantage that I was accountable to nobody other than myself and the customers. I didn't have to placate some nutcase head chef or worry about some weak-link co-worker. I didn't have to consult spec sheets to make sure that the plate was exactly as it should be. I also knew exactly what had and had not been done prep-wise.

I was always angsty about prep. Some chefs, and some very good ones at that, were very gung-ho in a kind of 'it'll be all right on the night' way. I wasn't.

It is always nightmarish when you open a tub that should contain, say, pickled aubergine, to find it empty, when the dish it goes with is sitting three-quarters assembled in front of you and you have to rack your brains to think of an adequate way out while more cheques arrive and the head chef is calling for X, Y and Z to be done at the same time. So many things to do it feels like your head is going to explode, and all the while more orders are flooding into the kitchen.

That was the plus side. Everything that should have been done, was done.

The minus side was that I had to do everything. I taught Francis to use the deep-fat fryer for the French fries and onion rings that went with the steak – so that was one job I didn't need to do, although he did spark concern with his habit of staring at the frothing oil as it bubbled precariously upwards, threatening to flood the kitchen with hot fat. He seemed transfixed, unable to move.

'Francis, for God's sake, lift that basket, that oil's about to go everywhere!'

He continued to stare in fascination at the 180-degree centigrade oil, rising ever upwards, a potential geyser of boiling oil, eight litres or so, ready to explode.

'FRANCIS!'

'FRANCIS, FFS!'

'Oh, sorry, chef.'

And so it went. Eventually the long day drew to a close and I patted Francis on his back and we agreed that the job was his. Watching him walk away across the yard outside the kitchen, I wondered if I'd made a terrible mistake.

Chapter Twelve

I leaned against the pass, stretched and yawned. I was tired and faintly depressed. It wasn't just the volume of food prep that was getting me down. Mrs Cope's legacy of duff machinery was getting to me, no matter how clean I managed to get it. Most people tend to think that professional kitchens are marvellously equipped with state-of-the-art machinery and gadgets. I have seen kitchens where this is true, but in general the money gets spent on what the customers see, the restaurant itself, leaving the chefs to struggle back stage. I so needed new equipment. At night I went online and drooled at industry equipment like a man staring avidly at hard-core porn.

I turned on the radio in the kitchen. Beech Tree FM news, the local radio station, was on.

'The mysterious death of a well-known local builder in the South Bucks area is being treated as suicide by the local police. A spokesman for Thames Valley Police said that nobody was being sought in connection with the incident.

Meanwhile, flood alerts have been issued along the Thames, particularly in Marlow and Cookham as water levels continue to rise. . . And now, here's Steps. . .'

I sighed and turned off the radio. So that was that. I was in the clear, although Whitfield still seemed an unlikely suicide victim, unless suicides in a field with a gun usually have an accomplice. I was thinking of the figure I had seen that morning running off into the distance. But it wasn't my problem. And that, thank God, was official. It was a big load off my mind. My mind then moved on to another mystery. I make my own stock for my own jus. It's time-consuming and costly and a fair bit of work, but the result – a dark, rich, flavoursome demi-glace, as the reduced stock is called – is well worth it. Escoffier was big on the virtues of a good stock, he said stock is everything. I kind of agree.

That's five to ten kilograms of beef bones, which I roast in the oven for twenty-five minutes in a shallow tray, for colour and flavour. Then I put them in an enormous stockpot together with a mirepoix of onions, celery and carrots, fill it up with water, add a bouquet garni – a bundle of parsley, thyme and bay leaves tied up with string – cover and leave it on the stove overnight, ticking over at a very low heat.

Then, in the morning, with a spider, which is a kind of hybrid of a sieve and a spoon, the size of a small badminton racquet, I remove all the bones and vegetables and bouquet garni and leave the liquid to cool. I had done that yesterday and, huffing and puffing – it weighed a ton – moved the gigantic pan. Where was Francis when you needed him?

He could have done that with one hand. I took it to the yard at the back of the kitchen where in addition to the bin area I have an out-house where there is a freezer and a dry store. The air temperature in the out-house was about five degrees, fridge temperature, so I was happy to leave it there for a bit. Today I went to fetch it from where I had left it. I couldn't find it.

I scratched my head; I was puzzled. I found the stockpot, cleaned and gleaming, but where was my stock?

At half past nine Francis arrived. His honest-looking face was freshly shaved and he'd smartened his clothes up, although they were badly rumpled – perhaps I should teach him how to iron. Nothing could be done about his blond hair which poked up and out like a bird's nest.

'Hi, chef, what do you want me to start with today?'

'Francis, where's the stock?' I asked.

He frowned. 'Stock, what stock, chef?'

For a moment I wondered if I was going mad.

'The stuff that was in this pan.' I opened the cupboard and pointed to the stockpot.

'That dirty water?'

Icy fingers clutched around my heart.

'What did you do with it?' My voice was strangled.

'Well, I threw it away!' He looked both hurt and puzzled. He knew from my expression and tone of voice that he'd done something bad, but he wasn't sure quite what. His resemblance to a dog was even more marked: one that had let its master down in a way it simply couldn't understand. If he had had a tail it would have wagged apologetically.

I nearly wept. All that work, all that time, all that money, for nothing. Twenty litres of prime stock, literally down the plughole. I counted to ten, my lovely, lovely stock. . . gone! Francis's big, beefy red face looked at me with agonising remorse.

'Please, Francis,' I said through gritted teeth, 'I've already told you once: never throw anything away without asking me first!'

'I'm sorry, I didn't realise it was valuable. I'm sorry,' he apologised again. 'I'm as much use as a lead parachute.' He looked like he might burst into tears.

I sighed, amazingly I managed to control myself. I didn't know whether I wanted to cry or scream, but I did neither.

I thought of the artist Louise Bourgeois, one of my heroes. She wasn't a chef, but nobody's perfect. She admired spiders she said, not just for their industry but because when one of their intricate webs is destroyed, they don't make a scene or go to pieces, they get on and make another one.

That's what I'd have to do. Make some more. I felt my heart, not exactly break, but twinge alarmingly. Francis was killing me.

'Never mind,' I said, through teeth so gritted I could feel the enamel cracking, 'let's put it behind us and move on. Now. . .'

I pointed to the Hobart oven, a double oven with a steam function that, to me, had been one of the selling points of the restaurant. It was an amazingly good piece of kit, the kind of thing you might find in a much bigger kitchen.

'Could you give that a clean?' I gave him some degreaser and heavy rubber gloves and a face mask. 'Go easy with that stuff, it's toxic, and be gentle with the oven, it's quite delicate.'

'Will do, chef.' He opened the door, nearly tearing it off its hinges. He gave me an apologetic look. Don't say anything, I thought. I smiled encouragingly.

By ten o'clock, God knows how, Francis had broken it.

Storm clouds were beginning to gather around my new life.

First the dead Whitfield, now my dead oven.

I knew which one I would miss more.

Chapter Thirteen

The following day I got up early as usual. It was still dark and still raining. It had now been going on for days but in truth, it felt like forever. A flood warning had been broadcast on local radio before I actually got up. The upper Thames was swollen and high, and Marlow High Street and the church were threatened by the rising waters.

I got up off my mattress, shivering in the draughty, chilly bedroom with its malfunctioning, gurgling radiators. I'd tried draining them, to no effect. I needed a plumber, but I couldn't afford one.

I was safe, though, at least from flooding. Hampden Green lies on top of one of the Chiltern Hills and if it ever floods then the whole country will be more or less under water. I didn't feel like going out for a run, and the ground off-road would be horribly slippery with mud, so I did some yoga.

I lay on my back panting from exertion. The yoga made me think of Justin. Why hadn't he been in touch? Was it because I'd beaten up Whitfield and that had put him off? Maybe he didn't like women chefs – like Slattery, but without the emotional baggage. Maybe he was thinking of someone else for that catering contract. I don't like being pushy, but I really should get in touch with him. God knows I needed the money.

To take my mind off things, I showered in the icy bathroom.

There's a lot of talk these days about the health value of cold exposure. As I tremblingly pulled on my chef's whites, freezing after my wash I thought, I should live to be a hundred. But it was a high price to pay. I went down the stairs and into the kitchen.

I only had one small electric oven instead of my giant Hobart (you clumsy bastard, Francis) so I thought I'd better spread the load through the day. By nine o'clock I'd made two Victoria sponges, one lemon flavoured with zest and juice, the other a ginger cake with stem ginger in it. I had some Crabbies ginger wine and I thought I would either flavour some cream with it or maybe make a kind of syrup.

At 9.30 I had a fish delivery from the company I used, A Safe Plaice. Kenneth, the fish guy, had been to Harrow, not specifically the London borough, but the posh school, a rival to Eton. He was what they call an Old Harrovian, immensely tall, immensely posh. It kind of made you wonder what he was doing driving a fish van. Suspect somewhere along the line, life had gone horribly wrong for him. He should be on the moors grouse-stalking or in a posh London club, but here he was with a van full of dead fish. I worked in a fish restaurant once. After a month or so I couldn't get the smell off me. Not fish per se, just a weird kind of indefinable musty odour. I became very popular with cats.

His voice was incredibly upper-class, languid, as polished as the hand-made brogues he favoured. I've got a bit of a thing about shoes. So, clearly, had Kenneth.

'I've got a special on Cromer crab today,' he drawled. He made King Charles sound like he was from a sink housing estate. The vowel in 'crab' went on and on and on: 'craaaaaaa-aaab'.

'Are they good? Dressed or undressed?' I asked.

'They're whole crab, they're bloody good, bloody marvellous.' ('whole craaaaab. . . bloodgood. . . blooodmaaaaarvlous')

'I'll take four.'

'Good man,' said Kenneth gravely. I'm a woman, I'm not sure he'd noticed, maybe it's a public school thing.

'Are you off to the King's Head?' I asked. The aspirational Michelin place around the corner intrigued me. I was dying to see their kitchens and have a good nose around. The thing is, the star isn't just awarded for blinding food. It's everything: surroundings, service quality and above all consistency at that level.

I can cook competently, on occasion faultlessly, but when times are busy and there's only me in the kitchen, well, inevitably sometimes things are less than perfect. At Michelin level, however, everything should be faultless, not just sometimes. If you play tennis, you might play like Federer for one game. But to do it over and over and over again, that's a different matter.

'Yes, and then I'm popping in to see Ropey.'

'I'm sorry?' I said.

'Ropey, the Earl.' He looked down at me from his great

95

height, his brow furrowed. Oh, the Earl, I thought, of course, silly me!

Kenneth continued, 'D'you know him?'

'I can't say I do.' I was going to say, 'I don't mix in those circles,' but I didn't. The Earl was often to be found at the Three Bells.

'Bloody good bloke,' said Kenneth, 'bloody nice chap.'

And then, with that, he said his goodbyes and he was gone.

When Francis came in, I showed him how to cook and prep the crabs. Two would be for dressed crab and two for crab cannelloni.

'Why are we cling-filming the table?' asked Francis. He scratched his head in puzzlement.

'Because, Francis, when we crack the shells, crab juice is going to go everywhere and I don't want to waste my money and your time by you spending a couple of extra hours clearing the mess up,' I said patiently.

'Silly me,' said Francis, then added gravely, 'we don't want to get into a pickle, do we?'

I looked at him wonderingly. Swearing is not big and not clever but lots of people, including myself do it a lot, Francis, never. He really was the most mild-mannered person I'd ever met.

'No, Francis,' I said, 'we most certainly don't.'

I prised a shell open and pointed with the tip of my knife at the grey leathery protuberances near the head.

'These are called dead man's fingers,' I explained. Someone had told me they were toxic. I wasn't sure if that was the case but I wasn't going to take any chances. 'Now, Francis,

this is important. They're poisonous.' I thought if I emphasised this it might lodge in his head that they were definitely
to go. 'And I do not want them in the food. We don't want
to make anyone ill, do you understand?'

'Yes.'

'Yes, chef,' I corrected him.

'Yes, chef,' he repeated. Good, I thought, that's that.

'Good, and no bits of shell in the meat either.'

'No, chef.' His sweaty face beamed at me.

'Great,' I said, 'let's crack on.'

While Francis busied himself with the crabs, I busied
myself with the rest of the prep list, resisting the temptation
to deal with the crabs myself. He was so slow. But at least
he seemed to be coping. I carried on thinking about the
difference between the Old Forge Café, my place, and the
King's Head, the wannabe Michelin place round the corner.

A VW Golf is a perfectly good car that wins awards,
sells well and will get you from A to B. A Rolls Royce is
also equally good at getting from A to B and, like the Golf,
wins awards and sells well. But there is a difference.
Obviously.

You can have venison at the Old Forge Café, and very
nice it is too. At the King's Head around the corner, you
can have venison saddle with snails, a mousseline of girolles,
chervil infused pommes puree and glazed, blow-torched
mandarin. It's three times the price of mine and deservedly
so. It's a luxury dish. I am a one-man band; the brigade at
the King's Head is probably round about ten persons in
total. You have a chef for sauces, a chef for meat, a chef
for fish, a chef for veg, and so on.

They can do stuff like that. I can't.

The King's Head currently has four rosettes. Four rosettes means that the restaurant deserves national recognition for culinary technical expertise and skill together with other elements that go to make up a restaurant: ambience, wine list, service. But basically it's down to the cooking. At four rosette level fame, a Michelin star is lurking in the wings – you're perpetually on edge because any, every, customer could be that inspector. That all important, anonymous person who can make you famous and rich. It makes for a very tetchy head chef.

I wasn't on edge because of an inspection, I was on edge because I was having to do everything via the small plug-in oven that I normally used for baking cakes. It was a hell of a nuisance, to say the least.

A repair-man for the Hobart was on his way. Every time Francis looked at the oven or saw me look at it, his face fell and he washed dishes in silence. His body language was like a dog who'd done something wrong, ears down, tail swishing low and apologetically. He was feeling terribly guilty over the incident.

And so he bloody well should, I thought.

So when Graeme Strickland, the King's Head head chef arrived for lunch, it was an event. I had looked his menu up on the internet several times, envious of both the technical skill that the dishes implied and his imagination, his originality.

Jess bustled into the kitchen in great excitement. Her dark eyes were alight.

'It's Graeme Strickland!' she hissed at me.

I was confused. 'What, just walked in?'

'No, he came in ages ago. He's just had a toad in the hole and then Victoria sponge with plum compote and Chantilly cream, the one that you flavoured with that weird Swiss liqueur.'

Pflümli. And she was right, it was weird-tasting stuff. Someone had given it to me as a holiday present. Every so often I'd use it. It was taking ages to get rid of. That's how weird it was.

'I'm so sorry, I should have recognised him earlier.' Jess was furious with herself.

'No, it's fine,' I said, and it really was. Many of my fellow chefs would have quite frankly gone ape-shit if a waitress had failed to spot someone they felt they should know about, like a rival chef or, more importantly, a critic. I was so calm because I suspected I might have gone to pieces if I'd known it was him and cocked it up – or worse, panicked and sent out something ridiculously over-garnished.

There was also the happy accident that the toad in the hole had succeeded perfectly as a restaurant dish. I had once worked in a place that had it on the menu by making them in advance and reheating, with predictably poor results. I was going down the par-cooked sausage, fresh batter route and telling customers it would take twenty minutes. Doing each one more or less from scratch. Luckily they all seemed happy with that.

I remembered sending the toad in the hole out: the sausages had been chestnut brown and gleaming, the batter light and perfectly risen, the onion gravy rich with a buttery sheen. Perfection.

If the experiment hadn't worked well, or if I hadn't been happy with the quality of the Victoria sponge that I had served Strickland, or if I hadn't seen, before service started, the disaster that Francis had made of the Chantilly cream, over-beating it until it practically turned into butter – 'I'm sorry, chef,' staring at the jagged, congealed yellow mess, 'No, it's fine, Francis,' (sigh), another disaster but inconsequential compared to Oven-gate, 'gentle peaks was what we were aiming for' – and redone it myself, I wouldn't have been so gentle with Jess.

'He wants to know if he can come and say hello,' Jess added.

I looked up at the clock, an automatic habit for any chef. Quarter past two.

I took my apron off. There was quite a bit of batter stuck to it and more than a smear of blueberry coulis after a Francis-related incident when he had spilt half a bowl of it over me ('ooops a daisy, sorry, chef') and there was onion gravy as well. I wasn't just cooking the menu, I was wearing a great deal of it too. Not a good look. I threw it in the laundry basket outside the door that led upstairs and grabbed a new one in snazzy red and white stripes.

'Sure,' I said, tying the pristine clean one tight around me, 'bring him in.'

Two minutes later Jess reappeared with the chef in tow.

Strickland and I eyed each other from over the barrier of the shiny, hot steel surface of the pass, that part of a kitchen where the chef hands the food over to the waiters.

We were a bit like dogs sniffing each other, friendly but wary.

I saw a small, slim man, very erect on his feet, in his mid-thirties, self-consciously good-looking, his features sharp and regular, with short brown hair and a very determined chin. He put his hand through the hot plate gap to shake mine, careful to avoid making contact with any of the metal surfaces or the powerful lights. He was wearing a dark green jacket and as he put his hand to mine and the sleeve rode up, I could see powerful wrists, the dark hairs criss-crossed here and there by old scars and a couple of nasty-looking fresh burns.

I hadn't doubted that he would be anything but a hands-on chef but it was still good to have my guess confirmed. I have only met a few chefs who refused to get their hands dirty. I find it hard to have any respect for a chef who doesn't actually cook. I have met a few executive chefs who say things like, 'I'm conceptual', or words to that effect. They're not my kind of people.

And what would he have made of me? I was regarded as reasonably attractive, but I was knocking on a bit and my body that I was so proud of was invisible under the apron and chef's whites. I could have been as knobbly and bulging as the sack of spuds by the kitchen door awaiting peeling at the hands of Francis.

We finished shaking hands and he said, 'I enjoyed my lunch. I thought your bread was good. Make it yourself?'

'Yes.'

'The hard crust?'

'Dutch oven.'

'So, not steam?'

And we were already hitting it off. Excited, animated

conversation about food. The great thing about catering is that even at my lowly level you can meet the top rank of chefs fairly easily and they tend to be pleasant, affable people, once they're out of their kitchens, keen to share their knowledge. It's a bit like playing football for a minor team and regularly bumping into Premier League players.

Half an hour later he left to walk back to the King's Head which was on the outskirts of the village. He would be getting ready for the evening shift. Strickland's hours were roughly Monday to Saturday, from eight o'clock in the morning to midnight. A ninety-hour week. On Sunday he got drunk and slept. Over our food talk he'd had a coffee, complimentary petits fours that I had made, two glasses of brandy and (here I'm making an educated guess, based on his suddenly glazed eyes and an equally sudden outbreak of sniffing after he had used my bathroom) a huge line of coke.

I watched him go with affection and a certain amount of reflected glory that I wasn't indifferent to. Strickland's verdict was a huge ego boost.

And Francis managed to peel the potatoes without fucking it up.

I went to bed happy that night. It wasn't going to last.

Chapter Fourteen

It wasn't only success that I had to cope with. I had failure too. My Hobart oven was as dead as my relationship with Andrea. The repair-man had been most apologetic. I hadn't understood the technicalities but I did understand this much.

When Francis was cleaning it, he had shorted it and blown the fuse. That, in itself was no problem; what was a problem was the bodged repair job from a few months previously that had wrecked the circuitry leaving it an accident waiting to happen. The damage caused by Francis had simply brought this to light sooner rather than later.

'How much would it cost to repair?' I asked through gritted teeth.

'You can't, well, you could,' he admitted, 'but it would cost more than buying a new model. It'd be a waste of time and money.'

'How much would a replacement cost, like for like?'

'With VAT and installation' – he screwed his face up; it's not going to be cheap, I thought – 'oh, five K. Probably nearer six.'

Six thousand I did not have.

'Actually,' he added. Go on, I thought, stupidly hopeful until he spoke, 'Better make that seven, to be on the safe side.'

Thank you, Mrs Cope.

I felt both angry and sick with worry at the same time. I really did not have the money. Neither could I live without the oven. I went upstairs to my flat, toyed with the idea of crying, then remembered Louise Bourgeois and the spider, so I did some exercise to wind down after the excitement of the day. Despite the suicide verdict, I was still slightly worried in case Slattery managed to connect me with Whitfield's body. I was convinced he would be trying. Failure to notify police of a crime, a charge I could hardly deny. I couldn't really say I hadn't noticed the headless corpse as I reached the stile. But, as yet, no return visit from Slattery. Nothing had happened so far. No news was good news.

The work situation was grinding me down too.

I had cast Jess in the role of friend and confidante. She seemed happy to do that and I had grown to like her hugely. But now I was worried that Francis might be coming between us.

He was spectacularly useless. I couldn't really rely on him to do anything. Today he had ruined a couple of kilos of broccoli. Like most restaurants, I precook my vegetables and microwave them to order. But if there is one thing I hate it's overcooked veg.

I'd got Francis to take the heads of broccoli and cut them off the stalk into identical, or as near as possible, sized florets. I'd watched him like a hawk as he did this, and he'd managed fine. I was relieved. Then we put a big pan of water on to boil.

We'd filled a sink with iced water. He was to boil the broccoli for three minutes, drain it, then plunge it into the iced water to stop it cooking and bring the temperature way down.

He listened intently. 'We want to avoid soggy broccoli, Francis, don't let me down.'

'No, chef, I won't.'

'What don't we want, Francis?' I asked, to check he had understood.

He screwed his face up with effort. 'Soggy broccoli, chef.'

'Three minutes, in boiling water.' It seemed simple enough.

'Yes, chef.'

'No more, then into the ice ok?'

'Ok, got that!'

I left him to get on with it and went outside into the yard and into the store room and checked on my dry-store goods: tinned tomatoes, dried pasta, olive oil, salt, things like that. I walked back into the kitchen. Francis was cleaning the large double-handed pan in the pot-wash area. There was nothing on the stove. I walked over to the sink.

That's when alarm bells started to ring.

The colour was wrong. The broccoli floating in the sink should have been a vibrant green, a kind of emerald. It wasn't. It was a dull, lifeless green. I put my hand in the water and picked up a floret. It was not al dente, it was soggy mush.

105

'Francis, this broccoli is no good,' I said, quietly, masking my fury. How could he have been so unbelievably stupid? 'Take it out and throw it away.'

'What's wrong with it?' he asked, in an annoyingly challenging way.

What I wanted to do was scream at him, throw a handful of the stuff at the wall and shout about how it shouldn't explode like that on impact. I wanted two burly chefs to hold him down while I stuffed chunks of it into his mouth yelling, 'Eat it! Eat it, you incompetent bastard!' as I had once seen happen. I was truly upset and what made it even worse was that he seemed to have no conception of what he had done wrong.

It would be disgusting to eat and he hadn't noticed.

I liked Francis. He was good-natured, hard-working, eager to please but he was a terrible, terrible chef. If I had a larger brigade and all he had to do was wash up, I'd be – we'd both be – happy. But I needed an extra pair of hands. It was a real problem.

I was going to have to let him go.

How would Jess take it? She was very attached to Francis. I didn't want to upset her.

From below, there was a knocking on the back door and I went downstairs to open it. My guilty conscience made me think it was going to be DI Slattery come to interrogate me as to the fate of Whitfield for no other reason than the fact that his ex had run off with a chef. Oh, and the fact that I wasn't local and had had the temerity to move into his village.

I was a mess of irritable woe, falling far short of where I wanted to be mentally, spiritually and financially.

I opened the door. It wasn't Slattery.

'Hello,' said Justin. He looked great. I didn't. I was wearing old running tights and a T-shirt over a rugby shirt that had belonged to Andrea. I was covered in sweat. I looked tired and sweaty. Tired, sweaty and anxious, fearful of the future. Not gorgeous and fearless at all.

'Hello,' I said, politely, 'do come in.'

'Thanks,' he said.

I ushered him into the kitchen. I didn't have much provision for entertaining guests. There was the restaurant itself, obviously; plenty of tables and chairs, but it would have felt like sitting in a goldfish bowl. I was becoming very aware of how any action seemed to be seen by everyone who lived in the village. I could have turned the lights out, but then it would just have felt a bit strange.

Upstairs was out of the question. I thought of my lounge, bitterly cold, the two beer crates covered with towels that acted as chairs. 'Do take a crate, Justin. . .'

The contrast with his own warm, cosy, beautifully furnished living room would have been breathtaking. In a bad way.

I took his coat. I offered him a brandy which was pretty much all I had in the kitchen. I buy seasoned cooking wine for cooking. I couldn't give him that, and I couldn't really offer him the Pflümli. It was OK to cook with, but it was too weird to drink.

He settled in a corner of the kitchen, sitting on a work-surface as he sipped his brandy. He seemed happy enough with it.

I apologised for the seating arrangements. I apologised

for my mood. I explained about the oven. Justin made sympathetic noises.

Commercial kitchens are not great places for a cosy chat, no chairs. Justin was sitting next to the small plug-in oven that I used for desserts, and, of course, everything else now (curse you, Mrs Cope), and I leaned against the pass.

'Cheers!' I motioned with my glass.

I wondered what had brought him here. I hoped to God it wasn't to cancel the party I was supposed to cater for.

'I think someone killed Dave Whitfield,' said Justin. He looked at me to see my reaction. I suppose I could have said, I know. I saw someone running from the scene. I shrugged. To be honest, I was completely indifferent to how or why he had died.

'The police are going to treat it as an accident. I bumped into Slattery, he let me know.' He drained his glass and put it down hard on the metal surface on which he was sitting. I didn't like to tell him that I had heard it on the local radio. He obviously wasn't here to talk about his party for his New Age friends. What was it called, the Feast of Imbolc or some such title?

'Oh,' I said. I was mystified as to where all this was leading. I refilled his glass.

'Do you get the Hampden Green Facebook page on your devices?'

I shook my head. I dislike social media. I was going to get Jess to put together a Facebook page for my business. This required setting up a personal account which I didn't yet have, so no, I wasn't aware the village had one.

'You know you said you had an enemy in the village?'

I nodded, Go Home Townie Bitch. It was starting to feel like good advice.

'Well, they've started a rumour somewhere online that you were somehow implicated in Dave Whitfield's death.'

He looked at me sympathetically.

'But that's ridiculous!' I said, feeling angry and hurt.

He nodded. 'Obviously, most conspiracies are, and unfortunately this one has real traction. Someone else said you were probably having an affair with him.'

'WHAT!' I mimed vomiting. I'd seen his balls, that was bad enough. Let alone the moobs.

'Yeah,' he nodded supportively, 'village life, eh. There's a lot of speculation about you and the murder.'

'But,' I said, 'I'm innocent.' God, I thought, this will be bad for business.

'Everyone knows everything in a village, or thinks that they do. . .' he swirled the cognac around in the glass.

'I'm from London too,' I said. 'I suppose that makes things worse.'

'Undoubtedly.'

Bloody Slattery, I thought. He must have started this. Even if he hadn't, his suspicions had given this legs.

Justin continued. 'I knew Whitfield reasonably well, he could be an idiot but he would not have gone walking with a loaded shotgun, safety catch off. He would not have done that, full stop.'

I know, I thought. I was beginning to feel really guilty now. I had seen someone running from Whitfield's body and I hadn't told the police officially and now I hadn't told Slattery unofficially. I had replayed the scene hundreds of times in my head. The horrid mess that was Whitfield, the cold rain, the biting wind and that figure, running away. It could have been a man or a woman. A fast, athletic run. I wished I had said something to Slattery. *Beware your sins will find you out.* I very nearly told him at that point, confessed I suppose, but I didn't.

'These rumours have spilled into the New Age community,' he said, 'people don't want you near their food.'

I stared at him in horror. First the oven thing, now this, like a coup de grace, a final bullet through the head to finish me off. I had been relying overmuch on this.

'But,' I almost whimpered, 'what can I do?'

He stood up.

'There's only one thing you can do, Charlie, find out who killed Dave Whitfield.'

Are you crazy? Was my first reaction.

'Why me?' I asked, plaintively. 'What makes you think I'd be able to do it or want to for that matter? I'm a chef, not a private detective.'

Justin walked over to me. He stood in front of me.

'Because you have to.' He then played his ace, 'Do you trust Slattery to find the killer?'

I shook my head.

'Exactly. You'll have to do it. I know people, Charlie. Whitfield was a hard bastard and you flattened him without blinking. You're intelligent and resourceful, and I think. . .' he took a long, appraising look at me, 'I think you're very tough and very capable. And I think you are desperate for this place to succeed. And I know you've got other worries, I can see that you don't have very much money. It's in your eyes, I know that look – a worried-about-bills look,

I've had it myself. I've been poor in my life and now I'm not. I'll pay for the oven.'

I stared at him with a mixture of hope – I really needed the money – and apprehension; I didn't want to owe anyone money or favours, were there strings attached? Money and friendship do not make good companions.

'I don't want your money,' I lied.

'You need a new oven,' he smiled. 'I am doing quite well financially, so this is my thank you to karma. When you're on your feet you can pay me back.'

'I don't know what to say,' I said.

'I do,' he smiled again, 'you say, yes, Justin, I will find Whitfield's killer and silence the haters and then you say, yes I will accept your no strings attached offer; and when the time comes and you are flush with money, as you will be one day, hopefully soon, you can pay me back and maybe do the same thing as I've done. Help someone who really needs it who is as deserving as you are.'

I looked at him with gratitude. I definitely needed an oven, and I definitely couldn't afford to buy one myself. Well, I thought, even if I didn't find the person who had run away, the killer, at least I can show that Whitfield was murdered, and the police can re-open the case; that should suffice. And I was hard-working, and I wouldn't rip him off.

'Done,' I said. We shook hands solemnly.

'Hobart oven?' I asked hopefully.

'Why not?' he said.

'Can I come round tomorrow night at nine,' I said, 'I'll need to take notes on Whitfield, learn as much as I can about his background.'

'Sounds good,' he said, 'I know a fair amount about him and I've got a lot of local connections, I'll ask around. I'll see you then.'

He added, 'I look forward to it.'

I let him out and wondered what I had let myself in for.

Practical Cookery, Seventh Edition, the industry bible, did not, as far as I know, cover sleuthing.

Oh well, I thought, I'll just have to wing it. It can't be too hard.

Which shows just how little I knew.

Chapter Fifteen

The very next day I killed Ollie Scott, the local drug dealer.

Or thought I had.

At five o'clock in the afternoon, while I was going through my mise en place list for the following day, there was a knock on the kitchen door. It was DI Slattery, a faint smirk on his lips, and he was not alone. He was accompanied by a tall, slim, pleasant-looking middle-aged woman with blond hair and slightly prominent teeth.

My heart sank. What was going on now?

She introduced herself. 'Hello, I'm Sandra Burke, EHO, and I'm here to look around your kitchen.'

'Feel free,' I said. I could feel an icy hand tighten around my heart. The Environmental Health Officer does not need to make an appointment, like Death they can arrive unannounced.

Sandra Burke fired a volley of questions at me as she walked around the kitchen opening cupboards, peering under things and checking the clipboards that I have hanging up detailing things like fridge and freezer readings. Luckily, in many ways, I'm an EHO's dream. I take cleanliness and hygiene very seriously. To be honest it's no great effort on my part, I'm a naturally tidy person anyway. I show due diligence and I had the records to prove it. It helps that my pessimistic nature ensures that I am continually preparing for the worst and now it had arrived, she was impressed.

Fridge and freezer temperature logs where twice daily the temperatures had been recorded. Records to show I temperature-probed my cooked food. Everything was dated and labelled. I had records for everything, I thought smugly. Slattery stood watching, his face grim. I could imagine he was annoyed by my meticulous standards.

She looked in fridges – all was clean and tidy including the seals (a notorious place for grime to build up). She even made me pull them out so she could check behind them to make sure that I'd been cleaning there. I had. Though I say it myself, it was impressive. Not just my opinion: 'This is very impressive,' Sandra Burke said, echoing my own thoughts. 'I wish all the kitchens I look at were this clean.'

Slattery watched, a slight frown on his face. I could feel his disappointment growing. I bet he was thinking, 'If only there were a cockroach or two. . .'

'What's all this about?' I asked him as Burke started photographing my kitchen and making notes about the storage and started poking around the hazardous chemicals for cleaning. That got me thinking. Dear God, I thought, I let Francis do some simple prep – I hope to God he didn't confuse salt with sink cleanser. Or drain unblocker!

'You know Ollie Scott?' the DI said. I cast around in

my memory: Ollie Scott the drug dealer. I almost called him that but stopped myself. Slattery would probably assume that I was one of his customers.

'Yes, he was here for lunch,' I said.

Slattery nodded grimly. 'Yes, he was,' he said. The penny dropped.

'He's not ill?'

'No,' Slattery's voice was accusing, 'he's dead.'

'Oh,' I raised my eyebrows. All sorts of possibilities flashed through my mind lightning-fast, but I think I had guessed what the DI was going to say before he said it.

'How did he—'

Slattery didn't wait for me to finish my question.

'He died of what looks suspiciously like food poisoning, which is why I am here with Ms Burke. Now, what exactly did he have to eat?'

All I could say was, 'Well, he didn't get it from here.'

'We'll be the judge of that,' Slattery said.

At least I was able to find his order. The tickets containing the food orders are duplicates; one is kept by Jess for the bill, the other goes to me. After I've sent the food I impale the tickets on a vicious-looking spike that juts out of a block of wood. We're old-fashioned, not yet electronic. That was on the to-do list.

There were twenty-five tickets from lunch. They were still there, on the long slim, needle-sharp piece of metal; I hadn't got round to throwing them away yet. Ollie Scott had been the only lone customer. I remembered Jess making a comment about him having no friends. I found his order. My heart sank: a starter of crab cannelloni, the only one I had sold that lunch, and a grilled chicken baguette with rice salad.

It could hardly have been worse. Chicken and crustacea and cooked, reheated rice. A terrible triumvirate when it comes to food safety. Like in some kind of horrible word association test, the related food-poisoning ailments neatly zoomed up in my mind and clicked into place. There certainly wasn't anything wrong with my memory, that was for sure.

Chicken was represented by salmonella, surely that wasn't fast-acting? The crab: shellfish are notoriously prone to contamination from sewage, could it have been that? I think you can get cholera from them too, but South Bucks was not exactly famous for cholera outbreaks. Rice I could dimly remember was bacillus cereus. Three very high-risk foods.

My heart sank. If only he had had a cheese sandwich.

'Do you have any of these foods left over?' asked Burke.

I nodded, opened the relevant fridge and handed her the containers.

'Oh, that's very good. Look,' she said to Slattery approvingly, 'clearly labelled, dated, day dotted, that's excellent work, Ms Hunter.'

Slattery's frown deepened. Another thought struck me. Oh, Francis, I thought, did you get rid of those dead man's fingers when you prepped the crab or are they in those cannelloni? Are they poisonous after all? Have we killed the drug dealer?

'I'm not going to serve a compulsory shutdown order on you, it's just a precautionary measure, you understand,' Burke said brightly. 'Overall, I'm more than satisfied with the standards that you maintain in this kitchen.'

Slattery looked mutinous, as if he could not disagree more. But it wasn't his place to say anything.

She carried on. 'And, of course, it hasn't been proved yet exactly what killed Mr Scott although the symptoms he was exhibiting – nausea, diarrhoea, cramps. . .' She smiled at me. 'I'm sure you don't need me to spell it out.'

'Terrible way to go,' Slattery added. He was very eager to spell it out. 'Agonising death.'

Burke glared at him.

'As I was saying before I was interrupted, all his symptoms bear the hallmarks of food poisoning and unfortunately you appear to be the only place where he ate. In hospital, before he lost consciousness, he even blamed you for his condition, although' – here she looked at Slattery – 'I assume that's of doubtful relevance.'

'Too early to say, isn't it?' said Slattery with a malicious smile. The smile suggested that anything that might possibly implicate me would be taken down and used in evidence.

'So, what do you want me to do?' I asked.

'Well, it's Tuesday today, I'll get these off and analysed as soon as possible and let you know the results before the weekend, but I would like you to voluntarily cease trading until then. Take the rest of the week off.'

I nodded. That was going to cost a hell of a lot of money but what could I do?

I watched them leave and closed and locked the door.

I sat down heavily on the floor. 'Shit!' I said, out loud.

I decided to be positive. Let's assume neither I nor Francis had inadvertently killed Ollie Scott. Make that a given. Presumably, then, it was the same person who had killed Whitfield. Even a place as weird as Hampden Green couldn't produce two killers.

But now I definitely had to find who it was. Not only was the fate of my business at stake, but someone was trying to frame me.

And doubtless it would be all over bloody Facebook too.

I had to find the killer as soon as possible, I very much doubted that Slattery would.

If I didn't my business would end up as dead as the drug dealer.

Chapter Sixteen

I went straight round to Justin's. It didn't seem worth finishing my prep as I wasn't going to be open the following day. He opened the door. His long dark hair was wet and he was practically naked. He was wearing a towel wrapped around his waist, his muscular torso gleaming with water. His pecs were hard and looked like you could bounce a tennis ball off them; he was hairless except for a strip of dark hair running southwards from his navel into the white folds of the towel. I stared in fascination at his abs, hoping he wasn't noticing.

'I thought you were coming round at nine,' he said, looking slightly confused and certainly not best pleased. 'I'm just out of the shower.'

'I'm sorry, I should have phoned or texted, it's just that some really weird stuff's been going on. . .'

'Well, go and wait in the living room while I get changed and you can tell me about it.'

I just nodded mutely and did as I was told.

Later, Justin, dressed in jeans and a T-shirt sat cross-legged on a sofa. He got himself a glass of Merlot from a half-full bottle and offered me one. Usually I would have said no, because I would have had prep to do, but not tonight, maybe not for a while, so I said yes. He poured out the wine and I poured out my story. He tutted his sympathy as I explained what had happened.

He was an excellent listener, and wasn't one of those annoying breed of people who gives you unwanted advice.

'I'm sure that it's nothing to do with you,' was his comment. I concur, I thought. Facebook wouldn't. I bet I'd be all over social media, unfairly accused of being a poisoner. So we moved on to Dave Whitfield. I asked questions and made notes on my tablet.

They'd met about five years ago when Justin moved in. Like many ageing single men, he didn't have many friends and would often turn up at Justin's door, half-pissed with a bottle of wine, hoping for company.

'It's not that he was a bad builder, or set out to rip anyone off,' said Justin thoughtfully, 'it's just that he hated turning work down, so he was always overstretched and as a result there were overruns all the time. That invariably meant delays and clients got annoyed. Then there was the added problem that he'd never back down, could never admit he was wrong.' He sighed. 'An apology often goes a long way, and it's such a little thing, but he hated saying sorry.'

As he talked about Whitfield I got the impression of a driven man who had come tantalisingly close to making it big. He had been involved in some high-end projects, and he was well respected. But the great pay day, the golden deal, always slipped through his fingers.

'So what enemies did he have around here?' I asked. 'I

heard he had fallen out with a guy called Chris Edwards. What was all that about?' Jess had told me when I'd asked her earlier if Whitfield had any enemies. I remembered that it was Chris who had alerted Dave to the arson attack. Now I wondered if he'd maybe lit the fuse.

'Well, that's ancient history,' Justin said. ' Chris hired Dave to do the groundworks on a property he was extending. Dave gave him a definite date, but, Dave being Dave, had also given two other people definite dates and he was a fortnight late in starting and cost Chris a huge amount of money.'

'How much?'

Justin shifted his weight on the sofa and re-crossed his legs on the other side. He looked effortlessly comfortable sitting in padmasana, the lotus position. I admired his flexibility, but not as much as I admired that hard, gymnast's body. Concentrate, Charlie, I told myself sternly, you're becoming unhealthily obsessed with Justin.

'I don't know, thousands. But that's ancient history, as I said. They kissed and made up.'

'Did they?' I was a bit disappointed. Chris was the only suspect that I had. I was sorry to lose him.

'Yeah, in fact Dave said they were thinking of working together again. Business is business and Dave could make things happen. He did have vision. Chris is a good builder but he doesn't dream the dream. Dave would take risks; sometimes it worked, sometimes it didn't.'

'Any other enemies?' I asked.

'Only the Turner family,' said Justin. 'Your waitress's lot.' His voice was quite bitter. I guess maybe the aunt thing rankled.

'I heard he made a bit of a mess of her uncle's conservatory,' I said, moving to safer topics. Justin's face darkened.

'Is that what you heard?' he said. I could see that he was annoyed. 'John Turner screwed Dave royally on that. He changed the spec, claimed the work was sub-standard, wasn't going to pay him. . . you get the idea. You should keep a close eye on that girl, Jess, Charlie. She doesn't like me either. She tried to ruin my business by claiming I was having an affair with her aunt.'

'Oh,' I said. I could hardly ask, 'Were you?'

He took a mouthful of Merlot.

'Oh, indeed. Camilla Turner, Jess's mother was furious. She's got it in for me, big time.' He sighed. 'The people in this village, Jesus, Charlie, they think they can do anything they want, get anything they want, either just because they've been here forever, like the Turners or because they've got money like the Earl. They think they own the place. So yes, the Turners were certainly not Dave's friends, but, much as I'd like to, I can't see them dirtying their hands by killing him.'

'And do you know what projects he was working on at the moment?' I pressed my head into the back of my armchair. I was having trouble concentrating. And that was not simply because of his stylish surroundings which were not like my Spartan existence – a mattress on the floor, my clothes in plastic crates. The man had taste, everything was beautifully arranged. Curated. No, it was more than that – I was aware of a growing attraction towards him.

'Not really,' he said. He reached behind his head and

twisted his long hair into a top-knot, patting it into place. It was a strangely intimate gesture.

I stared at the ceiling. No cracks, not like mine. 'How well did he know Ollie Scott?' I asked. The two deaths had to be linked. Hampden Green was definitely the strangest place that I'd ever lived but surely two deaths in such a short period of time had to be connected. So if he had been killed, rather than died of food poisoning, then there was almost certainly a connection with Whitfield.

'Dave bought coke off Ollie.' Justin pulled a face. 'Dave could take it or leave it – well, I say that, but come to think of it, I know he was doing a gram a day, maybe more; it's a lot of money. And I'm sure it was making a mess of his head' – he shook his own head – 'but not enough to shoot himself. He had a very high sense of his own worth.'

'So who would benefit from Dave being dead?' I asked. 'I mean, there wasn't a jealous husband around, was there?' *Cherchez la femme!* I thought. That was the extent of my knowledge of detection.

'Dave wasn't one for womanising,' said Justin, shaking his head again. 'Believe me, I'd know. He'd have boasted about it. No, his life was dull. He'd work, go to the pub, do some sniff with Ollie or buy it and take it home, get pissed and sleep. A sympathetic barmaid was Dave's idea of a perfect girlfriend; lager with benefits.'

Justin smiled at the thought. He looked very attractive when he did that.

They say the way to a man's heart is through his stomach, but Justin was impregnable. He didn't like the kind of food

I cooked, he liked biome-friendly fermented kimchi and fibre rich brown rice and partially cooked kale. Oh well.

I brought my attention back to Dave Whitfield.

I asked, 'So Dave wasn't having an affair with someone?'

'No,' he shook his head. 'Try asking Chris Edwards, he might know something.'

There was an unmistakable note in his voice that my time was up.

'I'll give it a try,' I said, standing up. 'Hopefully I'll get lucky.'

'I'm sure you will, Charlie, just keep digging.'

In my dreams, I thought, as he gently closed the door behind me.

Chapter Seventeen

It was twelve o'clock on Friday. I should have begun to see the restaurant fill up for lunch. Instead there was a sad note on my front door: 'Due to unforeseen circumstances. . .' How I'd hated putting that there! It was a strange sensation for me, not being in the kitchen, not one that I relished. I felt disassociated from life. It was hard to concentrate on anything. I kept thinking about the EHO and her tests. I was ninety-nine per cent sure they would exonerate me but there was still a niggling doubt at the back of my mind. I also had a paranoid worry in case Slattery somehow fitted me up. It was slightly mad, but then how sane was Slattery? Or anyone in this bloody village? I was feeling decidedly twitchy.

Just keep digging, I decided to follow Justin's advice.

Courtesy of Jess – font of knowledge of all things local and sworn enemy of Justin – I found Chris at the top of a ladder doing up the roof on a cottage that he was restoring. There was a lull in the rain and they were obviously making the most of it. He was replacing a whole section that was missing and you could see the timber frame that held the slates up.

I waved at him and he smiled and climbed down the ladder with an easy grace. Then he crossed over to where I was standing via a walkway they'd made out of planks. Because of the rain, the building site was a sea of claggy mud. Their wheelbarrows would have sunk axle-deep in the stuff.

He stood there in a plaid jacket, old torn jeans and work boots, looking lean and elegant. Why do builders wear so much plaid? They can't all have Scottish ancestry?

'Hiya, Charlie.' He continued, 'I heard about the Ollie Scott incident, sorry to hear that you got the blame. Bet it's nothing to do with you.'

God, that got around quickly, I thought, there's a surprise. I had a vision of my village enemy (who could it be?) typing away at a keyboard. Spreading false information.

A fatal poisoning. Just the publicity a restaurant needs. Hopefully, when it's revealed it was nothing to do with me, that'll go round just as speedily. Bet it doesn't though.

'That's nice of you to say so. Chris, could I interest you in lunch? I'd like to pick your brains on something?'

'What are you offering me? Not crab, I hope, Charlie, sorry,' he laughed in a good-natured way, but there was a malicious edge to it. I suddenly found myself wondering if I liked Chris. There was a certain contemptuous air about him, as if he were my superior, doing me a big favour whenever I spoke with him.

Then he asked, 'I thought you were closed?'

'Commercially, yes. . . don't worry, I'm not going to charge you, or offer high risk food,' I said, forcing a smile.

A flashback to Whitfield lying dead by the stile. *The figure running off in the distance.* If only I had given chase. Had they been tall? My eyes measured Chris, six two, six three? But it had been dark, and raining hard. . .

They had run quickly, they were fit. . .

If only I could remember, if only I had been able to see them better. Chris looked very fit. If he'd wanted to take Whitfield's gun away from him, he could have. I thought back. The rain in my eyes and the biting wind and the horrible mess that was Whitfield. . . *But whoever it was could run. . .* I think that would have excluded Ollie, he'd have been too wrecked. Besides, he was too short.

How had he known that Ollie had been eaten the crab? Was it Francis again? I had called him the night before to tell him we were closed over the weekend.

'*I hope we're not in any kind of a pickle?*'

His voice had sounded worried over the phone. A guilty conscience?

'*No, everything will be fine. . .*'

Or had it been Slattery? I had seen him the other night and he'd been with Ollie Scott. I began to seriously wonder about him as a suspect. There was very little that I wouldn't put past DI Slattery. Was all this hostility towards me, trying to implicate me in things, part of a long term plan so he could frame me?

I looked at Chris who returned my glance with what I thought was a certain amount of condescension. I remembered what Jess had said about him. 'You don't mess with Chris.'

Chris and Whitfield had worked together. *'Dave, could I have a look at your gun? Sure Chris. . .'* It was plausible.

I smiled politely at him. 'Steak, sourdough baguette with caramelised red onions on a bed of rocket and horseradish cream.'

I decided not to tell him the crab had been impounded, pending analysis.

He grinned. 'I've got cheese and pickle sandwiches on sliced white. I'll take you up on your kind offer,' he paused, 'so long as you don't poison me.'

I gave a tight smile. Ha, bloody, ha, oh my aching ribs. 'I'll try not to.'

He addressed the two workmen who were on the roof, shouting up to them, 'You two carry on with those roof trusses, I'll be back later, and Pete?'

'Yes, boss?'

'Make sure they're secure, OK, not like last time.' His voice was hard with warning and he suddenly looked very aggressive. I mentally flinched; I wouldn't want to get on the wrong side of Chris. I looked at him with renewed interest. His stock as a potential killer was rising.

'Sure, Chris,' shouted Pete.

'I'm surrounded by idiots,' said Chris loudly as he turned away. I could sympathise. Evidently I wasn't the only one with employee problems. The two men carried on with the roof and Chris and I walked away, squelching through the Chiltern mud.

Chapter Eighteen

Back at the restaurant I busied myself at the stove, char-grilling the steak. I drew a blank asking Chris about Ollie Scott. He said he knew him, of course, but avoided him like the plague.

'Couldn't stand the bastard, next question.' He was reluctant to even speculate about who might have had it in for him. It was an abrupt, dismissive shutdown of my line of questioning.

I persisted. 'But lots of people knew he was a dealer, so who do you reckon killed him?'

He frowned, annoyed at my persistence. 'It could be anyone, couldn't it? But if you ask me, he was poisoned, or given an overdose.' He leaned back in his chair. 'I mean they cut the stuff, don't they, so if you gave him something that was ninety per cent pure instead of ten, twenty per cent, or whatever, he could easily have OD'd. So, I'd guess his fellow scumbag criminals.'

And with that, he drew a line under Ollie Scott's death.

I prodded the steak. You can tell how well a steak is cooked by pushing the ball of your right thumb with your left index finger and comparing how they feel. All fingers open, rare. Right thumb to tip of right index finger, medium rare. Right thumb to middle finger, medium, to ring finger, well done. You can feel the muscle tighten as you prod it. That's quite literally a rule of thumb. It's not always perfect. Another problem with steak for the chef is that if the service is busy, even though the food may have left the stove perfectly cooked, if it's been left on a hot plate under the lights it'll carry on cooking. You can't always get it right with the best will in the world. What saves us chefs a lot of the time is that, on the whole, people don't like to make a fuss, provided you haven't screwed things up too much.

The reason I mention that is I can tell a great deal about meat when I prod it, but I haven't got a clue when it comes to prodding people for the truth.

Although Chris was reluctant to even speculate about who might have had it in for Ollie Scott, Dave Whitfield was a different matter. He was happy to discuss him.

I cut up the steak: it was perfectly cooked, seared on the outside, rosy pink on the inside, and I filled the baguette which had a bed of caramelised red onion in it. I ran some horseradish cream down it, job done. I said, 'I hear from some people he was a bad builder, others say he was good. What do you think?'

Chris shook his head. 'He wasn't bad, we all have our off days though. . .'

I finished plating his lunch – a little garnish of salad, a couple of onion rings, some fries – and asked casually, 'Didn't you two have a bit of a bust-up once. . .?'

Chris looked at me shrewdly and when he spoke it was

in very measured tones, the way you speak when you don't want to implicate yourself.

'I have to spend so much time monitoring work now that I employ a few people. I have to make sure it's done properly. I think that's why I've got a lot more respect for Dave Whitfield now than I did when we had our bust-up.'

'Did Whitfield screw things up?' I asked.

'I said I've got a lot more respect for him because he had to rely on other people. And that's hard. Because the people who work for you can't necessarily be trusted to do a good job,' said Chris.

Too true, I thought, mournfully. *Francis!*

He swallowed a mouthful of his steak. 'This is good!'

'Don't sound so surprised,' I said, irritated.

He laughed. 'Fair enough.' He returned to his theme of the building trade. 'No, there are a lot of thickos in construction. Sometimes I feel like I'm surrounded by fools.'

'So you made up with Whitfield?' I asked. Mrs Perceptive.

He nodded. 'Yeah. It wasn't just about money, but it's no secret we were going to be working together again. He was offering me in on something very tasty. He was going to be starting a big, fifty-home new-build project, a social and private housing development. Obviously something like that's worth millions.' He took another bite of his baguette. 'Particularly around here.'

'Whereabouts was that?' I asked.

'Chandler's Ford, near Aylesbury. I don't know exactly whereabouts in relation to the village.'

I ate some of my food thoughtfully. 'What was your role in this going to be?'

'Basically he wanted me as the site manager' – he smiled ruefully – 'it's a shame that he's gone because I'll probably never get to do it now. Whoever takes over from Whitfield Construction when it goes out to re-tender has probably got their own man lined up for the job.'

'Did you want the job?' I asked.

'Christ, yes. Regular hours, great pay, and, well, it's the kind of thing I do very well. I've got the practical knowledge, I can do most construction jobs myself – not electrics obviously – so you can't bullshit me.' He paused, ate a bit more steak and continued, 'And I don't get intimidated and equally, I don't lose my temper. And I can keep to budget and time, so it would have been well-paid and enjoyable, but now' – he shrugged expressively – 'well, that's all gone tits up.'

We sat in silence for a bit, contemplating what might have been. What he said had the ring of truth.

'Do you think he killed himself?'

Chris snorted derisively. 'With a massive thing like this going on?' He shook his head emphatically. 'No way. It's what he'd worked all his life for, the big deal.' He looked at me almost angrily. 'All his life he wanted to be someone, you know, to be looked up to. That's why I think he had that stupid blue pillar, it was like reassurance that he was important. *I* don't give a monkey's for stuff like that, so long as I've got money, but Dave wanted everyone to know. He wanted to be seen to be successful, that was so important to him, he really wanted that. . .' He fell silent, both of us lost in our memories of Whitfield, mine unfortunately fixated on his big hairy balls in the celeriac remoulade, presumably (hopefully) Chris's somewhat different. 'And that Chandler's Ford project would have done it for him. Of course he didn't kill himself.'

I nodded.

'DI Slattery thinks it was suicide,' I remarked. Chris blew his cheeks out contemptuously at the thought.

'He was always boasting, Dave was,' said Chris. 'Suicides don't boast. And as for Slattery,' Chris spoke with contempt, 'don't talk to me about Slattery. There are stories about him in the village. People say his wife didn't leave him for nothing. . . And he's a violent bastard. I've had it on good authority people have been injured while' – his fingers made air quotation marks – 'resisting arrest.'

So Slattery was a bent copper. Then I thought, in all fairness to Slattery, lurid stories about me were also swirling around. But it would explain the dinner with Scott.

My mind moved back to my scenario of Whitfield obligingly handing over his shotgun to his companion who had pulled the trigger.

Did Slattery shoot? I bet he did.

'Let's go and get some pheasants, Dave. . . meet up early?' Then later, *'Dave, could I see your gun?'*

Of course you'd hand over your firearm to a policeman, and who better than a CID officer to arrange a body to make it look accidental? And then to be placed in charge of investigating a crime that you had committed yourself. Fox-henhouse. No wonder the evidence pointed to suicide.

Anyway. What seemed obvious was that Whitfield had died at the point he was about to pull off something really big. Once again, the golden deal had slipped through his fingers. Chris's point sounded very likely. Whitfield with his longing for public recognition, his Ferrari: why would he kill himself now? I moved back to the development. Maybe it was a rival for that who had killed him? Get rid of Whitfield. Maybe they thought they would pick up the contract.

'What form did the bidding take, do you know?'

Chris nodded. 'It was sealed bids that had to be submitted by such-and-such a date. I don't know when the cut-off point was exactly. It was public/private partnership, overseen by the council. Everything had to be just so, even the plans on paper had to be of a certain size and folded a certain way. But there wasn't just the price criteria, otherwise everything would go to the large firms. With this it was also energy efficiency, local impact, green issues; all those had to be dealt with, and there was a certain amount of preference to be given to smaller, local firms rather than the big national boys.'

I looked at Chris, relaxed on his stool. His shock of iron-grey hair was belied by a young-looking, good-humoured face, and his long legs and arms looked immensely powerful. He was an impressive man.

'So,' I said, choosing my words carefully, 'the decision process wasn't at all straightforward. It did not simply boil down to price.'

'Exactly,' confirmed Chris.

'And Whitfield would qualify as a smaller, local firm.'

'That's right,' said Chris, 'and he was utterly confident that he had got it.'

And both Chris and I could guess how he knew he'd got the contract. We both knew that Dave Whitfield was friendly with Luke Montfort. There was the tower that he'd put up in his front garden, almost like a beacon that illuminated not just his company, but also signified the power that he managed to exert over the council planners who must have granted permission for what most people in the village regarded as an excrescence.

Was it a rival who had pulled the trigger?

Maybe one of his sleeping partners? Had Whitfield been too greedy?

Was it the same person who had been persecuting Whitfield or had someone else jumped on the bandwagon? And, a thought suddenly struck me, was it the same person that was persecuting me? Two people were already dead, might I be on a list?

That was not a good thought.

Chris finished his baguette.

'That was great,' he said. 'I hope you get the business with Ollie cleared up, I bet it was drugs that killed him, not your crab.'

'How did you know it was crab?' I couldn't help myself. Go on, Chris, say it, name names. . . Slattery! He's trying to kill my business off, drive me out.

'It's a village, Charlie,' his tone was kindly, speaking to the stupid townie. 'You're from London, you wouldn't understand, word gets around.'

I looked at his rather smug face, patronising me again. 'Well, Chris' – I felt I wanted to make some kind of point – 'if word gets around so much, how can a drug dealer like Ollie function? How come he's not been nicked, busted, grassed up or otherwise inconvenienced?'

Yes, Slattery, why are you so inactive on that front?

'Because,' Chris answered, pulling on his jacket, 'he might be a dealer, but he's *our* drug dealer, it's that simple. Now I'd better get back to work, check on those two muppets I've got working for me.'

So, I thought as I watched him through the restaurant window, walk lithely away across the green: local Ollie Scott can deal drugs and Slattery will look the other way, while non-local me sells food and he tries to run me out of town.

I seemed to hear Justin's comment from the other day ringing in my ears: '*Everyone knows everything in a village, or thinks they do.*'

Except, I thought angrily, except who killed the local builder and who killed the local drug dealer. Or worse, everyone knows, but me.

Chapter Nineteen

Brooding on injustice wasn't going to help, I needed to find Whitfield's killer. And soon – if my business wasn't going to be as dead as he was.

I got a piece of paper and a pen. When I need to think, I prefer to physically write it down rather than use a keyboard. Jess wouldn't approve. She could be scathing about my reluctance to embrace technology – every day I had some comment about it. Yesterday's lecture had been about passwords.

'Password1 is not a password, it's not secure.' She had shaken her head angrily, she was genuinely cross. 'It's like leaving your front door wide open, with the keys in the lock. Use a bloody Password manager. . . look I'll install one for you.'

I mulishly wrote: 'SUSPECTS' in blue biro and underlined it in red. Suck on that, Bill Gates, I thought. Using a ruler I added some columns.

I started writing a list of people and things to investigate, a sort of MEP list. I put Chris down and, under the column marked Reasons, wrote: *disliked Whitfield, involved in shady property deal.*

I could imagine Chris being quite violent; Jess had hinted that he had a history of it.

I added: *violent*. I thought of the running figure I had seen: *athletic*, I added.

Next I put Montfort. To be honest, I couldn't see him blowing Whitfield's head off. He was a pen pusher, not a man of action. I also found it hard to picture him as the person I had seen running away. I obviously hadn't been able to form any opinion of what they'd looked like, but the way they'd moved had been fast and athletic. Neither of those qualities applied to Montfort.

But. . . he was in Whitfield's pocket, from the minor (the obelisk), to the major (the housing development). All major building projects in South Bucks passed through Luke Montfort's sweaty paws. He had a great deal of power and even if he couldn't rubber-stamp something himself, he would know whom to approach. Even if he hadn't killed the builder, he might know who did.

Devious, I put, *corrupt*. I remembered what Jess had said about him: *perv*, I added.

Then I added Slattery to my list. The DI had the right character for crime: arrogant, judgemental, contemptuous and, I suspected, violent. I remembered him at the Raj restaurant with Ollie Scott and Montfort. They were not the sort of people I could imagine him socialising with; that left business. Was he involved in their deal?

Slattery looked like the kind of detective who had joined up at eighteen, so he must be coming up for retirement. Was this part of saving for his retirement?

I put: *Chris says he's bent and violent*. But Chris was a suspect too.

Ollie Scott next. Ollie Scott was dead but he was a criminal; he too had been involved in violence, albeit on the receiving end. He could have killed Whitfield. If he was close enough to sell and do drugs with Whitfield, he was close enough to blow his head off.

I put: *unstable, not athletic*.

I added a question mark. I thought of all the previous incidents – the fire, the damage to his car – all designed to enrage and humiliate the builder. Was his murder the culmination of an escalating campaign waged against him? Was his death due to someone just hating him?

And where did that leave me, I thought. I was experiencing an escalating campaign against me, was I in danger?

Lastly and reluctantly, more in the spirit of even-handedness than because I believed it to be true, I put Jess's name down. According to Justin, the Turners did not like Whitfield one bit. And while I couldn't imagine for one minute Jess's parents shooting the builder, someone had.

Well, I thought, it's not going to be them. I scored their name out.

Where to begin?

With the weakest link. Montfort.

I thought I must speak to Montfort next. Then I thought, if Montfort had really been in the pocket of Dave Whitfield he was hardly going to confess all to me. And I could scarcely insist he talk to me: I wasn't DI Slattery, able to go marching into people's lives and workplaces. But equally, I had to make some kind of effort.

Any meeting was better with Montfort than no meeting at all. Mousse, I thought, Montfort loves mousses. I shall lower myself to inviting Montfort round, and to catch a rat, you need bait.

Put mousse on the menu and I'll come.

His words.

I also thought of the way he had surreptitiously tried looking down inside my blouse when he'd wandered over in the restaurant, another couple of reasons why Montfort would come.

I folded my piece of paper away and tucked it at the bottom of my overfull in-tray on my desk and got on with the mousse.

I fetched four eggs, 400 ml of double cream, caster sugar and three sheets of leaf gelatine. I had three passionfruit in the fridge doing nothing, they'd work.

I cleansed a steel mixing bowl with boiling water; oil is the bane of any whisked egg white. I put another two mixing bowls out for the cream and the yolk/sugar mix and as I cracked and separated eggs, I thought of Louise Bourgeois's gigantic spider and I whispered to myself while the whisk whirred, *Come into my parlour, Mr Montfort.*

Chapter Twenty

The mousse was finished and I was extremely satisfied with it. It was beautiful. Its texture was ethereally light. It held a hint of sweetness and was full of the exotic, musky, perfumed flavour of the passionfruit. Passionfruit comes from South America so I toyed with the idea of maybe pairing it with something else South American. If I were in possession of a liquor licence I'd have suggested a rum-based cocktail.

My liquor licence application for the restaurant was languishing somewhere in the council offices in Aylesbury. I was far from sure if I was going to be given one. I was fairly sure that Slattery would object, he certainly seemed to have it in for me. And as an official of the law he would be listened to. I think it was a safe bet to assume that if he could make trouble for me, he would.

So while that rumbled on, I was restricted to non-alcoholic beverages, which, as I was only open at lunchtime, didn't really affect me too badly. It was probably, I reflected, just as well I didn't open at night so I wouldn't sigh over a large amount of lost revenue.

Well, I thought, no use brooding over possibilities. I put the passionfruit mousse, covered, clingfilmed, labelled and dated, in the dessert section of one of my fridges. I decided to go to the Three Bells. I needed a change of scenery, however grim.

I pulled my coat on, locked the kitchen door behind me and went through the yard into the road outside. It had started raining again and the January sky was cold, grey and bleak. It matched my mood. There was no one on the common and only the odd car around.

The pub fronted on to the far end of the common on the left. I could see its sign swaying in the stiff breeze. Opposite the pub was the little access road for the houses where Justin and Slattery lived that overlooked the common on the far side from where I was standing.

The quickest way to the Three Bells was diagonally across the grass, but as this was so waterlogged I stuck to the pavements, doing two sides of a triangle, walking past the village hall that doubled as a fitness studio for Justin's yoga classes. A few doors further on was the pub.

It had a little strip of grass around it and some rickety garden furniture that looked none too sturdy.

There was a picket fence, the paint fading and peeling and a short concrete path to the door. There was a snow-drift of discarded cigarette ends outside. Above the door, as if to mock me, and my lack of a liquor licence, it said:

Malcolm Nowell, Licensed to sell beer and spirits

I went in and walked across the reddish carpet, sticky with spilt drinks and pockmarked with burns from the time not so long ago when smoking was still allowed in pubs.

'Afternoon, Malcolm,' I said to the cadaverous pub land-lord with his very red face. He nodded a silent greeting.

'Usual, Charlie,' his voice hoarsely whispered from beyond the grave. If a film crew ever turned up here to make a zombie film, Malcolm would be a natural fit for one of the undead. His jerky movements, the horrid, hoarse quality of his voice, the way he swivelled his head slowly to look at things, his weird rheumy eyes, all were those of a reanimated corpse.

He fetched me my usual. I had been in every day since the beginning of January, as it was a convenient five-minute walk away from the Old Forge Café where I was spending far too much time. Horrible it may have been, but it was a welcome break.

I normally drink white wine when I'm out but I'd tried Malcolm's Chardonnay and it was like paint stripper, so I stuck to drinks that couldn't be screwed up. I sipped my Diet Coke, ice and a slice and looked around Malcolm's shabby, shadowy establishment. The Kingdom of the Dead. The Underworld. There was no sign of the split shift chefs from the King's Head up the road who were doubtless right now having to hurriedly replace whatever had run low during the lunch service. No break for them today. Split shift had turned into what is known as an AFD shift. All ****ing day. I'd spoken on my mobile earlier to Francis who had driven past at twelve and said that their car park was rammed.

My restaurant was, of course, empty.

The only other customer was a girl that I recognised as Ollie's girlfriend, well, former girlfriend now. A widowette.

ALEX COOMBS

She came up to the bar and stood in front of me.

'You're the chef, right?' Her voice was slurred and her eyes slightly unfocused. For a moment I thought that she might be going to have a go for poisoning her beau. Either that or collapse, she was swaying slightly on her feet. Then she smiled uncertainly at me and I relaxed slightly, free to assess her as a person rather than a threat.

She was much younger than Ollie, who I think had been in his mid-thirties. She looked about twenty. She was quite small, but voluptuous, with short blond hair and wearing a red dress that showed a lot of cleavage and incongruously (to my eyes) fishnet tights and high-sided blue Dr Martens boots. She certainly wasn't dressed for a freezing January. She was half 1950s glamour girl and half punk. It was a look she managed to pull off very successfully. A tattoo of a snake coiled around a tree ran up her left arm. There were Hebrew (of all things) letters and an apple tattooed on her right upper arm.

'I'm Bryony, with a y.' She put her hand out, long red-varnished nails the same colour as her dress and her lipstick (how else would you dress up for a village pub in the country?) and we shook hands.

She said, consolingly, 'I don't blame you for Ollie, it probably wasn't your fault. . . He wasn't in the best of shape.'

No, I thought, I'm sure he wasn't, what with the drugs and the booze and the smoking and, presumably, a reckless lack of exercise. But I felt it wasn't my place to offer health advice. Bryony blinked huge grey eyes at me. She seemed to have difficulty focusing. Her chest heaved. There was a lot of it, a great deal of it was on view.

I stared at the tattoos on her arm, at the intricate Hebrew lettering.

'What does it say?' I asked. Curious despite myself.

She turned her head down to look at the letters. 'That bit' – a blood-red fingernail traced the cursive script – 'says, *the serpent beguiled me and I ate*' – how appropriate, I thought – 'and that bit. . .' her finger moved along, 'says *Exodus 3.13*.' She looked at me with her dilated pupils. 'It's from the Bible. Eve said it.'

'Oh, that's nice.' Sunday school had clearly paid off in Bryony's case. The serpent beguiled me and I ate. I thought of me and the other man and Andrea. It was uncomfortably close to home. Let who is without guilt throw the first stone. I was in no position to judge Bryony, that was for sure.

'I bet I know who poisoned him,' she lurched a little on her feet and grabbed my arm to steady herself. I could smell strong, musky perfume and sweat and a faint hint of grass.

Good, I thought to myself, a lead!

She steadied herself and leaned upwards so she could whisper in my ear.

'Shall I tell you who did it?' she slurred, her pupils were massive, her eyes looked like they had been double-glazed.

'If you wouldn't mind. . .'

'The Earl,' she whispered dramatically. 'He's the killer.'

145

Chapter Twenty-One

When I returned home from the Three Bells, I looked up the Earl on Google. According to Wikipedia, the title had been created in the nineteenth century by Lord Salisbury for now obscure governmental services. Even then, scandal dogged the family. Seemingly, the first Earl had been accused of buying the title, not from Salisbury, who was wealthy enough, but from a fellow minister. There had also been rumours of actresses, frolics with the Prince of Wales, gambling debts unpaid. The present Earl had led a similarly chequered life.

James Rupert Harrington Winslow, born in 1961, had been educated at Eton, St John's College Oxford and had served in the Guards. He had, during the late 1970s and 80s, been arrested for drug possession, and had also been found guilty (suspended sentence) of tax evasion and attempted bribery. He had become a bit of a tabloid darling, what with his entitled high-jinks.

The words 'vice' and 'high' in the newspapers became inextricably linked with his name. 'Vice Romps at Aristo's Palace', 'High Times at Henley, Earl of Hampden caught with joint', 'Happy Birthday to You! Drug Earl in Vice Girl Orgy on Estate!'

That kind of thing.

I turned off the computer and added the Earl to my list of suspects. I knew it couldn't have been him the day I had found Whitfield, he was far too old to have run away like the person I had seen. But that would not have prevented him contracting the job out, if he were involved.

Why would he have wanted Whitfield dead? Or Scott, come to that? Bryony hadn't said. After she had accused the Earl, the pub had started to fill up and she'd joined a group of youngsters by the pool table, occasionally glancing over meaningfully at me, in between endless messaging on her phone. I speculated it was maybe because of the housing project, 'worth millions' according to Chris. Even earls need money, high-class call girls don't come cheap.

'We'll talk later,' she'd promised before joining her friends.

Could Bryony be the key to the whole thing? If the Earl had killed or caused Ollie Scott to die then I strongly suspected he would be involved in Whitfield's death. I thought to myself, I'll get her phone number or address from Jess, she'll know how to find her.

In the interim, there was the housing development itself to look at. I texted Jess to see if she was free the following day. It was time to pay a visit to Chandler's Ford to have a look around. At the very least it would give me something to tell Justin when he asked me how my investigation was going.

My phone buzzed, it was an immediate reply – Jess was free and would be round at eleven o'clock. This was followed by another text: could I lend her a rolling pin?

Sure.

I wondered why as I looked in the drawer where I keep my baking things. There was a choice. I had a really big one from Italy that I used for pasta, a couple of polyethylene 46 centimetre long ones, a couple of small ones that I used for pastry work and fiddly things like Chinese dumplings and two 30 centimetre ones. I scratched my head and picked up a 30 centimetre one. I shoved it in the inside pocket of my jacket so I wouldn't forget it in the morning.

I went to bed early that night.

It was now Saturday morning and as I drove I brought Jess up to date on developments with the food poisoning investigation.

'I'm hoping to hear from Sandra Burke today,' I said, 'but it's a long shot. The lab requires three working days so it'll probably be Monday before I hear and I'm given the all clear.'

'I'm sure it'll be fine,' said Jess, checking her phone for messages as she did every few minutes.

I made a noncommittal noise as the car splashed through puddles.

'I met Ollie Scott's ex yesterday,' I said, casually. I was curious to get Jess's opinion of her.

Jess grimaced. 'Bryony Mogg. God, that girl.'

'Do you know her?'

'Mm, I was at school with her, she dropped out in year twelve. She was quite bright but. . .' There was silence. It was obviously a big 'but'. Too much to tell.

'Did she show you her tattoos?' she asked me.

149

'Yes, they're very biblical.'

'Aren't they just,' said Jess sniffily. 'I bet she's got *"For what we are about to receive. . ."* tattooed here,' she indicated just below her navel. 'Slut,' she added, for good measure.

Things were not looking good for casually finding out how to contact Bryony.

'I'm sure she's a very nice girl, deep down,' I said, 'deeply moral, all those Bible studies. . .'

'And I can assure you,' said Jess, emphatically, her thumbs darting over the keypad of her phone and glancing over at me, 'that she is not.'

We were now on our way to look at the site in Chandler's Ford, the place where Whitfield had laid his plans to make his fortune with the multi-million-pound development. We drove along country roads that would be pretty in the spring but were now lined with brown hedgerows and muddy, stubbly fields. The trees stood gaunt and bare. The only sign of life were depressed, bedraggled crows.

Jess now filled me in on the Earl. From the village point of view.

'He's a bit of a scandal, really.'

'Still?' I asked. I would have thought his grey hairs would have brought respectability.

'Still,' confirmed Jess. 'He's got all these tarty Eastern European girls young enough to be his granddaughters drooling all over him' – she shook her head in disapproval, her dark curls flying – 'people say that he hosts these sort of orgies up at the Hall, and he certainly hung around with Ollie. I'd say I'd agree with Bryony. If anyone poisoned Ollie it'd probably be him.'

'Why would he do that?' I asked.

'Because he's an evil old bastard,' was Jess's reply. It seemed a bit nebulous.

'Does he still do drugs?' I asked. Perhaps he'd been behind Ollie's punishment beating, perhaps he was Ollie's backer. 'At his age?'

'Bound to,' said Jess with youthful certainty, 'leopards don't change their spots. Even if he doesn't – his girls will.'

We drove on in companionable silence. Occasionally the car juddered badly as we hit another pothole that, filled with water from the recent rains, looked deceptively like just another puddle. Then as we were driving alongside the main railway line that ran to Aylesbury, Jess pointed with her finger.

'You see those trees down there?'

Across the fields was a line of pollarded willows. I nodded.

'That's the river Bourne. Chandler's Ford is about a mile away.'

A couple of minutes later I drove into the village. To call it a village was a bit misleading, it was more a collection of houses along a road that looped off the main road and re-joined it a mile or so further westwards.

They didn't have a green like we did, I thought smugly. This was followed by the thought, Oh My God, I just thought, 'we'. I'm turning into one of them, a villager. Turning into a villager would be like unwittingly becoming a vampire. You'd start by thinking, oh, sun's a bit bright today, I'll pull the curtains. Later, I'll just go out for a stroll now it's dark. Mmm, some blood would be nice. Before you knew it there you were. With a villager it would be,

'You're not from around here are you?' followed by a hatred of change and suspicion of incomers. Particularly people from London. Pushing up property prices. Filling local schools with their children, a kind of Trojan Horse approach.

I looked around this new village.

There was a church and a car park and a pub. There were two rows of houses, one between the church and the pub, one after the pub. I parked the car and we got out.

'It's down here,' said Jess. I followed her down a muddy path to the river. Like 'village', 'river' was a bit of a misnomer; it was a clear stream, maybe three metres across, if that. It was edged with reeds and the occasional brown, dead, bulrush.

The drizzle continued to fall and the water flowed fast, swollen by the seemingly endless rain.

We looked out across the water to the fields on the opposite side. We could see large pools that had formed in the sodden ground.

That was where, according to the page I had downloaded from the council website, planning permission had been granted to build the 200-house development.

I pointed with my finger. 'It's supposed to be over there, in those fields.'

'It doesn't look very suitable for houses,' Jess commented, 'it'd be like a rubbish version of Venice.'

I had to agree. It looked far too watery for building. As if to confirm that, a couple of ducks splashed down on a vast puddle in the middle of one of the fields.

'Look,' said Jess, 'they've landed smack bang on Number seventeen's conservatory.'

We stared at the quagmire opposite. It was wildly unsuitable for a housing estate.

'Let's go and ask at the pub,' I said, 'see what the locals have to say.'

If the river flooded much more, you would be able to row up to the Greyhound's back door. That was no exaggeration. Its beer garden faced on to the Bourne and it was mostly under water. The pub looked dispirited and shabby. It made the Three Bells look like Harry's Bar, the epitome of luxury drinking. The paint was flaking away from the grimy windows and the pub sign was cracked and battered. We walked into the porch.

The Greyhound, unusual for these days, still had two bars, a saloon and a public bar. That's how it used to be, the saloon for the white-collar drinkers and the ladies, and the public for the blue-collar workers. Mostly all gone now, a thing of the past; like schooners of sherry, brown ale and 'gin and it'.

I chose the saloon bar. Strangers were rarely welcome in public bars. They were very much a place for locals, and interlopers were not made to feel at home. I didn't want to upset anyone. I looked around as we walked in. Unlike the Three Bells which was like a grotty inner city pub in terms of decor – you could have uprooted it to Kentish Town without anyone being any the wiser – this was a typical grotty country pub, dusty, musty, borderline dirty. It was low-beamed, and bric-à-brac like horse brasses and pieces of old farm machinery whose original function, now long forgotten, adorned the walls, and there was a pervasive smell of damp. Chandler's Ford certainly didn't lack for water.

There was a man of about fifty behind the bar with a heavy drinker's reddened features and strawberry nose. He took my order without comment, eyeing me with dislike. What is it with country pub landlords? I thought.

He poured me a bitter lemon with an icy disdain and leered at Jess as he gave her a J2O.

'We're doing food,' he said (snarled), indicating a black-board in the corner.

I glanced at it politely. I'd seen it as I walked in, of course, but 'liver and bacon' and 'sausage casserole' had sounded more of a threat than a promise, as did the 'all-day Bucks English Breakfast', which I suspected to be a grease-fest drowned in cheap baked beans. It would almost certainly contain that nasty, cut-price bacon with white flecks of God knows what in and probably deep-fried sausages that looked like unwholesome penises when the casings shrank back in the hot fat.

'I'm fine,' I said, suppressing a shudder.

'I'm fine too,' said Jess.

The landlord gave us a venomous stare and went through to the side where the public bar was. It was mostly cut off from our view by a partition wall that ran three quarters of the length of the bar but I could see his back turned to us and hear the hum of conversation as he chatted to a couple of regulars on the other side.

'Lovely day,' said the only other customer sarcastically. He was an old man sitting in the corner with his dog, an ageing springer spaniel, that banged its tail on the floor in a friendly fashion.

Jess went over and stroked the dog. The man smiled at

her. He must have been in his late seventies, tall and cadaverous, with powerful bony wrists clutching a tall walking stick. He was sitting ramrod straight in his chair. He had one of the old-fashioned Bucks accents that have a country burr to them. You don't hear it now in anyone younger than people of his age. I suppose it's TV that has killed it off.

'What are you two doing here?' he asked. Strangers were obviously a novelty in the Greyhound. Customers I guess would be a novelty in the Greyhound. It smelt not only of damp, but failure.

'I came to look at the site for the new housing development,' I said. 'Do you know anything about it?'

Jess was engrossed with the dog who had rolled over to have his stomach rubbed, wheezing with pleasure. His owner looked at me rather oddly.

'Friend of Paul Harding's are you?' he asked, suspiciously.

'Um, I don't know the gentleman in question,' I replied, politely. Harding sounded like he was clued up on the development project. 'Is he around?'

The old guy smiled rather grimly. 'You'll find him in the churchyard, six feet under. He was interested in the new houses too.'

I gave him an inquisitive look. He was clearly warning me off the subject. It was having the opposite effect; now I was intrigued.

'Who owns the land?' I asked. The old man looked nervously at the bar. I turned around and, as I had guessed, there was the landlord. It was obvious that the topic of the housing development was not an item of conversation welcome in the Greyhound.

He rang the bell used to call last orders. Normally it's rather a cheery sound but it had quite a threatening toll to it. A sound of ominous finality.

'I'm afraid we're closing now,' he said.

I looked at the time on the clock above the bar: 12.45. A very odd time to close.

'If I can have your glasses.' It was a demand, not a request. Basically an order to get out of the pub.

The old man lifted his pint. 'No, you're fine, Tom,' said the landlord, 'it's just these two. I'm sure they've got things to do.' His voice was polite, but it carried an undisguised threatening tone.

I realised that the public bar, the other side of the serving area, had fallen silent. The absence of sound carried an undercurrent of menace that washed through to our half of the pub. He went back to the other side of the bar. I suddenly wanted very much to be out of the Greyhound. I stood up, as did Jess, from where she had been squatting stroking the dog.

I noticed Jess was about to speak, she was quite a combative person. I caught her eye and shook my head.

'Sure,' I said and finished my drink.

I nodded a goodbye to the old man and the dog, and Jess and I left the pub.

We emerged into the cold, overcast grey of the January afternoon and as we walked back to the car, Jess said, 'Well, what was that all about?'

'I don't think asking questions about the Chandler's Ford housing development project is particularly popular. Not in the Greyhound anyway.'

I led Jess into the churchyard through the wooden gate that had a kind of portico above it. The spire was very tall and had gargoyles protruding from it. It was quite impressive.

'I didn't know you were religious?'

'I'm not,' I replied, 'we're going to see someone who, I guess, opposed the project.'

The graves in the churchyard were neat and well-kept and the grass short. I quickly found what I was looking for: a fresh grave, fading flowers still heaped upon it. The inscription on the temporary marker read:

Paul Harding, Loved this Village.
Et in Arcadia Ego

His dates followed. He had died in December. He had been sixty-six.

We walked back to the car.

'Is that the man Tom told you about?' asked Jess. I nodded.

'I guess he asked the wrong questions too,' I said. That made three dead people recently – two of whom were linked to the proposed housing development – Whitfield by virtue of the consortium and Harding, for reasons that I didn't yet know.

As we left the church precincts en route to the car, the door of the Greyhound opened and two men started striding purposefully and menacingly in our direction. They were swinging their arms aggressively as they approached. I guessed they were the regulars from the pub, the ones I had heard.

But not seen, in the public bar. Jess saw them too. I don't think it occurred to her that we might be in any danger. Why should it? In twenty years on this planet I don't think anything bad had ever happened to her.

Well, it had to me.

'Jess.'

I tried to keep my voice calm but there was obviously an edge to it. I was very fond of Jess and it looked like I was about to get her involved in some unpleasantness. I would have left her behind if I had suspected for one instant that something like this might happen.

'Could you get in the car please while I have a word with these two gentlemen?'

Jess nodded and did as I asked. I looked around at the two men who were now rapidly approaching.

One of them was sixty if he was a day. He was of middle height, with a white Colonel Sanders-style beard and a black hat, the kind a cowboy might wear, if he was the kind of cowboy who wanted to look ridiculous. He was dressed head to toe in black, a Chilterns version of Johnny Cash, but without the charisma, charm or looks. Also, we weren't in Kansas, we were in Buckinghamshire. That certainly didn't help. The other one was trouble, the muscle. He was twenty years younger than his companion, short, stocky, aggressive in his movements, with a sneering kind of face. It wasn't a sneering look, his whole face was built that way.

'Can I help you two gentlemen?' I asked politely.

'*Can I help you two gentlemen?*' said the short guy in a kind of mincing parody of my voice.

The one with the hat laughed unpleasantly. His function was obviously to act as a kind of cheerleader to the thug. It was all very playground, the school bully and his hangers on.

'Yeah, give us a kiss, darling,' he said, puckering his mouth repulsively.

'Sorry, I'm taken,' I said, smiling sweetly, 'my heart belongs to Daddy.'

'Stay away from our village, and keep your nose where it's not wanted, ain't that right, Eamonn.'

I very much did not like the way that the conversation was headed. I slipped my right hand inside my jacket and my fingers closed around the cold polyethylene of the rolling pin that I'd put there the night before and not got round to giving Jess.

Eamonn, the tough guy, looked me in the eye.

'Fuck off, bitch,' he said.

I'd had enough of him and his threatening behaviour.

'Mind your language, short-arse,' I said, staring down at him, 'there's a lady present.'

I don't think Eamonn liked being called a short-arse. He screwed his face up for effort and drew his fist back to menace me. Semaphoring a punch. It wasn't the best of ideas.

I don't think Eamonn was an ideas man. He wasn't very much of a fighter either. He obviously planned to either punch me, or frighten me. Well, that was his plan, but as Mike Tyson famously said, everyone's got a plan until they get hit in the face.

He seemed woefully slow in his movements. I wasn't. And I most certainly wasn't going to stand there obligingly and get punched. With one smooth movement I drew the rolling pin and swung it in a short arc from jacket pocket to the bridge of his nose. The rolling pin weighed about half a kilo. His head snapped backwards and he squawked with pain and buried his face in his hands. Blood trickled through his fingers. It must have hurt like hell.

I hadn't really thought things through but, in for a penny. . . I stepped forward and hit Hat Man in the gut with it.

I don't think there was much in the way of muscle there and he doubled up in pain. I snatched the hat from his head.

'Ha!' I said, mainly for effect. I enjoyed saying it, so I said it again, this time for dramatic emphasis. 'Ha!'

As I suspected, he was as bald as a billiard ball but with a kind of side fringe of wispy white hair. I skimmed his hat in the direction of their insignificant river. To my intense satisfaction it soared up like a Frisbee and landed in the water.

A startled duck squawked and flew away.

The hat floated off downstream borne away swiftly by the current.

Eamonn was standing up now, trying to stem the blood that was flowing from his smashed nose. He made no move to challenge me. Hat Man was still bent double, gasping for breath. I had beaten the two of them. Well, I thought with satisfaction, Daddy would have approved.

I stood there a moment tapping the rolling pin in my left hand. It wasn't so white anymore, it was now slightly smeared at the end with Eamonn's blood. They backed away. They'd had enough. I opened my car door. Eamonn swore at me, unpleasantly. I tossed my hair back in a deliberately provocative way, got in the car and we drove off.

'Wow!' Jess said, her eyes were shining, 'I can't believe you just did that!' She shook her head admiringly. 'That was amazing.'

I smiled at her. 'Serves him right for attacking a defenceless woman. . . you should see me when I'm really cross,' I said.

But as we left the village, the adrenaline subsiding, the euphoria fading, I thought to myself, have I been unbelievably stupid? Whitfield was dead, Paul Harding was dead and those two muppets I had just hit were, I suspected, connected with the development I had just been asking about. Ollie Scott was also dead and I was beginning to believe that that was something to do with Chandler's Ford too.

I thought, I've been very unwise.

Eamonn and Hat Man might be rubbish in a fist fight but they certainly looked mean enough to be able to pull a trigger, or spike drinks. The freshly dug grave in the churchyard and the old man's reluctance to talk freely to me spoke volumes. I thought, if there's a next time, they'll plan it a lot better.

Chapter Twenty-Two

'There's been a complaint about you.'

It was DI Slattery, who else? I had dropped Jess at her house on the outskirts of the village, promising to lend her a different rolling pin, one not coated in blood. Her mother, in a rare fit of *Bake Off* inspired enthusiasm, was going to try to make biscuits. Jess was highly sceptical.

I drove back to the restaurant. I checked my email. No word from any of the official bodies involved in the 'food poisoning incident', Public Health and police.

I was now totally sure that Ollie's death was nothing to do with me. I had other suspects in the frame. There was nothing that I could do, however, business-wise, until I had some form of clearance from the powers that be. I emailed the office of Sandra Burke, the EHO, to ask if the toxicology reports were back on my food samples. In Viking mythology a man's fate is held in the hands of the Norns, shadowy mysterious figures who live at the foot of Yggdrasil. My fate was controlled by shadowy, mysterious food analysts who lived in a lab in Colindale in North London.

I added Eamonn, Hat Man and the landlord to my suspects list for Whitfield's death and I wrote Paul Harding's name down beside Ollie's. The tally of the guilty was growing, unfortunately the bodies were stacking up too. However, I felt I was making progress, of sorts. I looked at what I'd accomplished with satisfaction. When Justin had suggested I find out what was happening, I'd thought he was crazy, but it seemed he'd spotted something in me, a talent or whatever, that I had never suspected I possessed. I felt I owed him a lot, and not just for the oven. My self-esteem was rebuilding itself.

Now, here was the long arm of the law, again. I had invited him in, fully expecting some kind of official exoneration, and now this. I had never imagined that a person who had instigated an assault would have the nerve to claim to be the victim, but my naivety was about to be exposed.

'I'm sorry, what kind of complaint?'

He took out his notebook, although I'm sure that he didn't need it.

'Mr Eamonn Farson from Chandler's Ford claimed that you attacked him and his friend, Lawrence "Jacko" Jackson. At the station in Aylesbury, he made a statement saying that you broke his nose – by way of corroboration, he showed a date-stamped picture that his friend had taken, of the bloodied organ together with you, clearly visible at the wheel of your car, fleeing the scene. It was quite spectacular. . . You're very handy with a weapon, aren't you, Ms Hunter? First Dave Whitfield, now this.'

Was it my imagination or did I detect a trace of admiration in his voice?

164

I said, outraged, 'It was self-defence; he attacked me,' I was going to add – a defenceless woman but that was demonstrably untrue – 'you can ask Jessica Turner, she was there with me. I think you would have to agree that she is a much more reliable witness than Mr Farson. Or his so-called friend.'

It was true and Slattery knew it. I would bet a substantial amount of money on Farson being known to the police.

'But she works for you,' said Slattery, with an air of desperation, 'she might be swayed. . .'

I laughed despite myself. The idea of Jess being financially dependent on me was ridiculous, and he knew it.

'My God, DI Slattery! Will you listen to yourself? Have you seen Jess's house?' Of course you have, I thought.

'Of course I have.'

'I know you have,' I said. 'It was a rhetorical question.'

You could hardly miss Jess's house, it was a vast thing like a mansion, set off the main road from the village. To his credit, Slattery looked sheepish.

'And how might I be swaying her, Detective Inspector?' I said, sarcastically, driving home the point. 'With my limitless wealth? Or my sparkling personality?'

'There is such a thing as personal loyalty,' he pointed out stiffly.

'Sure, and there is such a thing as credibility. Who do you think is more likely to be telling the truth, him, or her?'

'OK, fair comment, I apologise.' There was no trace of anything in his voice other than of genuine regret.

Now that was a surprise. I looked at him in astonishment.

'So what happens now,' I asked, 'about Mr Farson's complaint? Are you going to nick me?'

Slattery scratched his head. 'No, nothing so drastic. We're not going to take any action. He wasn't seriously hurt. And as you say, it was self-defence.' He stood up. 'I'm here to officially reprimand you, but unofficially, you couldn't have picked a better target.'

I nodded. 'Thank you,' I said. I felt unexpectedly touched by this semi-thaw in Slattery's relentless hostility.

'What were you doing in Chandler's Ford anyway?' asked Slattery. All my mistrust of him came flooding back immediately. I looked at him combatively. This is why you're here really, I thought to myself. Do you have links with the building consortium, DI Slattery? What do you know about Whitfield's death? Was it you who got it dismissed as a 'suicide' or an 'accident'?

'Jess was showing me some of the lovely South Bucks countryside,' I replied.

'Is that so?' Slattery leaned over my work-surface, his solid bulk an imposing threat.

'It is so,' I said. 'It's very pretty down there, the river and all.'

He leaned in towards me. 'I heard that you were asking questions about Arcadian Valley?'

'I'm sorry?'

Slattery looked impatient. 'The housing development, Arcadian Valley is what it's called.'

'Really? That's a bit grandiose, isn't it?' I looked at him innocently. 'I can't see what bearing any question I might or might not have asked has on the so-called assault.'

Slattery leaned forwards a bit more. I noticed he seemed to like encroaching on personal space.

'Were you nosing around it? I would hate to think you were involved in some sort of vigilante investigation of the death of Dave Whitfield.'

It was uncomfortably close to the truth. It was exactly what I was doing. I had no intention of admitting it, though. Instead I slipped the punch.

'I thought Whitfield's death was an accident?'

Slattery's face was hard and menacing.

'You know what I'm talking about, Charlie Hunter. Keep out of it' – he opened the kitchen back door – 'oh, by the way, I've seen the tox report on Ollie Scott.'

'Oh, yes?' The million dollar question.

He nodded. 'Methanol poisoning, so unless you've been selling anti-freeze cocktails or setting it in aspic, you're in the clear.'

'Methanol?' I repeated. I was so delighted, it was definitely not the crab; I was off the hook.

'Yep. Methyl alcohol,' he said. 'So this one is going down as suspicious. Like I said, watch your step.'

Aspic! So old-fashioned!

He closed the door behind him. 'Watch your step!' For once, I don't think he was referring to himself. He sounded genuinely concerned for my welfare. Somehow, that was quite alarming.

I had been warned.

Chapter Twenty-Three

I'm not good at many things – singing, formal cake decoration and talking about football or cars are just some of them. Heeding warnings is another. I emailed the Land Registry office in Coventry and paid for a copy of the report on the ownership details of Arcadian Valley and also details of the flood report for the Chandler's Ford area where the Arcadia development was situated.

Sod you, Slattery, I thought as I was doing this. Mind you, in fairness, he had backed away from the Farson claim of assault, not that he would have got very far with it.

I also hunted for information about the deceased Paul Harding on the internet. It wasn't hard but it took a great deal of time. It was the usual problem: an excess of information. It's a fairly common name and despite trying to refine the search, I waded through a lot of extraneous Hardings. Did you know there is a famous Paul Harding, a Pulitzer prize-winning author? Me neither, but I do now. There are quite a few others, too. But I persevered and, in the end, I found what I wanted.

My one, Chandler's Ford Paul Harding, newly deceased,

had been a stalwart champion of the community, an elderly, left-wing eco-activist and, reading between the lines, a champion pain in the ass.

He had been active in the Chiltern Society, a tireless fundraiser for local causes and had been given an OBE. That was not his only official recognition. He had also been arrested several times and had restraining orders placed on him, banning him from a mile's radius of three out-of-town supermarkets after vigorously protesting in their aisles and car parks. He hated supermarkets. He was against development of all kinds. There was a wealth of pictorial evidence available.

Harding was into bondage, but not in a sexual way. He loved chains. He had chained himself to trees, lamp-posts and, one time, a digger. He had no truck with the modern trend for glue, he wasn't a polymer guy, he liked rocking the vibe of good old fashioned steel. I found umpteen photos of him, thin, bald with a fringe of silver hair and glasses, corduroy jacket and tie, being carried away by policemen.

If it was made of concrete, he opposed it. If it had room for a chain, even better.

I found an obituary from the local paper. It mentioned his opposition to HS2, the railway line (or, 'a dagger through the beautiful heart of the Chilterns' as Harding put it – lots of diggers to chain himself to) but no mention of any other causes he had been championing at the time of his death.

He had been killed by a hit-and-run driver as he walked his dog, a miniature Schnauzer called Cobbett. I thought the chances of Paul Harding welcoming an executive housing development in the village he lived were infinitesimal. Conversely, the chances of Paul Harding leading a successful protest movement against a housing development on the land were fairly high.

Was it just coincidence? But I bet it wasn't the developers and builders of HS2, Balfour Beatty, McAlpine or whoever, or the owners of Tesco or Lidl, who had mown him down in a car and failed to stop.

I spent more time reading on my computer screen. Harding had been killed by a dark hatchback. I wondered what car Farson drove. Well, only one way to find out.

I looked at the clock: 6.00. By 7 o'clock I was in the car park again at Chandler's Ford, this time in Justin's Audi A3 which I had borrowed for the occasion. I had explained why. I didn't want to use my own vehicle in case anyone saw it. I suspected that even Farson, maybe not the brightest of men, might well be able to remember the make of car belonging to the woman who had knocked him down earlier in the day.

I thought that I stood a fairly good chance of finding him in the Greyhound at that time of the evening. There was something about Farson that gave more than a hint he was not married. He seemed an unpleasant little thug and at his age, mid-forties I guess, any woman dumb or unlucky enough to have formed a relationship with him would surely have moved out. I assumed he would live alone, sustained by porn and booze. Of course he would be in the pub, where else could he go? Who else would have him?

I parked the Audi by the church and walked to the Greyhound. I was warmly dressed but I shivered in the cold wind. As if on cue it started raining heavily. There were lights on only in the public bar. How disappointed non-regulars would be, I thought, who might want to enjoy the warm welcome of the landlord in the luxurious and welcoming saloon.

Its car park only held four cars, none a dark hatchback. Well, I wasn't too surprised. The vehicle must have been quite dented after hitting Harding and it would have been a bit much to have blithely driven round in it afterwards, even in Chandler's Ford. I doubted they would have got it fixed. Turning up at a local garage with a massively dented car after the death of a prominent citizen in a hit and run might be somewhat risky.

I wondered if Slattery had investigated the murder. I wondered again about his proximity to Whitfield and Montfort.

In fact, I was beginning to think quite a bit about Slattery. He seemed very zealous when it came to investigating me and very lethargic when it came to anyone else.

As I walked in the darkness, I realised that there were no streetlights in Chandler's Ford; it struck me how surprisingly insular the villages round here could be. We were probably only about thirty or forty miles from where I had lived in North London, but out here in the Chilterns at times was like being in the middle of nowhere. There was a certain crazed and, to my mind, utterly misplaced, pride in this isolation, too, from the local populace.

In the Three Bells I had seen two men nearly come to

blows over who was more local. One, aged twenty-three, had said he'd lived in the village all his life, that is, twenty-three years; the other, aged forty, had pointed out he'd lived here thirty years, thus making him seven years more local. Being 'local' was worn like a badge of honour. I knew their respective ages because they were central to the (very loud) drunken argument. The other had said, maybe, but you weren't *born* here, you grew up for ten years in Yarlsdene, and that's five miles away. Therefore, you are obviously a foreigner.

Like angels dancing on pinheads. Who cared? They did, and it could be funny, and it could be scary. Like Morris Men are. They may look ridiculous, but what they're doing is very dark indeed. But that's the countryside for you. The thing was, not so many people lived in Chandler's Ford, but I would bet a week's takings that, even if they knew who had run Harding over, they'd rally round, clam up and say nothing.

Local murders for local people.

I reached the pub and looked in the dirty window. Sure enough, there was Farson and Hat Man propping up the bar. The latter was wearing a trilby tonight, as his cowboy-style hat floated along down the Bourne somewhere. I'd looked that up too, when I was on Google. Seemingly, it disappeared into a sinkhole some five miles away. I wondered if his hat had gone too, disappearing with the waters down into the bowels of the earth. Like the Styx.

A hat for Charon.

I hoped so.

They were with another two ageing, seedy macho men. What a crummy clientele the Greyhound had! One wearing a cracked faux-leather jacket and slicked-back Brylcreemed hair, improbably black, and another, tall and skinny with bottle thick glasses. These two were about fifty. There were no women in the pub, unsurprisingly. They were playing some sort of card game with the landlord that involved a lot of shouting, waving of arms and banging the cards down.

Probably not contract bridge then, nothing intellectually more complex than Happy Families. I peered through the glass at them, useless lowlifes perpetually on the lookout for people they could intimidate.

I could easily believe any of them capable of running an OAP over. They would probably find it funny. I was glad I'd broken Farson's nose, I just wish I'd hit him a few more times. Maybe kicked him in the balls while I was at it.

When it came to Whitfield's death I wasn't so sure about their role. For a start, I didn't think any of this lot seemed man enough to do it. I'd hit Whitfield, but I knew what I was doing and Whitfield was drunk, and confused; angry, yes, but his heart hadn't really been in it. He could have taken any two of this lot on, probably all of them, and won handsomely. For Whitfield to have been killed with his own gun implied that whoever was with him had Whitfield's trust. None of this lot would have had that. A prickly, suspicious individual like him wouldn't have passed someone as obviously untrustworthy as Farson or Hat Man a loaded shotgun.

Slattery, though. . . or the Earl, whose land he had been on when he died.

Also, Whitfield's killer had the ability to run athletically.

I must have played the scene over and over again in my mind like a gif. Over and over again, on a loop in my brain.

Like now.

The body lying there, the field, the horses in the far corner, the stile, and in the distance the figure running away with speed and grace.

Could the Earl have done it? He was probably on performance-enhancing drugs for his Eastern European floozies – maybe he'd taken a handful of amphetamines that fateful morning instead of Viagra?

I crouched outside impotently in the darkness wondering what to do. So far I had ascertained that Farson knew some unpleasant-looking people, which was hardly a break-through. Who else would hang out with him?

I think when I left Hampden Green I had some vague idea of following him back to his home and finding his car. It was now obvious to me that was going to be pretty impossible. I might have been able to tail him down a motorway but not along a single-track road with passing places. Talk about obvious.

I scratched my head and then was forced to move fairly quickly for cover as I saw the headlights of a car approaching the pub. I ran across the strip of car park and crouched behind the three wheelie bins that stood there. The bins were overflowing and stank to high heaven. They were also very close to the wall and I was jammed between their metal sides and rough brick. The bins weren't just over-flowing with refuse; dirty smelly water was running off them and on to me. It was foul. Like a hideous shower. The landlord was obviously not in the habit of washing them out very often and the smell of rotting vegetables with an overlay of off-fish was so strong you could almost touch it. I wondered when they were last emptied as bin juice effluvia trickled off my head and down my neck.

I saw the headlights wash over them, and heard the loud throbbing of a powerful engine. The car stopped and the door opened and closed with a solid-sounding thunk. I peered round my bin.

Despite my considerable automobile-ignorance, I recognised the car immediately by the distinctive trident on the grille. It was a Maserati.

I also recognised the man who was driving the car and my eyes widened in surprise. What was he doing here?

Chapter Twenty-Four

'So, what do you think the Earl was doing there?' asked Justin. He had kindly lent me his bathroom after I had dropped his car back. I could see his nose wrinkling from the stench that I'd imported from the Greyhound's car park.

Justin's bathroom was everything I'd imagined it to be, and then some. A wonderful, a state- of-the-art shower, a big, deep bath, gleaming marble surfaces, heated towel rails and, neatly lined up, various male grooming products.

I wasn't complaining. All I had in my shower was some shampoo and a few other necessary products. Certainly nothing screaming luxury and pampering like his. My bathroom was so depressing it hardly seemed worthwhile investing in such things.

Not having much inclination to linger in my horrible shower, my shampoo doubled as body wash, or 'soap' as I liked to think of it. So I had spent a happy half hour in Justin's enormous bath scrubbing myself with exfoliating tropical shower gel (a kind of gritty fruity sludge) getting the smell of the Greyhound's bins off me.

'I don't know, it could be something as innocent as simply enjoying the company of Farson and his friends for the evening, but why would anyone want to do that?'

We were now sitting in his lounge while my clothes that he'd washed for me whirled around in his dryer. I was in the armchair, wearing one of his bathrobes and little else. He was on the sofa. I thought to myself what a kind man he was. Not many people had let me use their bathrooms and did my laundry for me. He poured himself another glass of Sancerre.

'So what do you think is happening? Would you like some of this?' he indicated the bottle.

'No thanks,' I said. 'When I get back to the restaurant I've got quite a lot of work to do. I've been given the green light to reopen. It's going to take me about eight hours to get all the prep ready.'

Sadly it was true. I looked at the clock on the wall: 8 o'clock. My heart sank. I thought, I'll work till two in the morning and get up at seven to finish off what's left, that should do it. Francis was in at ten, Jess at eleven and she'd get the restaurant set up.

I so didn't want to have to go back home. I was warm, comfortable and enjoying Justin's company. He was wearing a white baggy sweatshirt and black running tights. His shapely feet were bare.

Every now and then I could hear the percussive rattle of the buttons on my trousers against the drum of the dryer as they whirled around. It was a surprisingly soothing sound; I guess it was the sound of domesticity, something I hadn't known since Andrea and I had split up.

It reminded me of what I had been missing.

A life shared.

'What do I think's happening?' I said. 'I think that there's something very fishy about that housing development and I think Paul Harding was killed because of it and I think Whitfield probably was too.'

'What are you going to do about it?' he asked.

When he had first asked me to look into Whitfield's death, I had been reluctant – despite the oven. But I was actually beginning to, not exactly enjoy it, but become fascinated by what was happening, now I had lifted the lid on what looked like a criminal conspiracy. I felt compelled to go on. I had got so far, I really wanted to know the truth so strongly I surprised myself. I answered his question.

'When the Land Registry get back in touch with me then I'll know more. At least I'll know who owns the land, but I have a horrible feeling that basically any enquiry is eventually going to come up against DI Slattery.'

'What difference does it make whose fields they are?' he looked puzzled.

'I honestly don't know,' I replied, 'but if Whitfield's death has anything to do with the Arcadia development it probably is relevant.'

'It's strange,' he said, 'that the dead man, Paul Harding, should have that quotation on his tombstone; it's like someone is gloating.'

'Or boasting, or warning,' I said. 'It means "I too am in Arcadia" – it's some sort of classical reference. It's from a famous painting. Arcadia is some kind of countryside heaven. The other thing I was wondering, is, if I do discover

179

anything concrete, what do you think I should do about it: tell the police?'

I wasn't looking forward to going to Thames Valley CID. They'd probably refer me to Slattery.

'Eventually you'll have to, to clear your name,' said Justin. 'I think that you've done brilliantly so far.' He frowned. 'But I can understand your reluctance, I've got a funny feeling about Slattery. . . I heard stuff about him from Dave Whitfield occasionally. Rumours. . . I think he's on the take, a dirty cop.'

He drank some more and changed the subject. 'So, if I were you, I wouldn't go straight to him, you can't chance it. Let me know what you find out and we can decide together on what course of action to take.'

I nodded, that sounded good.

'I'm going to have to go in a minute,' I said.

'You're not really going to start work now, are you? Look at the time.'

I was only too aware of the time.

'I have to. I'm open tomorrow, I need to do the prep. I lost quite a bit of money being closed.'

'Well,' he pointed out, 'you've saved on the cost of a shower, plus shower gel.'

'And I smell of mango. That's always a bonus.'

He laughed. He had excellent teeth.

'That's true, I can smell you from here.' He swung his legs up on the sofa with an athletic movement and pushed a hand through his hair. He looked at me with an expression in his eyes that I couldn't really understand. I wanted to tell him how attractive I found him, but equally I didn't want to break the spell of happy togetherness that we were sharing. I didn't know what to do.

'It's often paired with lime,' I said.

'What is?' he looked confused.

'Mango,' I said.

'Is it really?' he said politely.

'Mango also goes well with scallops. . . it's because of the citrus overtones,' I added, in desperation. I really was losing the conversational thread.

'The dryer's stopped,' I said. 'I'd better get dressed and go.'

Part of me now was hoping he'd say, 'No, don't go' or words to that effect. 'Please stay' would have been good. I realised I was beginning to fall for Justin.

Instead, I got, 'I'll go and get them for you.'

In some ways I was relieved. I really liked him and I didn't want to risk our relationship. I felt it was so delicate. If we ended up having a relationship would that jeopardise our friendship? Or deepen it?

Was I even ready for a relationship with someone – especially after the end of the last one – or was I happier on my own? Seeing Andrea again had rocked me more than I would have thought possible. We'd been engaged, I had loved him. And then, due to my impetuousness, it had ended. I had experienced a lot of disappointment in my love life, such as it was, I didn't want to add to it.

Oh well, I thought, that's enough introspection. I can always make some chocolate éclairs. Choux pastry will always mend a broken heart.

And like choux pastry my hopes had reached dropping consistency.

Chapter Twenty-Five

The next couple of days I devoted to getting the Old Forge Café back on track after my enforced closure. Or sublimating my emotional frustration and growing feelings for Justin through cooking. One and the same.

I made choux pastry, I made éclairs. I remade my passion-fruit mousse and wondered how best to lure Luke Montfort over to the restaurant. My plan – to stupefy him with mousse and then get him to reveal the secrets of the Arcadia development – seemed optimistic to say the least, maybe even far-fetched.

It might not have been a great plan, but it was, undeniably, a plan.

I wondered if he knew Farson and Hat Man or if they were simply sidekicks of Whitfield and whoever else was involved with Arcadia. One thing was for certain, Farson was not the brains behind it. I doubted if Farson had any. I couldn't see him killing Whitfield – too cowardly, too stupid, too inept – but I could easily imagine him setting fire to things or vandalising a car.

I had added Farson and Hat Man – Slattery had told me

his name but I'd already forgotten it – to my growing suspect list together with the Greyhound's landlord. I put a circle around them and a line linking them to Montfort with a question mark. If they were connected I wondered if Farson had informed him of the incident outside the pub. Or worse, Slattery. Was the DI part of the cabal that was Arcadia? Was he hatching plans to supplement his police pension? They were all local. It made for plausibly cosy connections.

The scenario as I saw it so far was as follows.

Arcadia was a development consortium led by Dave Whitfield and others, as yet unknown. They had obtained land and managed to get planning permission for housing, despite the fact that (a) it was greenbelt and (b) prone to flooding. Whitfield had a contact in the local council – namely Luke Montfort who worked in planning – and already stood accused of bribing said official. For some reason the conspiracy had fractured. Whitfield had been harassed, the arson and the paint over his beloved car, threats designed to keep him in line. Whitfield had been murdered because he had finally, irrevocably, fallen out with his partner(s). They were obviously prepared to kill because they had already murdered a local campaigner who might have blocked their plans.

That all seemed perfectly plausible to me. But it was conjecture. I needed proof.

On Monday, I phoned the council, got through to the planning department and then a female voice asked who I wanted to speak to. I gave Montfort's name and then my own.

He took the call almost immediately, 'Hi, Charlie, how can I help you?' He sounded jolly, but in a strained kind of way.

'Hi, Luke. I remember you saying that you were a fan of mousse.'

There was a pause and then a relieved chuckle. That's one of the good things about food, it's reassuring.

'Well,' I continued, 'I've just made the most fantastic passionfruit mousse – light, amazingly flavoured and yours for free if you and a companion spend more than ten pounds between you at the Old Forge Café.'

I could sense his smile down the line.

'Do you phone up all your potential customers individually?' he asked.

'No,' I said, 'only the important ones who may have control over catering budgets for work-based events or who may be in the habit of meeting the movers and shakers in South Bucks.'

I felt that this combination of flattery, implying that he had a great deal of power, together with a slight implication of corruption, would appeal to Montfort. We're all men of the world together kind of thing. And so it proved to be.

'As it happens, I am being taken to lunch tomorrow and I will suggest your place.'

'Thank you,' I said politely, 'see you then.'

He hung up and so did I. Bingo!

I finished making a chicken liver parfait and, during service, tried Francis out on starters. I had taken photos of how they should look when finished and had printed them out. There were now ten photos of the cold starters and

185

sandwiches with a checklist which I fixed on to the tiled wall surface above where the starter ingredients were kept.

All Francis had to do was look at the picture, maybe read the description – a spec sheet as it's known – to make sure everything was there that should be there, and off we go, job done.

Foolproof.

But not Francis-proof.

The reality was proving a little bit tougher than I'd anticipated.

'That's great, Francis. Now if we could just make it look a bit more like the one in the picture. . . No, Francis, half a *tablespoon* of remoulade – that's half a *tea*spoon you've put there, it doesn't really look very much, does it?'

'I'm sorry, chef, it's so confusing, teaspoon, tablespoon' – woeful look – 'I'm as much use as a sponge lifebelt.'

'Never mind, Francis' – through gritted teeth – 'Rome wasn't built in a day.'

Service went smoothly. Francis didn't do too badly, although I did have to check more or less everything that he did. By the time we'd finished, he hadn't done anything disastrous and after we had cleared up – he was great at washing floors – I took him over the road to the Three Bells to buy him a pint to celebrate.

I saw in the car park the grey Maserati that belonged to the Earl. The same car that I'd seen pull up in the Greyhound car park.

What was it that Kenneth the fish man had called him? What nickname had he used for him?

'Ropey, a bloody good bloke. . .' I remembered now. We

walked in and I went up to the bar and got our drinks. The Earl was sitting at a table. He wasn't by himself.

I studied the controversial aristocrat closely. He was tall, with a full head of grey hair, and a clipped grey moustache. He was dressed smartly, in chinos and a jacket, wearing two-tone Oxford brogues, which gave him a raffish look.

The casually elegant look was bolstered by the company he was keeping. The last time I had seen him he had been with the Slavic call-girl. Today he was with someone closer to home. He was with Bryony, Ollie's ex. She waved blearily at me. Bryony looked stoned out of her mind. I recalled what I knew about the Earl and his penchant for drugs. Despite his past, he looked very trim, enviably fit for a man of his years. I suddenly wondered how fast the Earl might be capable of running. He certainly looked no stranger to exercise.

Did he look fit enough to run away at speed from a murder scene?

Yes he did.

Bryony was not dressed for the Carlton Club. She was wearing a micro mini-skirt, biker boots and a torn cashmere jumper under a denim jacket. She looked very punk today. I wondered what she was doing with the alleged killer of her boyfriend. She'd obviously decided he was a bloody good bloke too.

Francis and I sat down at a table near the bar. He picked up his pint of lager, raised it to his lips and tipped it back. He put it back on the table, three quarters empty. He turned and beamed at the pub in general. Francis was amazingly good-natured, an example to us all.

My kitchen porter somehow dominated the bar. He undeniably had presence. There wasn't a lot going on between Francis's ears but he was kind of eye-catching. His huge physique – when he bent his arm the fabric groaned – his startlingly blond hair, his slightly goggly eyes, his cheery red face; he was very noticeable.

The Earl had certainly noticed us. He stood up and came over. I rather arrogantly assumed that he would want to speak to me, but it was Francis that he addressed. He beamed up at him.

'Just came over to wish you good luck on Saturday – tough game you've got, I believe.' The Earl's voice was as precise and clipped as his moustache and it was as upper-class as might be guessed from the fact that he was an aristocrat.

Francis nodded happily. 'Beaconsfield are a good team,' he said, 'particularly in the line-outs, but, well, we're in with a chance.'

The Earl nodded. 'That's true,' he said. 'How's the leg?'

'Better now, thanks,' said Francis. 'I'm faster now than I ever was. When I get the ball those Beaconsfield boys will be hard put to catch me, I can tell you that. I'll be running like a bloody. . .' he scratched his head looking for a simile, 'salmon!'

'Good man,' said the Earl. He didn't speak to me but smiled in frosty politeness, and I nodded in acknowledgement. He returned to his table. For a moment I'd wondered what he had been talking about to Francis but then I remembered that Francis played for the local rugby team.

Francis leaned across the table.

'He's a bloody good bloke,' he said. Everyone seemed to like the Earl (with the notable exception of Jess) including Bryony. She obviously liked him a lot. I was getting good at being a detective, I had noticed that she was stroking his thigh.

'Is he?' I said.

'Yeah, the rugby club pavilion was badly damaged in a fire last year and the Earl stumped up about ten thousand himself in a donation to improve the shower facilities, 'cos the insurance were really dragging their feet.' He frowned at the memory. 'They were as much use as an underwater fish tank.'

So, the Earl was involved in good works in the local community. Maybe his taste for young women was just as innocent, part of an outreach programme. But I remained suspicious. There was his visit to the Greyhound that I had witnessed the other night. I couldn't see any reason for his being there other than to meet up with Farson. It was hardly the kind of pub you'd visit unless you had a bloody good reason to go in, either that, or you were a stranger. And Farson was, in my mind anyway, a potential killer. Not of Whitfield maybe, but of Paul Harding. If not that, a killer working on someone's instructions.

I doubted Farson could think his way out of a wet paper bag.

The Earl and Bryony stood up to go and she stumbled slightly and clutched at the table for support.

As they left the bar and the Earl started to open the door, Bryony, who was now supporting herself with an arm around his shoulders, leaned up and planted a passionate kiss on the dapper aristocrat, her tongue disappearing into his mouth.

It obviously wasn't an outreach programme.

Maybe he was just consoling her after her tragic loss.

Chapter Twenty-Six

That was enough excitement for one evening. I walked back across the green to the Old Forge Café. It was bitterly cold but I was quite glad of that. It helped to focus my thinking. Tonight, mercifully, it had stopped raining and I could even see stars through the scudding clouds. The ground under my feet was squelchy, treacherous. The weather until recently had been so wet and windy it was, according to Beech Tree FM – 'aaahnd now, here's the Weather Girls, hope it's not doing this over the Vale of Aylesbury. . . "It's Raining Men"' – setting new records. It was playing havoc with the trains. Trees' root systems were now anchored in wet ground and the high winds had blown several over and on to the track. At times, it seemed like South Bucks was predominantly made of mud.

Hampden Green had virtually no light pollution. For someone used to London, where obviously at night everything outside was illuminated, the darkness had come as a bit of a shock.

It still had the capacity to surprise me.

I looked up again at the stars and the constellations. I recognised the Plough and Orion's Belt. That was it, I was depressingly ignorant of the night sky.

My eyes might have been able to detect objects God-knows-how-many light years away but I didn't notice that I was being followed until I was nearly home. I turned around for some reason; I think it was simply that I wanted to see the effect of the village by starlight. Despite its inhabitants, it was a very pretty place.

There was the dark shape of Whitfield's house and the pillar that would never shine again. And there was DI Slattery's house. The lights were off downstairs but there was that light burning endlessly, it seemed, in the upstairs window. Again I had the fanciful notion that he was up there, surveying the village through night-vision binoculars. Like some dreadful vampire bat. Like Nosferatu.

I could see the lights of Justin's house and the others that lined the green on the far side from my restaurant. At first I didn't see the two men walking towards me as remotely threatening. Why should I? This was a Bucks village, not an underpass in Archway.

They were both wearing hoodies and when they noticed I had turned around and must have seen them, they quickened their pace. I still thought nothing of it. I just thought they were probably anxious to get home out of the cold. It was at this moment that the two started running towards me. It suddenly dawned on me that they were going to attack me.

I took to my heels and ran across the road. I opened the gate that led into the yard beside the kitchen.

I was now inside and I started to quickly push the gate shut. Ha! I thought. All that running in the morning has finally paid off. I began to feel a sense of overwhelming relief – I was home and safe – when I felt a massive blow in the small of my back.

It knocked me forwards and I slammed into the back of the gate.

I whirled around and saw the two men who had been waiting for me in my yard. I saw a hand raised with something in it, a pickaxe handle or a baseball bat, I guessed.

I had no time to think. I drove a fist into the face of one of them. They were wearing balaclavas so I couldn't see their features. The man I'd hit retreated, clutching his head. His sleeve rode up and I caught a glimpse of his wrist as he did so. Then the pickaxe handle that the other guy had, came down on my head and I pitched forwards. I can remember feeling a tremendous second blow – I almost heard it as a bang, rather than felt it – and then I was on the ground. I didn't feel any pain, that would come later, but I was very dazed.

Before I lost consciousness I heard one of them hiss as he pulled me off the ground by my collar.

'Stay away from Chandler's Ford, bitch!'

Chapter Twenty-Seven

I opened my eyes to find Francis bending over me; my body was on fire with pain.

'Jesus, are you OK? What happened?' His large face was full of concern; from where I lay on the flagstones outside the kitchen door his head looked enormous, like a full moon, looming over me.

He helped me to stand and we went into the kitchen. He supported me as we walked upstairs. My legs felt like rubber, and I sat down heavily on the mattress in my bedroom. I studied myself in the mirror on the wall.

I looked a real mess. The beanie I had been wearing had limited some of the damage, but not all. I touched my face gently. I could feel one eye swelling up, my jaw felt swollen and bruised, but my teeth appeared to be intact. Thank God for small mercies. I touched my nose, that was swollen too and was very painful, but all in all I had come off surprisingly lightly. I could breathe without pain so I guessed my ribs had survived the attack. I was lucky in that it was a freezing cold January night and I had a thick jumper and coat on which had absorbed a good deal of the punishment I had doubtless received. My hands were OK, nobody had stamped vindictively on them.

I remembered what they had said: 'Stay away from Chandler's Ford.'

This had been a warning. I thought of Whitfield. He'd had two warnings: two strikes and you're out. I could guess who the messengers were, Farson and his merry men, but who lay behind them?

Francis appeared with a wet towel and a basin of warm water. He crouched beside me and started cleaning up my face. He was touchingly gentle; he looked as if he were going to cry any minute. I felt more or less the same, I had to say.

'Shall I call an ambulance?' he asked, dabbing at my cheek.

'No, I think I'll be OK,' I said.

'What if you've got some sort of brain injury?' he said, looking really concerned.

'I think I'd be feeling a bit worse than this,' I suggested, wondering if that was true.

'How about the police?'

'I just can't be bothered with all the hassle, Francis. The police' – by that I really meant DI Slattery – 'closed me down thinking I'd poisoned Ollie Scott. I've only just re-opened. I don't want the general public thinking I'm involved in something I shouldn't be.'

I meant what I said. Police involvement is anathema to trade for a restaurant. If people see the police hanging around you, even if you're the victim, they associate you with bad things, crime, fraud. All of these negatives will come into play, consciously or unconsciously, especially when it comes to choosing somewhere to eat out. If the police keep turning up at your establishment, you're going to lose trust and custom. Besides, I also suspected that Slattery would not only be less than sympathetic, he'd end up arresting me on some spurious charge. Or maybe he'd just indulge in a surreptitious gloat.

I thought of the upstairs light in his house. Maybe he had been watching the whole thing. I wouldn't have put it past him.

I looked at Francis who was still cleaning me up. 'What brought you back here?' I asked.

'I left my wallet in my work trousers,' he said. 'You'd only been gone a bit. I got another drink and put my hand in my coat and then I realised it wasn't there, so I came back here. There was someone hanging around outside the gate and I thought it was you, so I shouted out and the next thing the gate bursts open and there's the four of them legging it down the road – two went across the common, two down Weston Lane.' That was the name of the road that led to Frampton End, the next village to us. 'So I ran in here, and there you were.'

God, I thought, they'd only just started. If Francis hadn't forgotten his wallet. . . well, I didn't like to think what could have happened.

'Thank God you did, I could have been dead by now. You saved my life, Francis. Thank you very much.'

He beamed at me delightedly. A thought struck me. 'Francis, was the kitchen door open? I mean, unlocked.'

He nodded.

God, the day's takings! Farson had come here to beat me up but I bet he would have taken my money too. I did have an old safe but I'd put the till drawer out of sight in the old oven. I hadn't got round to cashing up yet.

Francis helped me and we made our way downstairs, me gripping the banister like an eighty-year-old. I checked the oven, the till drawer was still there; I looked in the office, the safe was intact.

I was puzzled. I suspected that they'd been inside but why? If beating me up was the sole purpose, what had they been doing?

Francis's large, honest, red face looked at me in concern.

'So what are you going to do?'

I stood up. I actually felt not too bad, although my legs were still shaky. My face looked awful but I'd be hidden away in the kitchen so it wouldn't frighten any of the customers. I'd still be able to work tomorrow, thank God. I couldn't take much more financially of being closed.

I couldn't take much more of this, full stop.

'I think I'll go to bed,' I said.

'Not here.' Francis looked alarmed. 'What if they come back? I mean, if I hadn't turned up they might have killed you.'

He did have a point.

'I'll go and stay at a friend's,' I said, if he'll let me, I thought.

I can remember thinking when Justin was washing my

clothes for me how nice it would be to stay there, but this wasn't the way that I really wanted to be invited. Badly beaten up, certainly not looking my best.

Be careful what you wish for.

Chapter Twenty-Eight

By angling a hand mirror and using the one in the bathroom I could examine the cut on my forehead, near the hairline, where I'd been hit with whatever it was – pickaxe handle, baseball bat or piece of wood. The skin had split but the bleeding had stopped and Francis had criss-crossed it with sticking plaster so I looked a bit like Humpty Dumpty.

I felt quite ill, shaky but worst of all, I found it very hard to think straight. I couldn't seem to concentrate on anything. I felt very jittery. My mind was leaping around like a frenzied cat, jumping from thought to thought with no logical sequence. I also was puzzled by the kitchen door. I always lock doors behind me when I go out. I would no more have left it unlocked than gone out without my shoes. I always check it as well afterwards, just to make sure it is locked. Several times, if I'm honest. I think it's an age thing.

Someone had been inside the Old Forge Café and there had to be a reason. What could they have been looking for?

I told Francis that I would be all right and that he was to go home.

'Are you sure you'll be OK? You look terrible. . .'

'I'll be fine, Francis,' I said. 'I'll see you tomorrow.'

He had reluctantly gone home. He lived with his parents in a small cottage that belonged to the Earl, just on the outskirts of the village. Most places around here did, it seemed.

After he left, I prowled around the restaurant and the kitchen looking for anything that might be missing or out of the ordinary. I couldn't see anything out of place. I went outside into the yard and checked my two store rooms. I'm not sure if I knew what I was searching for there either.

Everything looked normal except that the washing machine door was ajar. I'd done a whites wash earlier: T-shirts, underwear, my chef's jackets, some aprons, and some old chef's jackets I'd accumulated that I let Francis use, and tea towels. I couldn't remember opening it. There was a basket sitting on the floor waiting for the damp laundry to be transferred to the dryer. Surely if I had opened the door I'd have finished the job? But I simply couldn't remember.

This was getting futile.

Upstairs seemed pristine too. In truth, there was very little to look through.

I went back into the kitchen and got my phone. I had forgotten it when I'd gone out, luckily. That would have been smashed up for sure in the mêlée.

It sat unscathed next to my PC. That reminded me I still hadn't got round to changing the password on the PC – well, I certainly wasn't going to do it now.

It was still only 8 o'clock in the evening. I was going to text Justin to ask if it was OK to come round but called him instead. It seemed easier to explain than type out the state I was in. He picked up immediately. His voice sounded slightly guarded, wary, like he didn't want to talk.

'I've got someone round,' he said. Momentarily I felt a sense of angry jealousy. Was 'someone' another woman?

Then I pulled myself together. It wasn't like he was my boyfriend or anything. A friend, maybe technically an employer. The idea that he might have a girlfriend had never crossed my mind, but why wouldn't he?

I suddenly realised I just wanted it to be me. I was surprised by how depressing the thought of him with someone else was.

'Oh,' I said, despondently. I have a way with words.

Justin must have sensed what I was thinking,

'It's nothing like that, I'm having a Tarot reading. Would you like to come round – you sound a bit odd?'

'I had a bit of a run-in with a couple of guys,' I warned him, 'I'm fine, but I'm a bit shaken up.'

'Oh my God! Are you hurt? Come over now,' he said, his voice full of tender concern. 'Anna's only just got here, I can reschedule. What happened?'

I gave him an abridged version of the events and told him I'd be over in a short while.

'I'll come and get you,' he said.

'No,' I said, 'I want air, I want to clear my head.'

'Well, if you're sure. . .' he sounded understandably doubtful.

'I'll see you soon,' I said.

I rather slowly pulled a pair of boots on and a clean coat. All my muscles ached. Bending forwards was particularly troublesome. It wasn't just the beating I'd taken, I felt slow and heavy and ponderous, like lead had been attached to my arms and legs. Shock, I guess. Or maybe concussion.

I left all the lights in the kitchen blazing, to deter anyone from coming back. It was a kind of primitive response I suppose to being attacked.

I locked the kitchen door with my key. That had still been in my trouser pocket when Francis had helped me back inside. They could have taken it out of my pocket, unlocked the door, gone in, then replaced it, but I doubted it. What had they been looking for and how had they got in? I went into the store room, took down the spare that I had hanging on an old nail out of sight behind a calendar advertising stock cubes and bouillon, and hid it under some tins of tomatoes that were on a shelf. It seemed a better hiding place. Just in case. Then I crossed the yard and opened the gate. I looked back, my eyes narrowed.

An hour or so ago I was lying unconscious down there, near my kitchen door.

Four attackers – Farson, Hat Man, definitely – but who were the two others? Maybe the other men I had seen in the Greyhound? But there was one detail that I did remember, or rather, I remember noticing something important. But I couldn't remember what. I knew it was something, maybe an accent, maybe a physical detail like a missing tooth or something, a scar? Whatever it was, it remained stubbornly hidden, like a name that's on the tip of your tongue. I gave up thinking. I knew that if I encountered it again I would know their identity for sure.

Five minutes later I was at Justin's gate. It seemed a lot longer. I was walking very slowly. At the outset, I kind of wished that I had Francis to help me across the common in case my legs gave way. But the cold night air was a great reviver and by the time I got to his place I was feeling considerably better.

But the main reason I'd walked was to show to myself that I wasn't scared. I don't back down from things (courtesy of Dad, another legacy), and I felt that if I hadn't faced my fears I would be damaged. I smiled with affection at the memory of my father. He had taught me how to box when I'd been bullied by a bigger, stronger girl (leader of the populars as the alpha girls were known – I never made the cut). 'Don't cry, Charlie, get even. Now, this is how you throw a hook. . .' And I had. It had been worth a week's suspension. Maybe stupid, but there it was.

I rested a minute or so, looking at the path that led to his front door. His Audi was parked in front of the low wall in front of his house and next to it was a BMW convertible that I guessed belonged to his Tarot psychic.

I looked at Whitfield's house, dark and mournful under the stars. There were bunches of flowers outside his section of the wall that villagers had left. A few doors further down was Slattery's. Earlier I'd imagined him watching while the assault happened. Now I wondered if he had been one of the men laying into me. I rather doubted it. Slattery wouldn't be so dumb as to associate with an idiot like Farson.

But someone had tipped them off as to when I had left the pub. Or had they just been waiting on the off-chance? Surely not. Someone had told them where I was earlier that evening.

Who knew? Was it someone in the pub? Or someone closer to home?

A vague thought drifted across my mind. It couldn't be Justin could it? I considered it as I breathed in the healing night air, the quintessential English country winter smell of damp soil and leaves, a hint of woodsmoke. But what possible motive could he have? Let alone the fact that he was such a nice guy. I smiled bitterly, I must have been hit on the head harder than I'd imagined to be thinking such thoughts.

I looked again at the flowers, just shapes in the darkness. I gingerly touched my damaged head. Would I have got so many floral tributes if I'd died? If I had been hit just that little bit harder it could well have happened.

Well, I was still alive and, I thought as I opened the gate, at least I'd be under the roof of a friend.

Chapter Twenty-Nine

'My God,' Justin said, opening the front door, his eyes widening as he looked at my face, 'you weren't kidding, you look just awful. Come in.'

He ushered me into the living room. He was wearing skinny jeans and a T-shirt, his dark hair was loose. I was feeling slightly lightheaded now. Despite my injuries, I admired the way the denim clung to him, Justin had an exemplary ass. As a trained chef I notice these quality points. Even if I can barely move. My God, I thought, as the word 'exemplary' swam around my brain, I am feeling weird.

The living room, as always, smelled exotic with its heady incense. There was only one light burning; the atmosphere was close, intimate. Shadows filled the room, a low fire burned red in the hearth. I wondered if I'd actually disturbed something I shouldn't have. To be honest, I was past caring. I felt safe and warm now, protected. That was what I wanted more than anything, I realised, to feel safe. There was another woman in the room. This had to be Anna, the Tarot reader. I sat down and Justin said to me, 'You must be in shock.'

'Got any Scotch?' I asked, slightly desperately.

'No alcohol for you,' Justin said, firmly, 'not in your state. I'll go and make you some herbal tea.'

Bloody yoga teachers, I thought. I wanted something a little less New Age. Something with a bit more oomph.

He disappeared off to the kitchen. My head hurt like hell.

I turned my attention to Anna.

'Hello,' I said.

She didn't look like my idea of a Tarot reader. She was dressed more for a boardroom than a gypsy fairground tent. She had white hair, cut short, was wearing an expensive-looking jacket and an above the knee skirt and heels. She had a couple of jade bracelets on her wrists and pearls at her throat. Her earrings were emeralds, and they glowed in the light of the fire. If I'd been asked to guess her job I'd have gone for something like investment banking. I'd met more than a few investment bankers, friends and colleagues of Andrea's, and Anna had that kind of vibe.

Fortune-telling must be well-paid; perhaps the spirits gave her hints about the stock market.

I was sitting on the sofa, she was in a chair opposite and between us was the solid oak coffee table that Whitfield had fallen on to when I'd hit him. I wondered irreverently if there was some psychic lingering phenomena there from the dead builder.

'I have a spirit here who would like the recipe for the celeriac remoulade. . .'

On the table was a pack of old Tarot cards.

'You look dreadful,' she said. Her eyes were piercing,

which made me feel uncomfortable. 'Do you know who did it?'

'No,' I replied. I touched my face gingerly. I was going to be panda-eyed in the morning.

'Do you know why they did it?'

Again I answered, 'No.' I obviously had a very shrewd idea but I didn't feel up to explaining everything, especially to someone I didn't know.

For some reason these questions seemed eminently reasonable. Anna was one of those people with an effortless ability to command your attention.

She nodded as if I had confirmed what she already knew.

'I'll do a reading for you,' she said, 'it'll take your mind off the shock, re-centre you.'

I groaned mentally. I'm not keen on mumbo-jumbo like that. But then, maybe it was what I needed, thinking about the future rather than dwelling on my attack. At least it would take my mind off things. Justin came in at that moment with my tea.

'Valerian and peppermint,' he announced. 'I've sweetened it with honey. That'll help you get over your shock.'

It sounded dreadful.

He looked at me closely. 'Shouldn't you go and see a doctor? I'm more than happy to drive you to A&E.'

Stoke Mandeville Hospital was the closest. Despite what I'd told Francis, I was tempted but the thought of being there for God-knows-how-long put me off.

'No, it's just cuts and bruises, I'm fine.'

'As you like,' he said, 'here's your tea.' He handed me a mug of murky, steaming liquid. It was certainly pungent.

'Thank you,' I said politely. I like tea, I drink a lot of it, but I like PG Tips, occasionally a more sophisticated tea like Darjeeling or Earl Grey, but generally it's PG Tips all the way. What I do not like is herbal tea. Or honey for that matter. I was beginning to regret accepting tea. I should have demanded, not asked for, Scotch.

The tea smelled horrible.

Anna caught my eye and smiled conspiratorially. It was as if she knew what was going on in my mind, but as a medium, so she should.

Justin said, 'Look, I'm going upstairs to run you a bath and make a bed up in the spare room for you. You can stay here tonight.'

'Thanks,' I said, 'I really appreciate that.'

Justin turned to Anna. 'Can you look after Charlie while I'm upstairs? I don't think she should be on her own.'

'I'd be delighted,' said Anna. Justin smiled at me, turned and disappeared through the living-room doorway. I heard his footsteps light on the staircase as he ran up it.

Anna looked at me sympathetically.

'I'm not a medium,' she said. I sort of jumped uncomfortably. How did she know what I'd been thinking? 'And I'm not telepathic and I don't know how the cards work.' She looked me in the eye. 'But when I see someone in need of guidance, I know that I should try to help them. And you look like a woman very much in need of guidance.'

'Do I?' I asked.

She laughed. 'Have you looked in a mirror lately!'

I smiled sheepishly. 'Touché!'

'Justin tells me that you are trying to find out the truth behind a man's death.'

'That's correct.'

'Maybe the cards will help,' said Anna. 'I can see you're a sceptic – no, don't apologise, they work better for non-believers for some reason, and don't say "no". Justin's already paid me for a reading and he's just cancelled, so you're in luck.'

'Am I?' I said.

'Well, maybe not,' she conceded. 'You might not hear what you want to hear. . . but we may as well do something while we wait for him to finish upstairs.'

I shifted in my seat,

'You could always reimburse him,' I suggested.

Anna looked at me. 'I'm not a charity, Charlie. The service on my BMW is due, and as a psychic I predict it's going to cost an arm and a leg and I need the money. Anyway, he can afford it. Now, let's begin.'

She handed me the pack and as I took them, the cards felt strangely warm. 'Shuffle, please.' Automatically I did so. 'But if you did ask me how the cards work,' she continued, 'I'd say that they act more as a guide to what you should be thinking about. They don't predict the future directly – they won't say, for example, you'll be run over by a bus tomorrow but they will say, pay attention when crossing the road, be careful of red objects.'

'Oh.'

I took a sip of tea and grimaced. It tasted much worse than it smelled, which was quite an achievement.

I laid out the cards as Anna instructed, face down, three rows of three. I was beginning to get interested despite

211

my scepticism. It certainly worked at taking my mind off the attack. The sofa was comfortable, the room was soothing in its semi-darkness and I felt warm and protected by these two friendly presences, Anna down here, Justin upstairs, like they were guardian angels. The fire was burning low and glowing in the grate. I was so glad I wasn't at home.

'Past, present and future,' she said, cheerfully. 'Now, let's have a look at the past. Turn the first three over.'

I did so and I looked at my cards – the ancient, evocative pictures calling down the ages: a youth, walking towards a canyon; a woman judge holding a scales and a sword; another woman, seated.

'Hmm,' said Anna, looking at the images. 'Well, here' – she tapped the card with a fingernail – 'we have the Blind Fool, walking to his doom, then' – me presumably, I thought – 'this here is Justice.' She looked at me, her gaze was disconcertingly shrewd.

'So, we've all done dumb things in our past but you've done something spectacularly stupid and paid a high price for it. Justifiably so, according to the cards, although you may think differently.'

'I've done a fair few stupid things,' I said. I thought about Andrea, splitting up with him; that was certainly dumb.

'I don't need to know, this isn't for my benefit,' she added, shutting down any attempt at self-justification.

I nodded, that was fair enough. Despite my initial scepticism I was beginning to get drawn into Anna's narrative, it was all ringing true.

She tapped the third card. 'This is interesting. The High Priestess. She can mean many things, but she guards the

Door to the Hidden Sanctuary' – she looked at me – 'in the past. I don't care how many or how few men there were in your life.' A kind of beauty parade of former lovers flickered through my mind. The ones from my teenage years would be my age now, some older, but to me they were still preserved forever unchanged in my memory, frozen in time, untouched by the passing years. I wasn't one for Facebook or keeping in touch with people.

Anna carried on. 'There is still one, a past love, a man you were deeply involved with, who reaches to you now, or will somehow affect your destiny.'

I thought of Andrea. His unannounced visit to the Old Forge Café. Was it him that the card referenced? He had certainly reached out to me but what on earth could it mean that he was going to affect my destiny?

'Now, moving on to today, the present, next three cards. . .'

I repeated the performance. Anna touched them gently, one by one.

'The Emperor, or the Stone Cube – well, this means the realisation of a dream in solid form.'

I nodded. It probably meant the Old Forge Café. My own place, that had always been my aim.

Anna moved on. 'This one' – she indicated the middle card – 'the Hierophant or Master of the Secrets. Just as the man who you don't know has the key to your future, so this man, powerful, probably rich since that's how we define power these days, more's the pity, he controls your present.'

I nodded, but I couldn't think of anyone. None of my friends are rich, none of my enemies either, come to that.

Then the last card of the present, the Hanged Man. He was hanging by one foot, suspended from a wooden frame made of leafy tree branches. The free leg had its knee bent and the foot rested on the other knee to form an inverted figure four. It was a deeply sinister card, I thought, it's bound to be allegorical or deceiving – though it's probably not as bad as it looks.

Anna regarded me. It was not a comforting look.

'I'm afraid you are facing a considerable personal danger – from whom I can't say, but you are.' She continued, 'What you experienced tonight is just a foretaste. You really will have to be very careful, Charlie Hunter. I don't want to be attending your funeral.'

I grimaced. I had forgotten by now that I didn't believe in Tarot readings; all of this made total sense and was extremely compelling. I didn't want to be attending my funeral either. I wanted to move on.

'And the future?'

Anna looked at me. 'Ready?'

I took a deep breath and turned the cards over.

'Ready,' I said.

Chapter Thirty

After Anna left I'd gone upstairs with Justin for the bath. At the top of the stairs, we stopped and, quite suddenly, we embraced and then I was kissing him passionately, guiding his hands to where I wanted them to be.

We'd made love twice, in quick succession. Justin had amazing powers of recovery, all that yoga I suppose. It was fantastic.

Now I was lying in the bath and under the bright light as I floated dreamily in the Radox infused water, both of us examined my own body with interest. There were angry red marks up and down the length of it that would soon turn into bruises.

'Sit up,' he said. I did so and he started to massage my back.

'So who were they?' he asked as I leaned forwards in the hot, soapy water while his skilled fingers worked my trapezius muscle.

'I assume it was Eamonn Farson, Hat Man, the pub landlord and Mr AN Other,' I said, 'warning me off looking at Arcadia Developments.'

'But surely it's all above board? I mean, the Arcadia deal.' His strong fingers dug deep into the muscle groups. I gasped. It was painful, maybe it was doing me good?

'You're very tense. . .'

'No shit, Sherlock,' I said.

He smiled ruefully. 'Sorry, that was a dumb thing to have said.' He moved back to his original point. 'Surely the council wouldn't let them go through with it otherwise. This is Buckinghamshire, South Bucks at that, not. . .' he searched for an example of somewhere famously corrupt. 'Not Sicily.'

'Is it?' I said. I was dubious. 'There are a lot of corrupt public officials, police, customs officials, you name it, and the same will apply in the council planning department.'

His strong fingers continued to work my muscles.

I slid down in the water.

'Don't put your head under, you'll open that cut,' warned Justin. I did as he suggested.

'I think,' I continued, 'that when I get that land report back, we'll find out that it was owned by a consortium including my friends from Chandler's Ford. We'll discover that they've got some dodgy financial backing and that your dead neighbour was part and parcel of it. I think too that Luke Montfort was bribed to grant them planning permission.'

'Will you be able to prove any of this?' he asked doubtfully.

'Not yet,' I said. 'Can you pass the mango body scrub? I've developed a taste for it.'

He smiled and did so.

I carried on. 'I think Montfort is the weakest link. I bet

Farson's been inside and knows the ropes, Hat Man will clam up and the pub landlord will phone a lawyer. But Montfort has got too much to lose and he doesn't look very brave. I shall lean on him.'

'So you think they killed Whitfield?' Justin had moved to the end of the bath (it was free standing! I'd only ever seen that sort of thing in TV adverts or in the style section of magazines) and was massaging my feet.

'Stop it!' I said. 'That tickles.'

'You have energy gateways here,' Justin explained, pressing my soles. 'They're called Yong Quan points. I'm stimulating them, it'll help unblock your meridian lines.'

He pressed and I squirmed, pulling my feet away from him.

'They'll have to stay blocked,' I said firmly.

'Be like that,' said Justin, with mock severity. 'Don't heal! Anyway, you haven't answered my question.'

'I'm pretty sure one of them killed Whitfield, and I think I can find out who did it. I hope so. You did buy me a new oven to find out.'

Justin didn't smile back.

'Charlie,' he said, his voice suddenly very serious, 'I want you to drop this. Anna said it was dangerous. Look at you, Charlie. You could be in intensive care, or worse. . . I thought back then it was a good idea, but now I've changed my mind. I hadn't realised, it was stupid of me, how serious this all is. Two men are dead, three if you include the protestor in the churchyard. You've been really badly beaten up. God knows what state you'd be in if Francis hadn't intervened.'

He did have a point.

I stood up in the bath and lathered myself with a different bottle of body scrub. 'Sandalwood – Pour Les Hommes' it said on the bottle. 'Pour Les Femmes' now, I thought.

'I'll be fine,' I said, with a confidence I didn't really feel. 'The thing is, Justin, I'm a very stubborn woman. Besides which, Farson is going to have to pay for this.' I gestured at my battered body. 'He'll be wearing his nads for earrings if I had my way.'

'Oh well. . . so be it, ' said Justin. He was staring at me in the bath as I slowly lowered myself back into the water. 'You've got a great body,' he observed, changing the subject.

'Thank you.' I felt flattered. All those sit-ups and crunches were finally paying off. 'Even with the bruises?'

'Even with the bruises.'

I nodded. 'You're right, it's fantastic. You're a lucky man to get your hands on it.'

'What did Anna say about your future, by the way?' he asked, changing the subject again.

I thought of the three cards, the Devil, sitting on his iron throne with a man and a woman in chains like his pet animals. There had been the Moon, the dogs baying at it, a mysterious crab-like creature crawling out of the water in the foreground, the ominous towers in the background and last of all Judgement, the angel blowing the horn for the last day, the graves yielding up their cargo of the dead.

Betrayal, a snare or a death, and last of all a judgement.

I felt reluctant to discuss it. 'It was shrouded in mystery, she said.'

Justin smiled. 'Well, mystery woman, I'm glad you are staying in my bed tonight. I think it'll be safer than going back to the Forge. At least I can keep an eye on you.'

'Thank you,' I said. 'I really mean it, Justin, thank you for everything.'

'Don't be stupid, if it wasn't for me, you wouldn't be in this position.' He smiled warmly at me. He had a lovely smile. I felt my heart melt. Don't, I told it. But it wasn't listening.

'If it wasn't for you,' I said, 'I wouldn't have a fantastic new oven and I wouldn't smell beguilingly of sandalwood!'

He laughed and stood up, pushed a hand through his hair.

'I'll go and put your clothes in the wash. I'll see you in bed.'

Later, we made love for a third time. I fell asleep with his strong arms wrapped around me.

The day hadn't been all bad then.

Chapter Thirty-One

Luke Montfort turned up for lunch with a woman called Linda Hargreaves, also from the planning department.

My face didn't look as bad as I had feared the night before. I had a black eye and a cut lip, but after my bath the previous night, I'd spent a profitable, although painfully uncomfortable, time with a bag of ice cubes on my face to reduce the swelling on my lips and cheekbones.

Jess was outraged by what had happened to me. But not as outraged if I had told her where I'd spent the night. The young are so judgemental, so easily shocked. So I didn't.

As for me, I was almost floating with happiness. I endlessly relived my amazing night with Justin. My chi energy seemed to be flowing incredibly well, it must have been the hard work on my Yong Quan foot-points that had made all the difference. It had certainly made me frisky.

'I think you're crazy not calling the police,' she'd said. I patiently explained my reasons again.

'Look, Jess,' I said, 'I don't want to make a big thing of it. I don't want customers thinking, "Old Forge Café, that's where crime lurks". I want them thinking, "Old Forge Café, great place to eat". And, Jess,' I pointed out, 'do you really think Slattery is going to investigate this thoroughly? If he found out who did it, he'd probably buy them a pint. No, it ends here.'

'I still think. . .'

'Let's just drop the subject.' I didn't like to say that I suspected Slattery of being involved, certainly at a planning level. Then I added, 'Besides, with the best will in the world, what could they do? I can't give a description of my attackers; they were all wearing gloves, there are no prints. . . no evidence to incriminate anyone. Even if I'd had CCTV, which I don't, there'd be nothing whatsoever to identify them. If anything my insurance premiums might go up. Anyway, I'm fine, I was rescued by Francis.'

Francis heard his name, turned around and grinned. He was so happy to have been useful.

As he did so, I reflected that actions often have the most unexpected consequences. Farson's attempt to inflict pain and alarm on me had brought me closer to Justin, an even greater desire to find out who had killed Whitfield, and had, oddly, saved Francis from being sacked. I could hardly get rid of him now, not after he had saved my life.

With my mind feeling a little sharper, I had checked the kitchen again this morning, and found nothing seemed to be missing. Maybe I *had* simply forgotten to lock the door.

I was feeling happy. Ecstatic. I thought, I'm in love! There, I thought, I've admitted it to myself. Wildly optimistic, although achievable plans for the future floated around my brain. I would open a wholefood café in Wycombe, restaurant downstairs – sell kombucha, kimchi, quinoa and kefir desserts – yoga space upstairs for Justin. I could move in with him, freeing up the living space at the Old Forge Café for staff, get a live-in chef and sous. I would build a small empire. I felt serene and confident. The memories of last night (the good bits) looped around and around in my mind. I felt like I was floating. Sometimes I would smile uncontrollably with delight. That hadn't happened for years. I felt like I was a teenager again, I felt like writing his name over and over again on the back of a lever arch file, like I had done when I was at school and in love with a boy called Danny Wilkes.

As a treat for Francis – a bit of light relief from potato preparation – I let him peel some quails' eggs that I was going to turn into Scotch eggs with homemade piccalilli. The eggs, small enough at the best of times, looked microscopic in Francis's clumsy paws. I gave him my Shun paring knife. It's Japanese; endless layers of folded steel, so you could see the grain when you held it up to the light. The cutting edge gleamed brilliantly, like a razor. The handle too I found alluring. It was just black wood, but there was an elegance and simplicity in its design that marked it and its companion boning knife out from my other knives.

'Careful with that,' I warned.

'Why, is it sharp?' asked Francis. I rolled my eyes.

'All my knives are sharp, Francis, but that one cost seventy-five quid. I'm more concerned about the knife than your fingers.'

Peeling boiled quails' eggs is a tedious business. The shell sticks like glue to the white and fragments into lots of tiny pieces. It takes forever.

While Francis got on with the task, I lined a heavy cast-iron terrine mould with clingfilm, then prosciutto, and in a bowl made the mix for a chicken and tarragon terrine with reduced stock, gelatine and chicken, with fresh tarragon. I filled the solid, metal container and folded the wafer-thin ham over, then the clingfilm. Then I weighted the whole thing down with a couple of cans to compress it and put it in the fridge to set. As I did so I thought if only I could get rid of my troubles so easily, pack them away in a sturdy Le Creuset terrine dish and put them where the sun doesn't shine. . . a Terrine of Troubles.

Service began, the cheques started to come. We were pleasantly busy.

Jess came in and handed me another cheque over the pass. When I started to make some money I would buy an EPOS system and we could move into the modern age by sending the cheques wirelessly; until then we'd have to make do with pen and paper, the old-fashioned way.

'Luke Montfort's order,' she said, with a grimace.

I looked at it: steak baguette/caramelised onions for him, chicken Caesar salad for her, w/a written on top. With anchovies. I felt a surge of love for Jess. It may sound trivial, the fact that the Caesar salad comes with anchovies, which is how it classically is; but, of course, many people can't stand them, so you have to ask, 'Would you like anchovies with that?' In my experience, many front of house staff will forget, but not Jess. If you told her something once, she never forgot.

'Ça marche! Cheque on,' I called to Francis, 'one chicken Caesar *with anchovies*. That's you, Francis. And one steak baguette, so a baguette plate and don't forget the fries!'

Francis had gained new-found confidence from saving my hide the night before, he had even made Montfort's guest lunch. I know that a Caesar salad isn't the hardest thing to assemble, but he had done it as it should be, and had saved me five minutes. And minutes are precious in a kitchen during service time. He'd also prepared the steak plate garnish: a little garnish of salad and the chips, which he'd remembered to season.

I had made his passionfruit mousse (and Linda's) look stunning. They came in individual glass bowls but I had glammed them up by judicious application of a fruit and cream garnish and some candied flower petals and orange dust. It looked very starry, Michelin starry.

'Service!' I called.

The dishes were taken away and then Jess returned with a ticket.

'That chef, Graeme Strickland's out there. He wants a steak baguette too, and he's pre-ordered dessert. He said he doesn't care what it is, he just wants whatever Montfort's having.'

I laughed. Think of the devil and he will come. I started work on his food.

When Jess cleared the Montfort table and had given me

his compliments, I said to her, 'Go and ask him to come in the kitchen. I've got something to ask him.'

Jess frowned in a slightly suspicious way and left the kitchen.

'Francis.'

'Yes, chef?'

I opened my locker fridge where I keep the food I need for mains and took out a bottle of Kirin. 'Would you mind going out in the yard for a minute? I'm just going to have a private word with Mr Montfort. Have a beer while you're waiting.'

'OK, oh, Japanese,' he said with delight, inspecting the bottle, 'like the knife.'

He bustled out happily holding his beer.

The kitchen door swung open. 'Hello,' said Montfort, 'the mousse was superb!'

'Good.' I smiled winningly at him. Montfort didn't comment on my dinged about face. Maybe it was just politeness on his part. But I knew it wasn't.

He was wearing a suit and tie and shoes that needed a polish. I'm a bit of a shoe girl myself. For work I wear black, high-sided Caterpillar work boots with a steel toe. Not only are they practical, durable and non-slip, they look good and take a good shine when you polish them.

I was disappointed in Montfort. As a public servant I felt he had a certain standard to uphold. Shoes maketh the man.

Montfort shot his cuffs and glanced down at his watch, as if to show me how busy he was, or maybe to show off the watch, which looked expensive. Either way, it was a terrible mistake on his part. I remembered the thing I'd forgotten the other night. It hit me like a lightning bolt. I had been planning to use reason on Montfort; all of that flew out of the window.

Now I wanted revenge.

'Would you like to come around this side of the pass?' I said. 'I've got something interesting that I'd like to show you.'

Montfort walked round. He had a kind of cocky strut and his eyes were full of a genial contempt. For some odd reason I thought of the hymn I'd sung at Sunday school, 'There is a Green Hill' with its lines, '*The rich man in his castle, the poor man at his gate*'. That more or less seemed to describe his attitude. And he was not the poor man. There was something condescending in his attitude, the Lord of the Manor.

I had nothing concrete on Montfort that I could use to coerce him, except fear. And I was going to make Montfort afraid of me.

I had no compunction for what I was about to do, Montfort had brought it upon himself. It was karma.

Montfort had to be the brains behind what had been happening. Here was the man who knew who had killed Dave Whitfield. Here was the man who was responsible for four men intent on beating me half to death. I thought too about a dead elderly environmental campaigner. And I hadn't forgotten he had tried to touch up a fifteen-year-old Jess. But above all he had almost certainly organised the attack on me the night before.

I beamed at him and drove my fist into his stomach.

It was a perfect uppercut. All the power from the sudden swivel of my left shoulder. Short, powerful, explosive. It must have hurt like hell.

It was certainly effective.

Montfort doubled up, gasping for breath. His eyes were standing out of his head, outrage vying with pain and shock. Then I booted him in the balls. Steel toes into his scrotum.

Montfort made a horrible noise and sank to his knees then toppled over on his side on the kitchen floor. He lay there cupping his balls moaning. Fleetingly I felt the approval of Dave Whitfield's ghost.

'Now I've got your attention,' I said, quietly and menacingly, prodding him with my steel-toed foot. 'You don't seem surprised by the state of my face, do you? That's because you saw it happen, didn't you?'

He looked up at me and then slowly, painfully got to his feet. His face was contorted with fear as well as pain. I doubt if anyone had ever hit him before. It was the kind of thing he had seen on TV but never experienced. Violence isn't pretty in real life. It hurts and it is shocking. As Montfort was finding out.

'I never. . .'

'Yes you did, Luke.' My voice was reasonable. I leaned closer towards him, his forehead was beginning to bead with sweat. He smelled of aftershave and fear.

'That's a very distinctive tattoo on your wrist and I remember it well. From last night. It also shows up nicely on my CCTV.'

Montfort wasn't to know I didn't have such a thing. But he was too frightened of me now to put up any resistance.

228

MURDER ON THE MENU

I knew he was mine then. He made no attempt to escape. He fell silent, standing miserably by the pass. Behind him, through the glass panel of the kitchen door I could see Jess making frantic faces at me. Her eyes were wide and I saw her mouth the three syllables, 'Slat-Ter-Ry.' God, I didn't want him bursting in. I obviously had to hurry. I carried on.

'You and your mate Farson have got it coming, Luke. Now, unless you want me to go to the police with this – you'll lose everything, Luke, house, wife, job, liberty. . . plus God knows what other things the inevitable internal investigation at work will come up with – this is what you'll do. You'll meet me tomorrow, before work and we'll have a chat and you can let me know all about Arcadia and who killed Dave Whitfield.'

He nodded. He rubbed his balls gently.

'Let me remind you again of what will happen if you're not my bitch, Luke,' I said. 'Just to make sure you got all of that, I'll go to the police with my CCTV recording and you'll be charged with assault, maybe attempted murder; either way it'll look terrible. They won't like it at Bucks County Council and, of course, it'll be all over the village. And, of course, they'll look for a motive and I'll tell them about Arcadia and even poor old Whitfield's obelisk and they'll start investigating your bank accounts and your work at the council and I rather imagine you'll be engulfed in a real shit-storm of a scandal.'

Montfort looked suitably worried. I decided to increase the pressure a little.

'And one more thing – no, don't stare at the floor, it's rude, look at me.' He did so and I looked him in the eyes. 'If you're not waiting for me in the car park – the other side of Church Woods, you know, the picnic area – at eight o'clock tomorrow morning, as well as the police, you'll have me to deal with' – I moved very close to him, intimidatingly so – 'and I'll really go to town on you, understand?'

'Yes,' he said miserably, 'I'll be there.'

'Thank you, you can go now,' I said dismissively. He started to walk away, unhappily, his shoulders slumped.

'I'm glad you liked the mousse,' I said.

He nodded again and smiled weakly. He visibly pulled himself together, straightened himself up, straightened his tie, smoothed his hair.

He walked towards the door and turned to me.

'I just want to say sorry. None of this should have happened. It just got out of hand.'

I nodded. I didn't give a rat's arse for his apologies.

'I'll see you tomorrow.'

As he pushed the door open I saw Slattery sitting at a table in the restaurant. He was staring directly at the kitchen, at us. It was an unguarded moment – it was pure fluke that the door should have opened at that instant and for me to have been standing where I was and catch a glimpse of him. I had seen that look on his face before, ten days ago, in another restaurant, when he'd been looking at Whitfield not long before Whitfield's death. I wondered what Slattery made of our faces now, Montfort looking worried, in pain and unhappy and me looking like I'd gone a few rounds in the ring with Triple G. The expression on his face was one of undisguised hostility and suspicion.

Later, after service, I picked up my phone and called Justin.

After I finished telling him how much I missed him, I gave him the good news about Luke Montfort, delighted I had something positive to share for once.

Tomorrow I'd know who killed Whitfield and the others.

Chapter Thirty-Two

I woke up about seven the next morning and lay in bed thinking about my eight o'clock meeting with Montfort.

I'd chosen the spot to meet because I didn't want him seen entering my premises by anyone. I didn't trust anyone in the village; either they would think I was having an affair with Montfort and I would be tarred with that brush, or Slattery might see him from the upstairs window of his house. By now I was convinced that he had me under continual supervision, which sounds paranoid, but who could blame me.

I had received the information from the Land Registry. The fields had been sold by the Earl of Hampden to the Arcadia consortium who were the current owners. I checked Companies House. Arcadia was a fairly common name, but after a bit of time searching I found an Arcadia whose registered company address was Number Four, the High Street, Chandler's Ford. It had two current registered officers. A director who was an Edward Musgrave and one resignation, a David Whitfield of Hampden Green. I had no way of knowing what had happened, short of asking

Anna Bruce to summon the shade of Whitfield, but in many ways, the why did not matter. The man was dead.

I suspect his resignation had led to having his head blown off with a twelve bore.

The Land Registry report also gave the land a flood rating of 'low risk' which I thought rather odd given the height of the river. It certainly hadn't looked 'low risk' when I was there a few days previously; it had looked like a paddy field.

I stared at the ceiling of my bedroom looking at the ominous cracks that had appeared since I'd taken the place over from Mrs Cope. There was obviously something highly illegal going on with the Arcadia deal, and of sufficient value to warrant the deaths of Paul Harding and Dave Whitfield.

Luke Montfort would know. And very soon so would I.

My guess was that Montfort had been bribed to greenlight the housing development and had got in above his head. Montfort didn't come across as a violent criminal; I guessed that someone, probably Farson, had made him participate in the attack on me to consolidate his hold on him. To emphasise the 'we're all in this together and don't you forget it' idea. And if Farson went down, he would. Guilt by association. I still thought it highly likely that Montfort was the brains of the outfit, possibly Musgrave – unless of course the Earl was involved.

I got up, did some sun salutations and a few Tai Chi exercises for my stiff, sore body, ate a banana, pulled on my running kit – the shoes were still filthy from the day before, I usually run them under the outside tap in the yard – and headed off across the green. I ran past Justin's house as I went. His curtains were drawn. He didn't want our affair to become common knowledge. Good luck with that in Hampden Green, I thought.

I jogged on through the rain in the dark early-morning greyness. It was only just above zero, colder than my fridges, and miserable and wet. As I ran I congratulated myself on arranging the meet at the church car park. I was beginning to feel that everything I did in Hampden Green was in the eye of the public, like *The Truman Show*.

I crossed the road and ran down the footpath by the allotments. It was unusually quiet; normally I meet a couple of people walking their dogs before going to work, but not today. I can't say I was surprised. It was bitterly cold and there was a northern wind slicing across the countryside. It didn't worry me too much. I was wearing gloves and a hat as well as a nylon windbreaker, designed (so it said) for arctic conditions. I settled down into the rhythm of the run once I reached the wood that lay between my village and the next one, Frampton End, where the church was. As I ran, it started raining in earnest; cold, hard, stinging my eyes.

The church gave its name to the woods surrounding it, Church Woods. The picnic area where I was to meet Montfort lay about a mile away on the far side of the wood. I was going to run past the church where there was another car park but too public for our meeting. From the church I would run along one of the many footpaths that went directly from it to the picnic area.

As the trees thinned I could see its tall spire. It was set back from the road, down a drive that led to a car park, invisible from the main road. I crossed the road – soon it would be snarled with traffic, it was a rat-run to the local primary school and it would be full of pushy Chiltern mothers in enormous 4x4s, Porsche Cayennes, Audis, Kias, Range Rovers, all jostling to park nearest the school in a display of aggressive Alpha Mum-dom. Now, it was empty.

My body felt tired and sore from the beating I'd taken. When I had been in bed with Justin the other night, it sang with joy; he was a fantastic lover. But now, running, it complained bitterly. Every step jarred and set my teeth on edge. I ignored the pain, running through it, but it was hard going. I jogged down the potholed track and into the car park. There was a red Audi A3 parked in one corner that I recognised as Montfort's. I wondered what on earth he was doing here. He knew where the picnic area was – not here but on the other side of the woods, he could hardly be lost. Here was too public, this was used a lot by the dog walkers. I crossed over to it. Sure enough, it was his car, and there was Montfort, sitting in the front seat. I rapped on the window.

He didn't move. Not even a twitch. He must have heard me. I suddenly felt very cold indeed and not from the weather.

For a heartbeat I stood there in the icy rain, water trickling down the windows of the Audi, the wind gusting. I looked around me: at the empty car park, the church with its very tall spire with gargoyles halfway up, where it began to taper upwards to a point. I had never noticed them before. They leered knowingly down at me.

I tried the door and it opened. Montfort looked straight

ahead glassily. He was sitting in the driver's seat, slightly slumped down. But he'd never need to worry about his posture ever again. I thought back to when I had first encountered Whitfield and momentarily fantasised about killing him.

For stabbing Whitfield to death I'd have gone for a long, thin but sturdy, boning knife. It would have slid in much easier. One can but dream.

As my old head chef used to say, 'Always choose the right tools for the right job.'

It was as if someone had been listening in telepathically.

I looked at what was sticking out of his chest.

Black handle, Japanese characters.

My very expensive Shun boning knife, companion to the knife I'd let Francis use the other day.

My knife had killed Luke Montfort.

Chapter Thirty-Three

I stared at the corpse in the car seat. Montfort was now the third dead man I had ever seen in my life and it was very disturbing. I think I may have been in shock.

You'd better do something, I told myself.

And quickly.

Things were looking very bad for me. Slattery himself had seen Montfort emerge from my kitchen the day before. He had seen my beaten-up face. He had seen Montfort looking shaky, shifty and frightened. It would almost certainly come out that was my knife. How many people would be in the Venn diagram of expensive, professional Japanese knife owners and people who knew Montfort? Motive, murder weapon, lack of an alibi, opportunity, none of this looked great.

If Slattery were bent, if this was his handiwork (or, as I suspected, his idea or the result of his tip-off) things looked even worse. God alone knows what other things beside my knife might be linking me to Montfort's body.

Think, I thought desperately to myself, *think and make it quick!*

As a chef, I was used to prioritising. Plenty of things to think about. But for now, I had the knife to deal with.

I pulled on the knife. Excalibur it wasn't. It slid out easily enough. Careful not to get any blood on me, I washed what little there was on the blade in a deep puddle, wrapped the knife in a plastic bag I had in my jacket pocket and ran across the car park into the wood, my feet needing no urging. At least I didn't need to worry about leaving finger-prints as I was wearing gloves.

Get rid of the evidence!

As I ran I thought to myself: so this is why they broke into the Old Forge Café. To find a weapon to kill Montfort to implicate me! It looked like Montfort's fate had been sealed before I had spoken to him. As had mine.

Once again, I was struck by the cool planning behind all of this. Montfort was well and truly out of the frame, step forward either the Earl or the DI.

The rain was now extremely heavy. The car park was a rough surface of impacted stones, but the path I was now running down through the wood was a mix of water, mud and leaves. I wouldn't be leaving any usable footprints. There was nobody about at all. The bare trees stretched out around me. A mile or so into the woods, a couple of hundred metres off the paths, virtually inaccessible, were a couple of ponds. I ran to the larger of the two and threw the knife into its centre.

It splashed into the gunmetal-grey water and sank beneath the surface.

As I ran home, a different way, making a kind of wide circle, my mind was working furiously.

How had Montfort been ambushed?

Who knew I was going to meet Montfort? He would hardly have told Farson or Musgrave, the director of Arcadia, that he was going to meet me. Justin knew of course, I had told him, but he wouldn't have told anyone.

His colleague Linda Hargreaves knew that I'd had a private chat with him and of course there was one other person who had seen Montfort emerge from my kitchen, DI Slattery. Slattery. Everything seemed to lead back to that man. God knows what Montfort had looked like when he had emerged from my kitchen but he must have looked shocked. Slattery, with all those years on the force, must have got good at reading the signs of tension and fear on peoples' faces. Had he guessed? How could he not?

Four men had attacked me, including Farson, Hat Man and a reluctant Montfort – I'd already worked out that Farson must have brought him along so Montfort would have been implicated in the assault. You can go to prison for GBH. It was extra insurance to make sure the man from the council kept his mouth shut. Montfort would never have dared come forward of his own accord after that. He would have been irrevocably bound to the Arcadia plot, whatever that was. But if they suspected Montfort was beginning to fall apart, steps would have to be taken. I's dotted, t's crossed.

Was Slattery the fourth man? Had he worked out that their hold on Montfort was slipping, and killed him – or was it more ruthless than that? Having played his part, got the development green-lighted, Montfort was no longer necessary. One person less to share the spoils with. Or the mysterious Mr Musgrave. I wondered who he was; he kept popping up in my mind every now and again. Did he even exist, was he like Mr Kipling, a made-up figure?

I could see the first houses of Hampden Green through the rain now. Lights were on. I ran faster at my mile pace, which for me meant a nine out of ten effort, heaving for breath. I wanted to get home without meeting anyone. *Please God*, I prayed, *let no one have seen me*. My mind was still turning over events and scenarios with furious speed.

The door to the kitchen had been open. I'd lied to Montfort: I didn't have CCTV, I didn't have a burglar alarm, but I did have a key and a lock and although I couldn't swear to it, I was pretty sure that when I left the Old Forge Café that door had been secure.

Slattery was the kind of man I suspected would have the ability to pick a lock, or know someone who could.

There was another possibility too, one that I hated to even think of. Someone who worked for me and who had conveniently turned up just in time to save me: Francis. He had a key, and he knew where the spare was.

Surely he couldn't be involved?

Could he?

Surely not Francis. . . he could have easily got hold of the knife.

Or worse, Jess. . .

No, I thought, I cannot believe that.

I got home, burnt the plastic bag that the knife had been in using an old bucket in the yard, just in case, showered and changed. It was now 9 o'clock and I busied myself with my prep list. I thought to myself, I must act normal.

I rehearsed my story:

Slattery: 'Where were you this morning?'

Me: 'I got up, went for a run, (but not to the church car park, obvs). Then I came home and started work.'

It sounded a bit thin.

I wondered when Montfort would be found. The church car park was used by dog walkers but it was a large area and they wouldn't necessarily see anything unusual in a man sitting in a car. He could be there for ages.

That thought was even worse. I could see now why people gave themselves up, this waiting was dreadful. I looked around the kitchen. I couldn't stay here, it would be torture. I even toyed with the idea of calling the police and saying what I'd found. Only the notion of telling Slattery kept me from doing that.

The day stretched in front of me in an uninviting way. Not only did I have the prospect of the police's visit hanging over me like the Sword of Damocles, I would have the presence of Francis working with me in the kitchen and have to act as if I had no suspicions of what was going on.

Jess would know immediately something was up.

Oh, God. . . 9 o'clock. Half an hour before Francis arrived, an hour before Jess was due in, two hours before opening. I felt faint and thought I was going to throw up.

The whole thing was intolerable.

So much for my Zen-like calm – my mind was hopping about like a cat on a hot chargrill. I tried to distract myself with work. Chicken liver parfait was the first thing on my prep list. I'd sold the one that I had made the other day.

I opened the tub of livers and one by one transferred them to a steel bowl so I could check to see that there were no gall bladders attached. The dark-crimson blood from the livers coated my fingers and I felt like Lady Macbeth. I lifted my bloodstained hands and stared at them. I thought of the thin line of blood that had run down the front of Montfort and my gorge rose. I ran to the toilet and threw up. I looked at my reflection in the mirror; cold sweat beading my forehead, eyes wild, pale face, bags under my eyes, one of which was badly bruised, hair a mess. I looked like someone who had just killed a man.

I kept expecting Slattery to turn up and haul me off to Aylesbury for questioning.

'The knife that killed Mr Montfort was a boning knife – a very unusual knife, mainly to be found in kitchens. Do you own one?'

'Yes.'

'Can I see it?'

'No.'

'Why not?'

'I can't find it.'

'You can't find it? Why's that then?'

'It went missing the night I was beaten up.'

'Did you report this alleged assault to the police?'

'No.'

God, it looked awful. If I could only work out myself what was happening. Slattery, even if he didn't try and pin the Montfort death on me, even if he were innocent, was unaware or uninterested in the Arcadia stuff, was bound to be suspicious.

244

And what else had been taken? I suddenly thought: the knife had been stolen to frame me, what else had they done?

The night I was beaten up, who knew I was going to the pub? I could easily have just stayed in, I often did. Someone had tipped them off! Who knew? Who could have known?

The phone rang and it was the Hobart installer: they'd had a cancellation, could they possibly come this morning?

I said yes and hung up. I clingfilmed what I was doing and put it away.

I came to a sudden decision. I simply couldn't face hanging around here waiting for the police, waiting for Slattery. The same thoughts were going around and around in my head like the Hobart mixer. I thought, only one thing can save me: if I find the killer, I'm in the clear.

When Francis arrived at nine thirty I had changed out of my chef's whites into a pair of jeans, sweatshirt and the pair of steel-toed Caterpillar boots in case I had to kick someone's head in. They'd certainly worked a treat on Montfort. Always dress appropriately.

I had done some Tai Chi breathing exercises to calm myself down; they were surprisingly effective. I managed to look at Francis with something like normality.

Francis regarded me in surprise, his eyes running up and down as he looked at my casual clothes.

'Off somewhere, chef?' he asked.

'Hobart are coming, Francis,' I said, nonchalantly. 'I'd like you to let them in. They know where the new oven is going and they're taking the old one away. We've got no bookings for lunch, so today we're closed. Can you text Jess, tell her not to come in. Keep an ear out for customers trying to get in. I've put an explanatory sign on the door but there'll always be someone who won't read it. Clean the restaurant, then when Hobart have gone, the kitchen.'

'When will you be back?' He looked worried, I could see his lips moving; it was a lot for him to take in.

'This evening, I guess. Lock up behind you and see you tomorrow.'

'But. . .' he started to say.

I contemplated him, his straw-blond hair, his goggle eyes, his air of agitation. Yes, Francis, I thought, why so worked up?

'Ciao, Francis,' I said and left him to it and got in my car. I headed in the direction of Chandler's Ford. Time to go and see Mr Musgrave. Whoever he might be. . .

Time to clear up this whole mess.

Before it buried me alive.

Chapter Thirty-Four

I pulled into Chandler's Ford and parked by the church. There was nobody around in the small village. I walked up towards the houses near the Greyhound, or rather I paddled through the flooded river. I was glad that the Caterpillar boots I was wearing were high-sided. The water had spread way beyond its banks and was now halfway over the field opposite. It was lapping around the church and surrounded the pub. I looked over to the far bank. The green fields of the proposed development were still visible but I could see the watery sun from the grey skies above glinting on the surface of gigantic puddles. It was obvious that the whole area was incredibly waterlogged, making a nonsense of the report that it was, in fact, flood safe.

The river was nearly up to the front door of the pub. There was only maybe a dozen or so buildings. I started looking for the address of Arcadia.

The terrace was numbered one to three, so I crossed over the road to the first of the other houses, number five. I went back to the pub. It had to be number four: the address from the Land Registry.

Over the door was the legend, '*Edward Musgrave. Licensed to sell beer and spirits.*'

So, the Managing Director of Arcadia, no less. And his corporate lair. It was hardly Shell House or the Lloyds Building.

Well, that was one mystery solved. I walked back to my car and I noticed the old guy I'd spoken to in the Greyhound, accompanied by his dog in the churchyard. He saw me and made no effort to move, just stood there stiffly as the spaniel, nose to the ground, excitedly snuffled around the headstones. I went over to him.

He was contemplating Paul Harding's grave.

'Morning,' he said to me. I noticed again how he had the old Bucks accent, now long defunct, an 'oo-arr' kind of burr.

'I'm Tom, they calls me Old Tom. . . course, I wasn't called that when I was young. . .' He laughed quietly to himself.

'I'm Charlie,' I said.

He looked closely at my face.

''Oo done that, Charlie?'

'Farson,' I said.

'Farson? All by 'isself?'

I shook my head. 'He had help.'

Old Tom laughed. 'Quite a lot of help, I should think. I saw you beat him the other day.' He looked at the grave. 'Shame you stopped when you did. Farson's a nasty piece of work, there's the proof if needs be.'

He nodded at the grave, the stone with its legend, '*Et in Arcadia Ego*'.

'So you think it was Farson who killed him?'

The old man nodded. 'I knows it, heard him laughing about it in the pub; it's a disgrace.'

Yes it was.

We stared some more at the grave. I liked the inscription. South Bucks was obviously Arcadia to Harding. It made poetic sense that it was chiselled there on the funerary stone since that's what Harding had campaigned for all his life. I wondered who had commissioned it. Harding could scarcely have predicted his own death.

It was a fine memorial to him, plain, highly polished granite, the inscription deeply cut. It had that deceptive air of simplicity that generally means very expensive.

'Who paid for that?' I asked.

Old Tom looked at me. His face was deeply lined but his eyes were still bright, his skin weathered like old leather from a lifetime of agricultural work. His dog still zigzagged around the churchyard, absorbed in whatever he was tracking.

I kind of knew the feeling: I felt I was picking up a scent so strong it was almost pulling me along, but unlike the dog I didn't really know who my quarry was.

'The Earl.'

'The Earl of Hampden?'

Old Tom rolled his eyes heavenwards as if to say, How many Earls are there in this part of South Bucks?

'He organised the funeral. Harding had no family, no real friends either come to that. Just his dog.' He contemplated his own animal. 'I knows the feeling.' He shook his head. 'Well, best be off, good luck to you.' He nodded in the direction of the pub. 'Be careful of Musgrave. I knew his dad, 'e was a chiseller but the boy, well, him, Ed, he's twenty times worse. And the next time you hit Farson, make it a good 'un.'

He whistled for the dog and they disappeared up the slope towards the cottages.

I got into the Volvo and started the engine.

Time to go and meet the Earl, then.

'Bloody good bloke.' I'm sure he was. I was going up in the world socially.

Perhaps I should have worn a dress rather than jeans.

Chapter Thirty-Five

I drove up the long and winding drive to Marlow House. I had never visited an earl before and was kind of curious. I was also wondering how I would be able to get him to talk. Montfort had been easy, but I had no hold whatsoever over the Earl. I would just have to trust to luck.

The house was not particularly grand. It was big and looked, to my eyes, like a small hotel; Victorian, lots of windows, posh, certainly, jaw-dropping, definitely not. I parked on the gravel next to the Maserati that I recognised. There was also a Range Rover and two BMWs. My car looked quite sad next to these; I felt I should be parked in the tradesman's entrance.

I crunched up to the door over the gravel and rang the bell. A volley of barks was followed by Bryony opening the door. Five dogs of various shapes and sizes ran out, none looked pure-bred. Most of them had seen better days. Bryony was wearing ripped jeans and a man's shirt with quite obviously nothing on underneath. As usual she looked quite stoned, with a faint aroma of weed hanging round her.

'Hi, Charlie!' The dogs sniffed me in a friendly way. I guess to a dog's ultra-sensitive nose, I smelled fantastic, a whole potpourri of exotic food smells. A miniature Schnauzer hung back and eyed me suspiciously, like an elderly major looking at some chav who'd dared try and enter his club. He cleared his throat and gave a disapproving bark.

'C'mon through. . .' said Bryony, gesturing vaguely with one hand, 'he's been expecting you.'

I followed her. Was he expecting me? Was that good or bad? I looked around as I followed Bryony. The hall of the house was marble tiled and hung with oil paintings – portraits and landscapes, nothing that looked particularly noteworthy. The impression was one of comfortable, family wealth. If the Earl was very rich he hadn't been spending his money on flash interior designers.

Again, I felt a bit let down. I wanted the Earl to be living in some riot of Gainsborough portraits in huge gilt frames and vast high ceilings and Gobelin tapestries, suits of armour, halberds, something really over the top aristocratic, not something that a mildly successful stockbroker might have. I was underwhelmed, like I'd been short-changed.

Bryony ushered me into the lounge. It was a large room, again comfortably, but not ostentatiously furnished. The Earl was sitting in an armchair, dressed in an elegant charcoal-grey three-piece suit. Bryony indicated a sofa facing him and I sat down. She went and stood by the Earl and put her arm around his shoulder. I thought, she's got over Ollie's death quite well, I wonder if she still thinks the Earl is behind it? If so, she's certainly come to terms with it.

He spoke to her. 'Please leave us now, dear.'

She nodded, then leaned forwards and kissed the Earl slowly, lasciviously, on the mouth. I thought, I guess she doesn't think the Earl killed Ollie.

She sashayed out, ignoring me. I thought, disapprovingly, bit of an age gap there. The Earl gave a wintry smile as if divining my thoughts.

'Does the age difference shock you?'

'To be honest, yes,' I said. I found it distasteful, I have to say.

'That's very conventional of you,' the Earl commented, 'I'm disappointed.' He sighed as if I had let him down.

'I would have expected you to have been a bit more broad-minded. Drink?' He indicated a small table on which were various bottles. I shook my head.

'I've got things to do,' I said. My face was grim. I had better things to do with my time than discuss sexual morality.

'I'm sure you have,' he said, drily.

I studied him frankly. He was slim, trim and dapper. He looked wealthy and assured, above all, he had poise. He had a kind of military look that was at odds with his hedonistic background: ramrod straight back, clipped moustache, silver hair brushed straight back. If someone had referred to him as 'the Colonel' I wouldn't have been surprised. But there was more to him than just a military, prosperous aura. There was a kind of raffishness. There is a book by a philosopher called Nietzsche whose title is *Beyond Good and Evil*. That's the kind of air that the Earl gave. Serenely floating above it all. I wished I was.

I wasn't floating above anything. I had another mental flash of the dead Montfort with my knife sticking in him. I was up to my neck in deep, deep shit, that was for sure.

'I'm here because of Arcadia,' I said. 'Do you know anything about it?'

The Earl steepled his fingers and looked at me, then he poured himself a cup of tea. He seemed faintly bored.

'Earl Grey,' he said. 'If you don't want an alcoholic drink are you sure you won't join me?'

I shook my head.

'Pity,' said the Earl, his piercing eyes looked at me over the rim of his cup. 'Well, I'll answer your question.'

I thought, thank God for that. I was, quite frankly, amazed. I hadn't expected honesty.

He put his cup down. 'Arcadia is a project of a consortium of locals. To be precise' – he held up his left hand and ticked them off with his right – 'Musgrave, Farson, Jackson and Whitfield. Part of it, but not officially, were Montfort and Ollie Scott. Montfort to ease things through with the planning and Ollie Scott, our esteemed local drug dealer, provided much of the finance.' He smiled frostily. 'Laundering his profits.'

'And two of these people are now dead,' I remarked.

'Indeed,' said the Earl, politely.

I wondered not for the first time who was the brains behind it all, who was guiding these people. I think I was still waiting to hear the name Slattery.

'And you sold them the land?' I asked.

'I did.' He sighed. 'That was a mistake on my part. I didn't think they'd get planning permission.'

'Why's that? I mean, why didn't you think they'd get planning permission – they obviously did.'

The Earl considered my question. 'First, it floods. As I'm sure you've noticed. But, historically, it didn't. What happened was this: about three years ago the Environment Agency and the council created a kind of sluice upstream of the village to speed the flow of the River Bourne, because they wanted to reduce flooding there. It did, but it moved the problem downstream. To Chandler's Ford. But the Land Registry report was based on figures of flow rates before the new development, so they don't reflect today's reality. The information the report is based on is hopelessly out of date.'

He picked his cup up again and drank more tea.

'The other reason was it was greenbelt land, or so I thought. It's ironic really. I thought I had ripped them off, when in reality it was the other way round. But I had reckoned without Montfort's cunning. He had it declared a brownfield site suitable for development because there used to be buildings on it long ago, an old paper mill. It burnt down fifty years ago and the land was ploughed up, but still. . .' he shrugged, 'there we go.'

'So Montfort fiddled the records?'

'No, he didn't "fiddle" anything.' He sounded exasperated at my inability to follow a simple explanation. 'Technically he was correct, but on paper, not in reality. But that's how the council works.'

'And Harding was going to point this out, I suppose. He was going to lead the fight against the development,' I said.

He nodded. 'He was going to point out the discrepancy

between the out-of-date report and the reality that it was an unsafe area to build on. Harding was an experienced campaigner, people listened to him. They obviously decided he was worth silencing.'

'Farson?' I asked.

He nodded. 'A disgusting little man. I heard you gave him a damn good hiding, well done you.' He sipped his tea. 'I felt very sorry for Harding when he died. I met him once or twice. We were both active in the South Bucks Conservation society. I didn't like him, and he certainly didn't like me, or aristocrats in general; he thought we were parasites and should be swept away. Strung up, I think he said. He's quite right of course.'

Eh? I thought.

He laughed, as though amused by the thought of the landed aristocracy dangling at the end of a rope. 'But I respected him. He was sincere. And he loved the Chilterns.'

I had thought that the Earl was going to be part of this. I wasn't prepared for this forensic dissection of the Arcadia group.

There was a knock on the door and Bryony came in with a phone. 'It's DI Slattery.' When she handed the phone to the Earl, my heart sank.

I knew immediately what it meant. Montfort had been found. The DI would have been round to the Old Forge Café like a shot. I guessed I was now very much wanted by the police. I wondered what Francis had said. I would have liked to have heard that exchange – when Francis was confused it was extremely difficult to work out what he was on about.

There was nothing to do but listen to the Earl's side of the conversation.

'Hello, Slattery. . . No. . . No, I haven't. . . Well, if I do, I'll be sure to let you know. . . Mm-hm. . . Luke Montfort, did you say. . . Poor chap. . . Certainly, bye.' He clicked off the phone and handed it to Bryony.

He looked at me. 'I assume you can work out what that's about.'

'Yes,' I said.

'Luke Montfort's dead. DI Slattery thinks you did it. He wants you to hand yourself in to the police.'

'How did he know I was here?' I asked, suspiciously.

The Earl shrugged. 'He doesn't, he wants me to tell my employees to keep an eye out for you, in case you try hiding out somewhere on the estate.'

He looked at me.

I looked at him.

Bryony looked beatifically into the middle distance.

Silence fell.

'The ball's in your court, Charlie,' the Earl said, politely.

Chapter Thirty-Six

The ball was in my court, but I didn't know what to do with it. I looked at the Earl for inspiration. So far, he had seemed to be on my side, but who could tell what was going on in his head. However, I believed what he said about the consortium and that he was no part of it.

'Did you kill Luke Montfort?' He spoke casually, as if out of politeness. His tone implied that he wouldn't care one way or another, but he felt he had to ask.

'No.' It did sound slightly unconvincing. I tried again. 'No I didn't kill him.'

'Did you know he was dead?' the Earl raised an inquisitive eyebrow, while Bryony stifled a yawn. Presumably she was inured to tragedy by now, after Ollie had been so cruelly taken.

'I did. I found his body. Are you going to turn me in to Slattery?' I asked.

The Earl considered the question. 'And you're sure you didn't kill him?' Now he sounded amused by the whole thing.

'He was going to tell me who had killed Dave Whitfield.'
I was getting irritated. 'No, of course I didn't.'

'I thought not,' said the Earl. 'I told Slattery I hadn't
seen you. Can you give Bryony your car keys, please?'

Bryony was staring into space with unfocused eyes. She
really did look very stoned indeed. One of the elderly dogs,
an Alsatian, had accompanied her and sat by her side and
she absentmindedly stroked its head. It panted and drooled,
its eyes half closed in bliss. The dog looked stoned too.
Perhaps it reminded her of Ollie.

'Why?' I asked. I was confused.

The Earl poured some more tea for himself.

'Slattery doesn't like you and he's not overly fond of me.'
He smiled coldly. 'He'll be round soon, or that wretchedly
noisy police helicopter will. Bloody thing. Bryony, will you
move our guest's car to the stables where it'll be out of
sight, dear?'

'What?' She looked startled. 'Oh sure, yeah, right, car,
stables.'

I gave her my keys and she disappeared. Should she be
handling heavy machinery? Then I thought, the fate of my
old Volvo was the least of my worries.

'Do you know who killed Harding and the other three?'
I asked the Earl.

'Farson almost certainly killed Harding. It's just the kind
of thing that repellent man would do. The others I blame
on a falling out between thieves. I really don't know and
quite frankly, I really don't care. As I said, Slattery thinks
you killed Montfort.'

'Why would I do that?' I said scornfully.

260

'A crime of passion,' he said, casually, smiling maliciously at me. 'If whoever's been posting about you on Facebook is to be believed. First Whitfield, now him.'

My gorge rose at the very thought. Doing it with Montfort? The Earl took his phone out of an inside pocket.

'It's got fifty likes,' he said; he looked again at the screen, 'make that fifty one. . . and rising.'

I wanted to tell the Earl that I didn't believe him, but I knew that I did. He noticed the expression on my face.

'Oh, didn't you know?' he said with mock shock. The malicious amusement in his eyes was obvious, unmistakable. 'Aren't you on social media?'

I stared at him in dislike as he drank his tea. Despite the fact he was helping me, he really was an evil old bastard. Jess had been right about him.

Farson, I thought, it had to be him who had killed Montfort. Killed him to shut him up and to implicate me. Two birds, one stone.

Farson must have followed his car – his distinctive red Audi – from Montfort's house. If he killed Montfort he would be free of a weak link in the chain. Montfort could never talk to the police now. Montfort alive had outlived his usefulness; dead, I would take the blame. I could imagine the scene, Montfort telling him of my threats, Farson: 'I'll come with you, I'll deal with it.' And he had, but not in the way that Montfort had envisaged.

So much for my peaceful country dream.

Et in Arcadia ego. And where was I now? A murder suspect, a jealous lover, and involved with a group of violent criminals.

Things had gone terribly wrong.

I looked at the Earl. It was hard to know if he was an ally or a slightly sadistic tormentor. Perhaps he was both. He was looking at me without compassion, a blend of good-natured contempt and interest, like I was a dim-witted but amusing insect, an ant, maybe.

'Why are you telling me all this?' I asked.

'I don't really like people all that much, I'm afraid, I'm too old to care,' said the Earl, in an offhand way. 'However, I do like nature and I like animals. I look after rescue dogs, I fund rescue centres. I do a lot with orang-utans. . . that's why I'm in the far East a lot, not for Thai brothels as people seem to think. . . I make money, I amuse myself and I support organisations that support my views. I admired Harding. He had a similar outlook to mine. Even if we were on different sides of the Dialectical theory of History. I paid for his funeral.'

'*Et in Arcadia Ego*? You had that put on the stone.'

The Earl gave a wintry smile. 'I did indeed. My idea of a joke. Musgrave was not amused. He threatened me with legal action, for bringing the name of his company into disrepute.' He frowned. 'I had to go round to his crappy pub the other night and read him the riot act.'

So that's what he was doing there, I thought. Not part of the conspiracy at all.

'Wasn't that a bit risky, after what had happened to Harding?'

The Earl smiled, a rather alarming smile.

'If I have a problem with wasps on my property, I have them dealt with, professionally. The same principle applies to people who try to do me harm, in business or otherwise. They know that. If they had been so stupid as to try anything with me. . . more fool they.'

'Why didn't you tell Slattery all of this?' I asked. If he had, the pressure would have been off me.

The Earl looked at me. 'Because I can't be bothered, and I don't want to get involved. It's up to you now. I don't care that much what happens. Personally, I didn't like Montfort, Scott or Whitfield. Harding, I had a soft spot for. That's why I'm helping you. Justice for Harding. The end of Arcadia as well, it's what he would have wanted. Don't kid yourself it's because I like you.' He looked at me, I must have looked hurt. 'Don't get me wrong, I don't dislike you,' he shrugged, 'I'm somewhat indifferent, if truth be told.'

Thanks a lot, I thought. He must have sensed what I was thinking for he added, 'Like I just said, I don't dislike you, not like that repellent trio at the pub. You can bring down Farson and whoever else is involved. I'm caring for his dog, Cobbett' – the Schnauzer, I thought, I knew he looked familiar – 'he's a nice little chap. But the rest is up to you.'

'But surely, all you have to do is tell the police what you know?' I asked. Pleaded, might be more accurate. I desperately wanted Slattery off my back.

'Where's the proof?' The Earl did have a point. It was all speculation.

'And you think I can get it?' I asked.

'You're doing quite well,' he said. 'You seem quite effective and you've physically injured two of them and

263

ALEX COOMBS

survived their revenge attack. Farson and Musgrave must
be panic-stricken. They don't know if Montfort told you
anything before they silenced him. They've got rid of
two potential blabber-mouths, that's all they can do.
Somewhere out there is Farson's car, essentially a murder
weapon, used to kill Harding. You could find that. Or
you could beat one of them up to get some information.
Slattery can't do that, much as he'd like to. Show some
spirit, woman! Stop snivelling, stop feeling sorry for yourself. Off you go.'

Go where? I wondered.

'And I suppose you have some idea of what I should do
next?' My tone was sarcastic.

He raised a bushy eyebrow. 'Of course I do.'

'Care to enlighten me?' I asked.

'I believe Anna Bruce read your Tarot?'

Everyone knows everything in a village, I thought to
myself. Even the Earl. Maybe especially the Earl. I nodded.

'She will have kept three cards back that she didn't
show you.'

She had. I wondered how he knew. Then scepticism
kicked in.

Oh great, I thought. The Earl's advice rests upon the
supernatural. Did I have a better idea? I thought for a
nanosecond, no. The ideas cupboard was bare.

'Go and see her, *she'll* tell you what to do. She's very
good.' He drank some more tea and then put his cup down
with an air of finality. My time with him was over.

I suddenly thought, he's the man in the reading that I
didn't recognise: the Hierophant, the Keeper of Secrets. It

described the Earl perfectly. Rich, powerful, secretive, a master manipulator. It was him, just as she had foretold.

I knew then that he was right, I had to see her.

It was a peculiar idea, but we live in peculiar times. Well, I certainly do.

'Where does she live?' I envisioned a Hansel and Gretel-style secluded cottage somewhere in the woods.

'In the centre of High Wycombe,' said the Earl, pulling a face. He tossed me a car key, attached to a heavy fob.

'Take the BMW, the i7. It's new; Slattery won't recognise it if he sees it, the police won't be looking for it. Anna's address is on the satnav, under Recents.'

I stood up. 'So you want me to go and be told what to do by a fortune teller?' I asked, just to clarify the situation.

The Earl laughed. 'Exactly that.' He raised an eyebrow. 'Do you have a better idea?' The situation was clear.

I didn't have a better idea.

Five minutes later, I was driving away from Marlow House (somewhat nervously, it looked an unbelievably expensive car, at least compared to my ten year old Volvo estate) behind the wheel of the BMWi7, following the measured, judicious tones of the satnav.

'Take the second exit and turn right in five hundred yards. . .'

At least she seemed to know what she was doing.

I certainly didn't.

Chapter Thirty-Seven

I followed the melodious instructions on the satnav as I drove out of the village and through the South Bucks countryside, along its dreadful road surfaces, wincing every time I hit a pothole. I winced a lot. Occasionally I saw the low-flying police helicopter, presumably looking for my old Volvo. Periodically the heavens opened and more heavy rain lashed down. I pressed the button marked 'Radio', tuned to Beech Tree FM and sang along to *Favourite Game* by the Cardigans. The news came on:

'. . . *waters still rising. Marlow High Street remains closed to traffic and the road is closed between Cookham and Cookham Dean. Meanwhile, more news on the Church Woods murder. A spokesman for Thames Valley Police says that they are not releasing the identity of the victim, a man believed to be in his early fifties, until the next of kin have been informed but they would urgently like to speak to a Ms Charlie Hunter who they believe has some information that may help them with their inquiries. Now, be careful driving in the rain, next up, the Venga Boys. . .Traffic after this. . .*'

I turned the radio off. I had been expecting that, but it wasn't what I wanted to hear. I didn't want to help the police with their inquiries at all. I kept driving. The countryside gradually gave way to housing and soon I found myself driving towards the ugly centre of Wycombe.

I drove through endless, anonymous housing, past pubs and schools and the occasional shop, then down the steep hill that led to the town centre. It was prosperous, it had high employment rates, several sought-after schools and on the whole was relatively crime-free, but it was ugly, it was boring and it was soulless. I wondered what on earth Anna Bruce was doing living here.

Driving as instructed, I eventually found myself in the middle of the town, outside an apartment block near the station. Handy for a commute to London or Oxford. The building was predominantly steel, glass and marble. It proclaimed edgy but classic modern design, or young, urban professional. It was the kind of place for wealthy, aspirant singles or young, childless couples – an odd place to find a fortune teller.

I left my car – the Earl's car, it was kind of him to have lent it to me (*'Bloody good bloke. . .'*) – in a multi-storey car park and walked back to the block. I found her name on the intercom by the entrance door, *A Bruce*, and pressed the button.

Five minutes later I was in her minimalist living room in the penthouse flat. One wall was entirely glass, leading out to a roof terrace.

She didn't seem remotely surprised to see me. Doubtless the Earl had messaged her, or maybe it was her psychic powers. Today she was wearing a severe hounds-tooth skirt and a dark green blouse with an expensive looking silver and pearl necklace. Her short, white hair looked expensively cut. I looked around the apartment; there was a signed Warhol Marilyn litho print on the wall.

'It's real,' she said. The furniture, sparse and again modernist in design, would not be available at Ikea or John Lewis.

We had a spectacular view of the unlovely town. She indicated it with proprietorial pride.

'It's great,' she enthused, 'I can see the house where I grew up, from here – it was a real dump.' She pointed out of the window. Wycombe is in a valley, a very long, thin valley, and all I could see were endless houses. Houses were built clinging on to the hills on either side of the valley and they snaked away into the distance. 'I get up in the morning and I think, thank God I'm not there on that crappy *Jeremy Kyle*-type estate where my parents' council house was! I love gratitude.' She smiled at me. 'You're probably not feeling very grateful today.'

Damn right, I thought.

'Do you want a drink, tea, coffee?'

'Tea please, Darjeeling if you've got it.'

Once again I reflected on what an unlikely medium or psychic she was. Anna was so matter of fact, and obviously intelligent. I had met a couple of self-professed psychics before, you would not apply the words impressive or charismatic to them.

She did have Darjeeling. I sat on a Bauhaus-inspired sofa while she sat on a matching one opposite, a glass and chrome coffee table between us.

'I like Brutalist design,' she said. 'People are surprised, they expect clairvoyants to be a bit, well, traditional. More chintzy. More Laura Ashley, maybe.'

I drank my tea. Clairvoyance must pay well, I thought, or maybe she can predict the Lottery.

'I have rich clients,' she looked at me and shook her head. 'You, however, fall under the category of charity.'

I got straight to the point. 'The Earl thinks you might be able to help me.' I resisted the temptation to say, 'But of course you already knew that.' I'm sure it was a joke she had heard a thousand times before.

'I need to know. . .' I started to say and she cut me short with a gesture.

'I'm afraid you get what you're given,' she said. 'You're here for the missing cards. I don't tell clients why they had to take another three cards, not unless they turn up and ask.' She smiled rather harshly. 'But by then, it's often too late.'

When she had finished telling my fortune that evening at Justin's, she had got me to put the picture cards back into the main pack, shuffle and then choose three more cards, face down. These she had looked at, photographed on her phone and put back into the pack without showing me and without comment. Now, here I was and asking what they were and why she did it like that.

'Most people I see don't have serious, life or death problems,' Anna said. 'It's usually career or relationships. But those who return are like you, in a bad way, and that's what that trio of cards are for.' She gestured with her hands. 'They're like the last chance saloon cards, they're for the lost and the desperate.'

'That pretty much describes me,' I said. I drank some more tea.

She looked at me. 'I know, or you wouldn't be here.'

Anna stood up and clicked across the tiled floor in her heels, opened a concealed cupboard in the wall and took out a rosewood box, then came back and placed it on the table.

'Can you touch it?'

I did so. It was icy cold. She looked at me questioningly. 'Well?'

'Well, what?' I said.

'What do you notice?'

'Do you keep it in the fridge?' I asked, baffled by the question. She didn't say anything, then checked her phone and riffled through the pack, removing three cards.

'Here are your cards; Typhon, or the Devil, the Twilight or the Moon, and one from the minor Arcana, the Jack of Spades.'

I looked at the cards, at the archetypal illustrations, the Devil with his horns, seated on his throne, lording it over the man and woman, helplessly shackled to an iron cube. I looked at the dog and the wolf baying at the moon while a crab-like creature (I thought of doomed Ollie Scott and his last meal) crawled from the water and the handsome, slightly arrogant, face of the dark Knave.

Anna tapped the cards with a shapely, clear lacquered fingernail.

'You may or may not remember that you actually picked two of these cards on the previous occasion. That is highly unusual. To choose the same cards twice from a shuffled deck.

271

It's what Jung would have called a synchronicity, a deeply
meaningful coincidence, that is, not a coincidence. We have
here then three distinct things. Betrayal; a snare or a trap –
that's the devil; then an attractive dark-haired knave, who can
be duplicitous. So, someone or something that you rely on,
that you trust, will betray you or otherwise let you down.
The moon, terror, deception. So, in a nutshell. You will be
lured or fall into danger and there is a dark-haired person in
your life who is very powerful and means a lot to you.' She
tapped the Jack. 'And that person will probably betray you.'

Justin? That's who it surely meant, but I couldn't believe
he could betray me. And in what way? No, I said to myself
with growing fear, no, it can't be.

'The cards are what you make them,' said Anna. 'They
don't necessarily predict, they can warn, they can advise'
– she made a kind of helpless gesture with her hands – 'even
if you don't believe, they can suggest different ways of
looking or thinking. Different courses of action. But there
is one thing that I will tell you.' She gathered up the beautiful, strange cards and put them back in the box and closed
the lid. 'Come here.'

We crossed her living room and she opened the cupboard.
It was small and had a wooden base.

'Put your hands inside and feel.' I did so. It was quite
warm.

'The cards were cold when you touched them,' she said.
'The Moon card also means Death. Whatever you decide
to do, be careful. You've drawn betrayal, danger and death.
I think that's fairly clear. Go carefully. Death is present.'

'Go where?' I said.

'I'd go to Slough, if I were you,' Anna Bruce said, matter-of-factly.

So I did.

Chapter Thirty-Eight

The cards can suggest courses of action, she had said. The mysterious Knave, was it Justin? I had to know.

Justin. The cards were pointing to Justin. Much to my disquiet.

Anna had said go to Slough. Slough meant Justin. He managed a health spa there, that much I knew. And Anna seemingly knew I knew.

From Wycombe it's only a twenty-minute drive to Slough, famous for the poet John Betjeman's line about bombs, and as the place where the comedy *The Office* was set. There's a lot more to Slough than that – there's the headquarters of Burger King, 'Home of the Whopper', as it says on the outside of the office block, for one – but it accurately sets the tone. It's probably safe to say Slough won't be a UNESCO World Heritage Site, despite the innovative, linked light traffic system, the country's first, to be more specific. It also boasted Europe's largest privately owned trading estate, the Mars factory and the stuffed dog in a display case at the railway station.

I drove through the endless road that led through Slough,

the heavy, slow traffic giving me ample time to savour its delights, and as I headed out towards West London and Heathrow on the A4, I found the Herschel Spa.

I pulled into the car park. It was the end of lunch, about half past two, and the place looked quiet.

I walked across the car park. A dozen or so cars were parked there; BMW, Mercedes, Jaguar. It was, as Jess had said, certainly based on the vehicles I could see, a place for the wealthy. I doubted though any of the vehicles was as expensive as mine. Rain was falling. Jets thundered overhead; Heathrow airport was within spitting distance. The building was one of those enormous roadhouse pubs that had been built in the 1930s beside the major new arterial roads that were constructed when motoring was beginning to take off. You can still see a few around: ugly; red brick; mostly turned into drive-through fast food outlets. They tend to be located in unappealing places; the romance of the road never really materialised.

The spa was no exception. It was an unusual place for somewhere specialising in wellness: four lanes of traffic outside, surrounded by warehouses and gigantic sheds selling building materials. The windows of the building were black, reflective smoked glass. I walked back to the car, got my phone out and looked at their website.

The first thing I noticed was that it was members only, then as I read, I started to feel acute discomfort. It offered 'discreet massages'; it catered for 'the stressed executive who needed to relax in a soothing, friendly ambience'; there were 'qualified relaxation hostesses'; 'expert, tactile de-stressing body rubs'; 'tête-à-tête romantic dining and champagne experiences'. The pictures showed attractive young women wearing bikinis, towels and knowing, practised smiles.

I clicked off my phone. It was what I took to be a thinly disguised brothel. Justin, how could you, I thought.

Then, maybe I should give him the benefit of the doubt. The main reason I was so suspicious was because Anna had told me to be and that was based purely on the strength of a playing card. Maybe it was an ok sort of place? I found it hard to believe. The best way, I thought, would be to ask someone who worked there.

I got out of my car and walked around to the back, past the bins, following my nose to the kitchen area. I knew it did food; I'd find a friendly chef and ask him.

There, as I knew I would, I found two young chefs, sitting on upturned plastic beer bottle crates and smoking post-lunch service cigarettes, shivering in their chefs' whites, sheltered from the drizzle by a gazebo. They looked up at me, curious as to what I was doing here since I wasn't staff or a delivery man.

'Hi, is the head chef in?' I asked.

The younger of the two said, 'Yeah, I'll go and get him. What's it about?'

'I'm head chef at the Old Forge Café, in Hampden Green' I said. Like they'd have heard of it, but there is quite a strong camaraderie among chefs born out of the incredibly long hours, stressful, back-breaking work and awful pay. We tend to help one another.

'I'm chasing up a reference on someone who says they're a manager here. I thought I'd check up their suitability in person.'

The young kid returned in a couple of minutes with the head chef. In my experience there are three kinds of chef, if we exclude the technical side of things and look at personality. The good, the bad and the ugly. The man standing in front of me, framed in the kitchen doorway, fell, I had no doubt whatsoever, into the latter two categories.

He was a huge guy, in his mid-forties, with a very round head and hostile, staring eyes. His expression was sour and his chef's whites – dirty blue and white checks, a jacket smeared with old food – not the result of a busy service but rather of not having washed it in ages. An absolute disgrace, both to him and the profession.

My heart sank. There was zero chance of empathy with this muppet.

'Who's it about?' he said. His voice was unfriendly.

'He's called Justin West,' I replied. From what I knew of Justin's lifestyle he was probably more a sleeping partner in the spa, or maybe, my heart leapt, Jess was wrong and he'd parted company with the place a while ago. Maybe it had gone bad after he'd left.

'Hang on a minute,' he said. He turned and spoke to one of the kids. I couldn't hear what he said, but his back was facing me I could see his arse cleavage as revealed by his saggy blue and white check trousers which had slipped down his hips. It was not rear of the year. Twin pale, hairy, globes, strangely fully rounded, which somehow made them worse, a ghastly parody of femininity, bisected by his bum crack. It drew your eyes in, the way horrible sights do. It was revolting. Black hair sprouted from it. Truly horrific, then. The thought of him touching food was stomach-churning.

His arse made Whitfield's balls look beautiful.

'Come into my office.'

He led me across the yard to an outhouse, half of which was a bottle store for the bar, the other half a rudimentary office with a table, an ashtray, an old swivel chair, an antique computer with a huge, bulky monitor on top – none of your flatscreen stuff, a genuine great, big clunky monitor out of the ark, and a dinged-up filing cabinet. The small room stank of cigarette smoke. A pornographic calendar was on the wall. It was the wrong month too. Or maybe he liked seeing a girl wearing a Santa hat and nothing else, not even a smile. Classy. The Dorchester it was not.

He sat in the swivel chair. 'Take a seat,' he said. I sat in the plastic chair opposite him. He looked at me malevolently and lit a cigarette.

'Justin West, eh?'

'That's right,' I said. 'I know what it says on LinkedIn but I'm after anecdotal info.' I smiled winningly.

'I see.' He stood up, dwarfing me, then walked round the desk and shut the door and leaned on it, blocking the exit.

'And who are you?' he said, with an air of menace, then, 'Bitch.'

I stared at him in disbelief. For a moment I was stunned by the insult.

'You what?' I said, stupidly.

'You heard,' he scowled at me, his voice unpleasantly aggressive. 'What's your name, you slag? Who are you?'

'That's not a very nice thing to say,' I looked him hard in the eye. He managed to mask his terror quite well.

'Yeah, well what're you going to do about it?'

The chef leaned his massive bulk forwards over me in a threatening way. He was one of those bullies whose sheer size makes them unstoppable. I guessed it had been years since anyone had stood up to him. He would have had a great time in the kitchens where the majority of his staff would be scrawny teenagers, over-awed by his title and position too.

Well, I had no intention of getting into a fight with him. He would probably rip me limb from limb. Anyway, I had other things that I needed to do that day which were a tad more pressing, such as finding a murderer.

I stood up; he towered over me.

'Let me out,' I said.

He shook his head. 'Who sent you?'

'Look,' I said, reasonably, 'I don't know what you think you're doing, but you're going to have to open this door. . .'

Just then there was a rap on the door from the other side.

'Ok then,' the head chef said, with an unpleasant smirk. He opened the door.

The guy framed in the doorway must have weighed about twenty stone. The badge on his jacket proclaimed him the head of security for the Bar and Grill.

'You,' he said, pointing a finger at me, 'get outside.'

Stony faced, I did so. Before I knew what was happening he spun me around and had me in a professional grip that I couldn't move out of. My arm twisted up behind my back, my wrist held by something approximating a vice.

'You're coming with me, girly,' he said in a gravelly East End accent. He looked like he'd been auditioning for a part in a film about the Kray Twins. In his fifties, dressed in a doorman's sombre two-piece suit and bow tie, a slab-like face and a powerful physique, but above all the kind of rock-solid self-confidence that comes from unlicensed boxing bouts and working the doors at troublesome establishments frequented by violent men and criminals.

The head chef followed us outside. He reached out a hand to grab me.

The security guy was having none of this. Handling trouble-makers was his turf. He fixed him with a basilisk stare. 'Leave it, Ray!' he barked, and the head chef backed away.

'Sorry, Cliff.' It was a heartfelt apology. Cliff was obviously not the kind of man you wanted to upset.

'C'mon you.' One hand held my shoulder, the other my right arm just above the elbow. There are a mass of nerve endings down there. His thumb pressed warningly on some of them. I felt any attempt to run away would end in tears, mine not his.

'Let go of me,' I said, angrily.

'Maybe later,' he growled. 'You're in a restricted area and it's management policy to detain trespassers.'

'Where are you taking her?' asked Ray, nervously.

'The beer cellar. It's soundproof and we won't be disturbed. Now, go back to yer pots and pans, Jamie Oliver, there's a good boy! Got that!'

'Yes, Cliff,' said the chastened Ray.

'Now, you,' he commanded me, 'move.'

Helpless, I was led off to my fate.

Chapter Thirty-Nine

Cliff marched me through the kitchen, everyone pointedly looking the other way. Don't stare at the condemned woman. Or possibly, 'No officer, I didn't see anything, I was looking at the RoboCoupe', as two of them were, their eyes fixed on the giant antique mixer, as if it was the most fascinating thing in the world and I didn't exist.

See no evil.

We went silently down a corridor to a locked door which my captor opened with a large key, then he switched on a light and pointed to a flight of precipitous stairs.

'Down you go!'

I did so, carefully, the wooden treads behind me creaking under Cliff's weight. He closed the door behind him and I heard him bolt it. There was the unmistakable smell of damp, bleach and stale beer that you get in a beer cellar. We reached the bottom and we faced each other. We were alone in the underground cellar. It struck me that it would be utterly sound-proof. He stood looking at me by the light of the naked bulb. Dozens of beer barrels surrounded us, the active ones connected to plastic tubing that ran upwards through the cellar roof to the bars above.

He took one of his black leather gloves off – Cliff – it read on his knuckles, and he started to unpeel the other. I knew what it was going to say, Yeats.

The moment had come.

We threw our arms around each other and banged each other on the back, overjoyed to see each other again.

'Uncle Cliff!'

'Charlie Hunter as I live and breathe. . .'

We grinned delightedly at each other. Cliff Yeats, former heavyweight Southern Area champion and part-time bare-knuckle boxer, and doorman par excellence in the Hayes and Uxbridge area, not to mention the West End, had been one of my dad's best friends. I'd known him since birth, but for the past few years it had been Christmas cards only and vague promises about meeting up. Now, here he was.

We sat down on empty barrels. Cliff drank brandy from a hip flask while I told him what had brought me here.

'But why all this heavy duty business?' I asked 'Why did that fat bastard chef get his knickers in such a twist? That was a bit uncalled for?'

'Do you know who owns this gaff?' asked Cliff, with obvious amusement.

'Nope,' I said.

'Thought not. The Herschel Spa is owned by the Anderson brothers,' he explained.

'Oh, I see!' Now I understood. The brothers, based in Edmonton, were one of North London's leading crime families. Any stranger, like me, snooping around, would be automatically suspect, to be warned off in no uncertain terms. I don't like to think about what might have happened if I hadn't known Cliff.

'Do you know anything about Justin West?' I asked. 'Did he really work here?'

'I know a lot about Justin West,' he said, 'and yes, he did work here. What's your connection to him?'

'I'm going out with him.'

'Seriously?'

'Seriously.'

He shook his head. 'You always had terrible taste in men, Charlie, apart from that Italian geezer; he was sound. What happened to him?'

'I'm afraid I let him slip through my fingers,' I said, sadly.

'Idiot.'

I nodded. 'I know.'

Cliff lit a cigarette and removed the cap he wore to hide his bald patch. He took a pull from his silver flask and started to talk.

'So, is this true, that he's asked you for a job?' Cliff asked. 'Tell him the position's filled, mate.'

'It's not that simple,' I said.

'You're not really dating him? Tell me that was a joke.' I shook my head. 'It's no joke.'

'In that case, mate,' Cliff patted me on my shoulder, 'you need your bloody head seeing to.'

Chapter Forty

I drove back to Hampden Green, slowly. I had a lot to think about. That was putting it mildly. What I had just learned almost pushed the fact that I was a prime suspect in the death of Luke Montfort out of my mind.

Basically this. The health club that Justin part-owned was owned by the London mafia. There was no way that he could not have known who his partners were. He was the public face of what was almost certainly a criminal organisation, almost certainly used as a conduit for money laundering. When you've got an ugly business, put a pretty face on it. In my opinion, not that pretty a face, but hey ho. That was obviously the thinking. And if there was one thing that Justin did have, it was charm.

'Take the next right,' the BMW satnav informed me. The onboard screen showed me my direction and destination on a map and, just to make sure, with German thoroughness, the instrument panel showed me too in its swanky way which way right was. If only I could get it to tell me what to do! A satnav for the soul. Anna Bruce had dropped heavy hints about Justin's reliability but that wasn't quite the same.

Even now, I could feel his charisma working on me; maybe he had been conned or forced into it somehow. . .

I drove into Hampden Green and past my restaurant. I noticed a police car parked in its small car park, almost certainly waiting for me to show up. I hadn't switched my phone on once since I had left the place earlier that morning. I guessed there would be umpteen messages telling me to get in touch with Slattery, or worse, 'give yourself up'. I felt that I'd rather plead ignorance.

The Earl's BMW would go unnoticed around here. I was quietly impressed by the way he quite casually flouted the law. I suppose that's one of the things about being rich, but then I thought, no, that's not necessarily the case. The Earl ('bloody good bloke') had that odd advantage of simply not caring about things.

I parked in front of Justin's house. I felt I was owed some kind of explanation. I suppose I was still in love with him. I wanted him to be innocent.

'You have reached your destination,' the car said. Well, that was true, in more ways than one.

His Audi was there so he'd be at home. I walked up to the door and rang the bell. I saw him coming through the opaque stained-glass of the door.

He opened it, his face fell when he saw it was me.

'Charlie,' he said, uncertainly, 'do come in.'

He was wearing ripped black skinny jeans and a figure-hugging Lycra top that emphasised his pecs and his gymnast's body. He looked great. He smiled at me and led me into the living room.

'I'm just having some tea,' he said, 'can I get you some?'

I nodded. 'Please do.' Normally by this time – it was now nearly four – I would probably have had about ten cups of the stuff. I was in tea withdrawal symptom mode.

He disappeared into the kitchen and came back with two cups and a ceramic teapot. He poured the tea, handed me a cup and sat cross-legged on the opposite end of the sofa.

'The police were round here looking for you,' he said. 'Luke Montfort is dead. It's all over the village.'

'Oh,' I said. I wasn't sure whether to add, 'I know' or not. I certainly didn't want to say that I had seen his body.

I drank some of my tea, I pulled a face, PG Tips it was not.

'Rooibos,' said Justin, seeing my expression. 'It's South African. It'll relax you.'

I doubted that. Since I had seen him the night before, I had experienced a somewhat stressful day: the body in the car; my knife in the body; disposing of a murder weapon; the Earl; Anna Bruce; the strip club; Ray. Most stressful at all, knowing that my beautiful, innocuous yoga teacher lover was connected to organised crime. It was all a bit much. I was way past relaxation. I doubted a fistful of temazepam would have relaxed me.

He, of course, knew nothing of all of this. The most stressful thing he had probably done today was arrange an appointment to meet a client or done pigeon pose.

Time to drop my bombshell.

'I was at the Herschel Spa today.'

His face hardened, his body stiffened.

'Oh, were you? Why's that then?' There was a sudden subtle but definite change in him. His voice became as hard as his face, I had never heard him sound like that before. I think it was at that point that I knew all that Cliff had said was true. All that Anna had said was true. The duplicitous, dark-haired Knave who would betray me. And I had fallen in love with him.

I ignored the question.

'Please, Justin, tell me what on earth is going on?'

'OK,' he said, in a kind of defeated way, 'I will.'

He stood up. 'Christ, I need a drink.' It was a very un-yoga-teacher-like thing to say.

'You've got tea,' I pointed out. I drank some of mine. 'It's very calming.'

'A proper drink,' he said, scornfully. I suddenly did not like the tone I could now hear in his voice. It wasn't the Justin that I knew. Scales began to fall from my eyes with a vengeance. The clothes he was wearing suddenly seemed a decade too young for him. There were lines on his face that I hadn't noticed before. He didn't look so boyish anymore, he looked like a man clinging to his youth by his fingertips.

What have I done? I thought.

He crossed the room and went to a cupboard, pulled out a bottle of Absolut.

He glared irritably at me and poured a large vodka into a glass. 'Want some?'

'I'd like answers, Justin,' I said, drinking more tea, 'not booze. That place is a front for organised crime, and you know it.'

'Well, you can wait a minute while I get some ice.'

He went into the kitchen and I heard the slam of the freezer compartment door, the tinkling sound of ice in a

290

glass, and then he returned and resumed his place at the end of the sofa. He took a big swig of his vodka.

'Right, now I'll begin.' He looked at me defiantly and took a deep breath. 'OK, Charlie, you want the truth, here it is.' He looked hard at me, it wasn't a nice look. 'I knew Ollie Scott from the Spa. He was one of the regulars, he had a lot of money, mostly in cash to spend.'

'Drug money?' I said brightly.

'No,' Justin said sarcastically, 'from a matured ISA. Of course it was drug money. Where else would it have come from? And occasionally, he'd turn up with Dave Whitfield when they wanted a night on the town and I'd comp them this or that. That's how I got to hear about this village. It was handy for Slough, but cheaper than where I was living. I sold my flat and moved here. I wanted a change.'

This was not what I wanted to hear, that he'd known Scott and the others. I didn't like where this was going. Despite everything, I was still giving him the benefit of the doubt. Please tell me you were an unwilling/unwitting accomplice, I silently pleaded.

'Who did you talk to when you were there?' he regarded me in a hostile way from over the rim of her glass.

'Cliff Yeats.'

He snorted contemptuously, 'Cliff Yeats! That fat old fool. Well, you'll know everything about me then. Not that it matters. Anyway, I introduced Ollie to Luke Montfort. He was a regular, obsessed with a couple of the girls who worked there. That's where Montfort's money went, on prostitutes, the younger the better, and together they created Arcadia. They bought the land off the Earl.'

'Why did they need those idiots from Chandler's Ford, Farson and Musgrave?' I couldn't see their part in it, why would they be needed?

'It gave the illusion of a community bid,' Justin explained. 'The Council are big on being seen to favour local enterprise – inclusivity – and the Earl wouldn't have sold them the land otherwise.'

'That's not what he told me,' I said. 'He said he was trying to rip them off.'

'Is that what he said?' Justin shrugged. 'It's hard to know with him. He pretends he's Mr Nasty but he does all this local charity shit. He's the reverse of most people who pretend they're nice and aren't.'

I was by now beginning to regret coming. It was becoming increasingly apparent that the sweet, caring, gentle man that I had fallen in love with didn't actually exist. They say that the truth makes you free, not that it's an enjoyable experience. I was not enjoying my new-found freedom. He carried on. 'Then Dave Whitfield, of all people, gets cold feet. Slattery has been nosing around.'

I was confused. 'But I thought Slattery was part of Arcadia. I thought he was on the take.'

Justin looked at me from over the rim of his glass. 'You know what your problem is, Charlie?' His voice was full of scorn. 'You're an idiot. That's why you're a chef, slaving away for peanuts, cooking food for a village that doesn't even like you. Slattery is as straight as they come and he really does care about this poxy village. He's had Ollie Scott in his sights for ages. He found out that Ollie was funding Arcadia, money laundering. He was going to pull Dave in and Dave had never been inside and he would be terrified of going down. If Slattery had leaned on Dave he would have crumbled like a biscuit. That's why Dave had to go, to shut his mouth.'

I looked at him in horror. 'So you've known. All along, you've known. . .Then why?'

'Why did I encourage you to find out who killed Whitfield? Because I needed someone to take the rap when Montfort died.'

I looked at him with even more horror.

'Oh, yes, Charlie, I set you up from the beginning. It's like a game of chess, but I've been two moves ahead all the time.'

I'd heard enough. I decided to leave.

'You needed. . .' I said, or tried to. The cup fell from my fingers on to the floor, it moved in slow motion. I tried to stand up, but my legs weren't working. I pitched forwards on the carpet.

'The tea. . .' I croaked, from my position on the floor. My head was swimming now, the room pitching like a boat on the sea.

'That's right,' Justin said, with contempt, 'it's the tea. You can almost see the wheels turn' – he shook his head pityingly – 'like I said before, you're an idiot. Who do you think could get close enough to Dave to carry his shotgun? Who do you think was with Ollie Scott and kept topping his vodka and coke up with methanol and who, when he started to cramp up, suggested to him he had food poisoning from your place?' He carried on. 'Who do you think saw you go into the Three Bells from their upstairs window and who do you think called Farson?'

He walked over to where I was sprawled and stood over me like a hunter standing over a piece of dying big game. He looked down at me contemptuously. I looked up at him through agonised eyes. I had loved him, and all this time he had just been using me. He prodded me with his toe.

'And you, Charlie, you moron, thinking you're so clever with your pathetic restaurant and that posh, slut student waitress of yours and that dimwit kitchen porter – you're the one that will take the rap for Montfort. That's why I slept with you. Do you honestly think someone like me would ever fancy someone like you? I did you to get the things I needed to make you a fall guy. Your knife killed him, and in my garage I've got one of your T-shirts with his blood on it. I'll put that back in the Old Forge Café tonight.'

He really hates me, I thought. The really horrible thing was, how much he was enjoying telling me all the shitty things he'd done. He was proud of them. And that was almost crueller than anything.

He carried on talking but I seemed to be sliding mentally into a dark tunnel. I was fighting a losing battle to stay awake and not to sink into unconsciousness. I thought, 'I'm not going to wake up.'

This was followed by 'I know what my problem is, I'm an idiot', then I managed one last thought, crystal clear.

'I have very questionable tastes in men.'

Lights out.

Chapter Forty-One

I came to as I was being dragged out of the back of a van by Farson and Hat Man. It was like I was drunk and they were helping me home. But I wasn't drunk, and this wasn't my home. The rain poured down around us, driven into our faces with stinging force by the high wind. I think that's what had revived me. I looked around. I was in Chandler's Ford. We made our way – me in the middle, they on either side supporting my weight – into the back garden of the Greyhound, the grass of the scabby lawn submerged by the flooding river.

Near the rear wall of the pub was a semi-circle of sand-bags put there in a vain attempt to keep the water out from the beer cellar trapdoor where the barrels were delivered by the draymen. The two heavy doors of the cellar, a double trapdoor, were flush with the sodden ground. They dropped me down on to the grass where I lay. I felt weak, incapacitated by whatever Justin had drugged me with. There were two recessed handles in the iron flaps and, bending their knees, Farson and Hat Man heaved them up, one at a time. Each door was a two-man job.

They dragged me to the gap that they had opened up. I could see the beer cellar was nine-tenths flooded. A couple of beer barrels were floating in the water; no wonder the bar had smelled damp when I was last there, it was as if the pub was sinking.

'Time for your swim, Fanny Cradock,' said Hat Man, a reference that really dated him, and they threw me in. I gasped as the icy water embraced my body. The cellar must have had a high ceiling, because I couldn't touch the floor. Momentarily I sank. I gulped water and inhaled some and came up coughing, my legs and arms thrashing around. I was still woozy and not really in control of my body. Then my foot made contact with the body of one of the beer barrels that must have been completely full and was still resting on the floor of the cellar. I stared up at Farson and Hat Man who were grinning down at me, their heads silhouetted against the lowering sky. I looked helplessly up at them. The heavens opened even more and it started to rain in monsoon-like strength. I narrowed my eyes against the torrential downpour.

'Sweet dreams,' said Farson and they heaved the doors over. They fell with a heavy crash and all light was extinguished. I was alone in the darkness in the flooded cellar.

I crouched on top of the barrel. Another few centimetres and I would be submerged.

Water was still seeping in through the cracks between door and brickwork.

The water stank. And it was bitterly cold. But above all was that overpowering smell. There was the beer that had leached from some of the real ale casks that were down there and there was a smell of sewage and rotting vegetation. I made my way, half swimming, my lips clamped shut against swallowing any of the foul liquid I was immersed in, until I was under the trapdoor.

I could see an outline of light that marked the edges. There was a kind of chute or slide, running from door to floor, where the delivery men slid the barrels up and down but it was at a steep angle and under water and I couldn't get any purchase on it. Every time I tried to stand on it to try to push the doors upwards, my feet slipped and I fell forwards. I swallowed a mouthful of river and retched. Water – its quantity increased dramatically by the apocalyptic downpour, I could hear it thundering against the metal above my head – cascaded through the edges of the cellar trapdoor and the central gap where the two doors met. The top of my head was pressed against the ceiling and the water was up to above my upper lip. Three or four more centimetres and I would start drowning.

I thought gloomily of the cards I had turned over for Anna Bruce: the Devil or Typhon, betrayal, the Moon, a snare or death. Well, I had been well and truly betrayed, ensnared and now it looked like I was going to die. She had been right.

I promised I would never sneer at fortune-telling again.

I thought of the list of the dead that had brought me to this place: Whitfield, Scott, Harding, Montfort. Dead men's names. I saw their faces, saw their hands beckoning me to join them. Dead men's hands, dead men's fingers.

Drowned in a beer cellar, and in a pub that did crappy all-day fry ups.

Despair, blacker than the cellar, washed over me.
I was going to die down here.
Down where the barrels roll. In a crappy country pub.

Chapter Forty-Two

Time passed. It probably wasn't long, but when you're facing drowning in icy cold darkness, time takes on a peculiar quality. I tried again to lift the heavy doors, but it was impossible. The only other option was the door that led to the bar. I crossed the flooded cellar, paddling through the foetid, freezing darkness, my feet using submerged barrels as stepping stones. The water was now so high I had to move with my head tilted back at an angle, my nose now occasionally brushing the rough, irregular roof. I found the stairs and the trapdoor that led up to the bar. Securely closed.

Slattery's words, 'Don't even think about going anywhere near the Greyhound', came back to me. Musgrave would say that he found me drowned in the cellar. He'd say I must have been trying to snoop around his pub again, got into the cellar and got trapped.

Slattery would believe him.

I thought some more about Justin.

I thought about why Justin had hired me to find Whitfield's murderer. As he had told me, it was to set me up as Montfort's killer. And hiring me as an investigator was a stroke of genius. My blundering investigations had served to fuel Slattery's suspicions that I was up to no good. I was certainly an obvious distraction to him in his quest to nail Ollie, the local Mr Big. Oh God, I thought, miserably.

How neatly Justin had set me up. It was almost certainly he who had taken my keys out of my pocket as I lay unconscious, taken my knife and my T-shirt. Running back across the green in time to meet Anna.

My head was tipped virtually completely back, my nose against the ceiling. What was it like to drown? I hoped it would be quick. . .

Why had Justin done all this? Killed three people and caused the death of a fourth, Paul Harding? Oh, and me. That made five. Money, I guessed. No, I thought, it was more than money. Justin just liked manipulating people. And cruelty. He could have just drugged me, but he didn't. He wanted me to suffer and he wanted me to know how clever he was.

How could he kill so many though? I suppose it's like olives. The first time you eat one you think yuck, then you develop a taste for them. He'd developed a taste for killing. A taste for death. Murder had been on Justin's menu for some time.

Waves of hatred towards him washed over me.

Then in the midst of darkness and my misery, came the sweetest sound I had ever heard in my life.

Over the noise of water running into the cellar I heard a voice shouting through the metal doors, a voice I knew well. 'Are you in there, chef?'

It was Francis, of all people.

'Help!' I shouted back. Then I coughed as water flooded my mouth and my windpipe. I was frantically dog-paddling my way back to the metal trapdoor so I could bang on it. My head was thrown back, my nose scraping the rough bricks of the ceiling as I moved towards Francis's voice. There was only a centimetre or so gap now before the water flooded the cellar completely. I felt a sense of panic that he might go away. I only had minutes left to me.

'Shout if you're in there!'

I realised, to my horror, that whereas I was in a relatively quiet place, the only sound the water flooding in, outside it was windy, pouring with rain and I couldn't be heard.

Then came Jess's voice: 'Francis, the police are coming, they'll get that door open.'

Please don't listen to her, I thought. I'll be dead. I can't wait. The tip of my nose was now resting against the metal of the trapdoor, the cold, filthy water practically at nostril level. I tried to slam my knuckles into the metal flap but all it did was produce a kind of dull thud that they would be unable to hear.

Then I heard Francis say firmly, 'Jess, they said they'd be here ten minutes ago, they're as much use as a chocolate teapot. Move out the way.'

It had taken two men to lift each of the two cellar doors, a job that they had barely managed. A job normally done by two large draymen who spend all day moving 80-kilo beer kegs around and are built to handle it, not by one man aided by a petite, non-weight-lifting girl.

But it wasn't a normal person outside the beer cellar. It was Francis doing the lifting. To my amazed delight, the metal door rose steadily, effortlessly and slowly upwards as if pulled smoothly by a machine. The crack of silvery daylight grew incrementally wider and wider, until the flap was at 90 degrees and then Francis let it go and it crashed down on the ground beside the trapdoor with a thud that seemed to make the cellar shake. My head broke fully free of the foul, scummy water and Jess and Francis peered down at me in astonishment, their heads framed by the grey sky.

I looked up from my watery tomb.

I felt like an aquatic Lazarus.

I croaked, 'Could you give me a hand out, Francis?'

He beamed down at me. 'Yes, chef!' He leaned forwards and extended a large leathery hand. It was like being enfolded by a wicket-keeper's glove.

He pulled me up in one massive jerk, like I was weightless, and I stood shivering in my sodden clothes. I felt ecstatically happy to be alive. I threw my arms around him, my fingertips barely touching, and kissed him. Francis blushed a fiery red.

I looked around me: the river had spread over the Arcadia development fields and the pub garden. The bare trees, and my saviours, Francis with his blond hair for once not sticking up but flattened against his head by the rain, and Jess peering out at me from under the hood of her parka.

'Francis,' I said solemnly, 'I love you.'

He grinned and shuffled his feet. 'Thank you, chef.'

Jess looked at me and shook her head. 'I told you that

man was bad news,' she said, and flung her arms around me. 'Thank God you're alive!'

Francis looked down at the cellar: no water was flowing into it now, its level had equalled that of the flooded beer garden.

'Crikey, that was close,' he said, mildly.

Chapter Forty-Three

I was putting out a row of brandy glasses that I was going to use for a dessert and listening to Beeches FM playing *Supernature* by Cerrone, in the background. Soon I'd be able to use them for what they were intended – brandy. Slattery had been by a couple of days before to tell me he'd green-lighted my liquor licence application. I think it was his way of saying sorry. He had also told me that a search of Justin's garage had revealed not just my bloodstained T-shirt but the car that had killed Paul Harding. Slattery had arrested Musgrave, Farson, Hat Man and, of course, Justin West. As far as I could gather they were all busy blaming each other. It very much looked like life sentences all round.

It was five days after my watery resurrection or baptism, maybe. I felt like I had been officially born again. I looked over with affection at the person in the corner of the kitchen.

Unlike the collective disaster zone that comprised the set known as my ex-boyfriends, here was a man I could trust, one that I was able to bare my soul to. My own chosen father confessor.

I stirred the lemon zest and juice into the simmering double cream and sugar that was on the stove. I was making a lemon posset that I was going to serve with finely diced stem ginger, some raspberries, toasted flaked almonds and accompanied with almond shortbread.

'Well,' my spiritual adviser said, ' that all looks very nice, Charlie. Low cal is it?'

The lemon juice worked its magic on the cream, it thickened almost as soon as the juice hit it. I had made the shortbread earlier and cut it up using a two-inch pastry cutter while it was still warm. Cliff Yeats was eating the latticework of shortbread that was left after I'd been at work with the cutter.

'No, Cliff,' I warned. 'That stuff is equal weight sugar and butter, with more sugar on top. I shudder to think of the calories. . .'

'Yeah, but it's got nuts in it, and they're good for you,' he countered. 'Besides, I chucked two kids out of a club in Bethnal Green on Tuesday night and they said they'd come back and shoot me.' He shrugged. 'I'd rather die of short-bread than a shotgun.'

'Fair enough.' I started ladling the posset into the large brandy glasses, in ten portions.

Cliff had come out to the country for the day to see me in my new environment. I showed him my restaurant, and pointed out the significant parts of the village. That didn't take long.

'You can meet my staff,' I said. 'The ones who saved my life.'

'How did they know you were there,' he asked, 'stuck in that cellar?'

I laughed. 'Jess had hacked Justin's phone. She got into it via my iPhone. My phone's backed up to my PC and she's got the password.'

'You gave your waitress your personal password?' He sounded shocked.

'No, she just knows it, God knows how.' I shrugged. I knew very well how she knew. I could remember her exact words from a few days ago: *'Password1' is not a password, it's not secure. . . it's like leaving your front door wide open, with the keys in the lock,. . .'*

'She got into Justin's messages. She'd had her suspicions about him for a while and she'd hacked into his phone. He had texted Farson to come and collect me and take me to the Greyhound. So Jess drove over with Francis. When they saw what was happening, they called the Old Bill.'

'How does she know how to hack into a phone?' said Cliff, admiringly.

'She does Ethical Hacking as part of her IT course at uni. I have absolutely no idea how any of it works. I guess she might have sent him some kind of malware purporting to be from me that he clicked on, but to be honest, I don't know and I can't say I care.'

'Good job she didn't study catering,' said Cliff, 'or you'd be brown bread, mate.'

'I know,' I agreed, 'and thank God it was Francis with her, able to lift that door up by himself.'

Jess came into the kitchen. 'Charlie, DI Slattery's in the restaurant,' she said, with a worried look.

'Send him in,' I shrugged. I had nothing to hide.

Slattery came in. He was wearing cords and a tweed jacket and I noticed how weather-beaten he looked. He really was a very outdoorsy kind of guy. With his powerful frame and dark hair he looked a bit like a gamekeeper played by Heathcliff.

'I just came by to let you know that we've arrested the guy who robbed Andy Simmonds,' he said, looking at me expectantly.

I stared at him in puzzlement. What was he on about? Then I remembered.

'The sausage thief,' I said.

'Exactly,' Slattery said, with a triumphant air. Cliff was looking at him open-mouthed with aggressive astonishment. I hoped there wasn't going to be a scene. Cliff and the law did not see eye to eye usually.

'Thought you'd like to know,' Slattery said. His phone pinged and he glanced down, frowning.

'Well, I'll see you later.' He gave Cliff a curt nod and walked out. The swing door to the restaurant closed behind him.

'What the f. . .' Cliff spluttered, too amazed to even manage to get the expletive out. 'That passes for crime round here? Someone nicking sausages! Hardly Brink's Mat or Hatton Garden, is it! What kind of a weird place is this, Charlie Hunter!'

I was now bent over a work station resting my forehead on the cool steel, suppressing hysterical laughter over Cliff's outrage.

'It all makes sense if you live here Cliff. . .'

'Dear God. . .'

A few moments later there was a knock on the kitchen door.

'What now!' groaned Cliff. I wondered that too; it couldn't be Slattery again, the knock sounded too polite. I opened it to find a UPS delivery man with a small parcel. I signed for it and carried it inside.

'What is it?' asked Cliff.

I shrugged. 'I've got no idea.'

I undid the packaging, a bottle of Veuve Cliquot '95 and a card with a mobile number on one side. I turned it over. '*In bocca al lupo*'. It was signed, Andrea. Underneath, 'Call me.'

Cliff picked the bottle up admiringly. 'I like fizz, I wouldn't mind some of this right now!'

I looked at him and said, 'Cliff, much as I love you, I'm not giving you a two-hundred pound vintage champagne. You can make do with PG Tips, and lager when the Three Bells opens.'

'Fair enough, mate.'

Cliff stood up and stretched. 'What does the card say?'

'It says, "*In the mouth of the wolf*". It means, "Good luck".'

I looked at the elegant, strong calligraphy on the card and I thought of Andrea. He was engaged now, to someone else. Should I call him? Did it just mean good luck or did it mean something else?

I decided to think about it later. Right now I would enjoy my day with Cliff – simple, uncomplicated friendship.

Cliff Yeats, unreconstructed, unrepentant Londoner and hardened sinner, looked through the door to the restaurant and beyond through the windows to the green and the houses opposite. For once it had stopped raining, and in the distance you could see the treeline that marked the edge of the cricket ground and a horse paddock.

'All these fields, gives me the creeps,' Cliff said.

'Now, now, it's my manor you're talking about,' I chided him.

He snorted in derision.

'Are you going to stay here?' he asked, 'after all this. . .' he searched for a word to describe several murders, the violence, the deceit, false imprisonment and a near fatal attempt on my life. He found one. 'Malarkey?'

'Why not?' I said. 'I like it here.' I patted the Hobart; by God, the price I'd ended up paying for it! Every cloud. . . I smiled. 'And besides, I'm local now.'

Bedford Square Publishers

Bedford Square Publishers is an independent publisher of fiction and non-fiction, founded in 2022 in the historic streets of Bedford Square London and the sea mist shrouded green of Bedford Square Brighton.

Our goal is to discover irresistible stories and voices that illuminate our world.

We are passionate about connecting our authors to readers across the globe and our independence allows us to do this in original and nimble ways.

The team at Bedford Square Publishers has years of experience and we aim to use that knowledge and creative insight, alongside evolving technology, to reach the right readers for our books. From the ones who read a lot, to the ones who don't consider themselves readers, we aim to find those who will love our books and talk about them as much as we do.

We are hunting for vital new voices from all backgrounds – with books that take the reader to new places and transform perceptions of the world we live in.

Follow us on social media for the latest Bedford Square Publishers news.

🐦 @bedsqpublishers
facebook.com/bedfordsq.publishers/
@bedfordsq.publishers

https://bedfordsquarepublishers.co.uk/